HURRICANE

BY

JACK STEWART

A BOOTLEG BOOK

A BOOTLEG BOOK
Published by
Bootleg Press
2431A NE Halsey
Portland, Oregon 97232

Bootleg Books may be purchased for educational, business, or sales promotional use. For information please e-mail, Kelly Irish at: kellyirish@bootlegprerss.com.

Bootleg Press is a registered trademark.

ISBN: 0974524670

Cover by Compass Graphics

Printed in the United States of America

November 2003

For my dear friends,
Ken Douglas and Vesta Irene

A writer's lot is a lonely one,
especially for a single man on a boat.
Your writer's group was a respite from that,
a great group of folks that helped keep me sane.

And I'd like to offer a special thanks to
Margaret Ashcroft Green
for her generous help with the manuscript.

///

Books by Jack Stewart

SCORPION
HURRICANE

With Ken Douglas

TANGERINE DREAM
DIAMOND SKY

HURRICANE

CHAPTER ONE

JULIE HAD THE THROTTLE WIDE OPEN. She saw something red out at the first of the Five Islands and wondered what it was.

"Mom, lookout!" Meiko shouted to be heard above the roar of the engine.

Julie pulled her eyes away from the small island and saw the log dead ahead. She shoved the throttle-tiller to the right and the dinghy jerked to the left.

Tammy screamed and fell over the side. She grabbed for the safety line, but her fingers found only air. Her scream was cut off when her head slid below the surface.

"Mom, she can't swim!"

Julie panicked and accelerated when she meant to back off the gas. The dinghy shot forward like a race horse given its head, increasing the distance between the rubber boat and the woman in the water.

"Mom, slow down!"

Julie backed off the gas.

"She's gonna be okay," Meiko said. With the engine at idle, shouting was no longer necessary.

"You sure?" Julie asked, turning the dinghy now that she had it under control.

"Yeah, she's dog paddling, but she's caught in the current," her daughter said.

Meiko stood in the dinghy and pointed to the floating log. Tammy saw it and started to paddle toward it. Meiko kept her eyes on the woman in the water, while Julie added power, and the engine died.

Tammy screamed, thrashing against the water, trying to stay afloat.

"And she was doing so well," Meiko said, kicking off her sandals. She dove over the side, swimming to Tammy with the long easy strokes of a professional swimmer. Meiko was twenty-one and her morning wasn't complete without a hundred laps.

"Damn," Julie said. She pulled on the starter cord and the Evinrude answered with a staccato sputter.

"Double damn." She pulled the cord again. This time, not even a sputter. She pulled out the choke and pulled it a third time, but the engine was too hot for the choke.

"Come on, Mom, hurry." Julie barely heard her daughter. She glanced up and saw that Meiko had an arm wrapped around Tammy's chest and she was pulling her away from the log, getting farther away from it with each powerful kick. Tammy wasn't over her panic and was still struggling. Julie pushed the choke in and yanked on the cord, but the grip slipped out of her hand without a whimper from the Evinrude.

"Hurry!" Meiko screamed.

Julie grabbed onto the grip and jerked hard on the cord. The motor sprang to life in a cloud of gray smoke. She gave it gas for a second because she didn't want it to die again, then she motored toward them.

"Are you okay?" Julie said, bringing the boat along side them.

"Yeah, we're gonna be fine," Meiko said. Julie put the Evinrude in neutral.

"You need help, Tammy?" Julie asked.

"Grab and pull," she sputtered. Julie grabbed onto the back of her blouse and pulled as Tammy struggled to get back into the dinghy. "Horrible," she said once she was inside.

Meiko shot out of the water with a strong scissor kick, sliding over the rubber tube and into the boat, like a seal shooting out of the water up onto the rocks.

"Not a log," Meiko said. She ran her fingers through her long hair and squeezed the saltwater out.

"Floater." Tammy shook her head and let the water fly from her short hair like a shaggy dog.

"What?" Julie said.

"Dead man," Meiko said.

That Julie understood and she motored over to the body.

"Do we have to?" Tammy said. "It's gross."

"We can't leave it out here," Julie said.

"It's a white man," Tammy said.

"Then it's probably murder," Julie said.

"Wow," Meiko said.

"Can you tell who it is?" Julie asked.

"Yuck. I don't want to look any more," Tammy said.

"Come on Tammy. It's dead. It's not going to hurt you," Meiko said.

"I don't care. Let's go." She turned away from the bloated body.

Julie started to take the line off the small anchor.

"What are you doing?" Tammy asked.

"We can't leave it out here."

"Sure we can," Tammy said. "We'll call the police when we get back. They'll take care of it." Tammy said. She was used to getting her way.

"By the time we get back the current will have the body halfway to the Bocas. And by the time the police get a hold of the coast guard and they get a launch out here, it'll be through and into the open sea. They'll never find it."

There was a light breeze working against the southern Caribbean sun, but it was still hot in the bobbing dinghy. "How do you know it was murder?" Meiko asked, watching her mother tie a small bowline loop in the end of the anchor line.

"A lot of African and Indian Trinidadians can't swim," Tammy said. "Sometimes they go too far out and get caught in the current. It's not uncommon."

"You're white and you can't swim," Meiko said.

"It's not racist if it's a fact," Tammy said.

"But you can't swim."

"I'm the exception, besides I would never go in the ocean, so I can't drown."

"You almost did," Meiko said.

"Touché," Julie said.

Julie fed the line back through the small bowline loop and turned the anchor line into a sort of cowboy's lasso. She pulled on it, testing its strength, before motoring over to the body. She put the engine in neutral as they approached. Tammy turned away and the dinghy bumped the dead man with a dull thud.

"You sure you want to do this?" Tammy asked.

"I don't think we have any choice." Julie reached over the side. She bit her lower lip, trying to take her mind off of her churning stomach. Up close the body stank. She held her breath and stretched her arm out, but her stomach heaved before she could get the line around the feet and she vomited over the side. The current had the body and by the time Julie stopped heaving it was several boat lengths away.

"I don't like this," Tammy said.

"Me either," Julie said. She splashed seawater on the side of the dinghy, cleaning it off. Then she looked out at the body again, frowned and turned toward Tammy. "We'll do it your way and leave it for the cops."

"We can't let it drift away," Meiko said.

"Oh, yes we can," Tammy said. "We'll just speed to the yacht club and call the coast guard. It's their problem, that's what they get paid for."

"Can't we tow it to one of the islands and tie it to a tree?" Meiko said.

"Even if we could get it there the corbeau birds would finish it off before we got to the yacht club. In fact I'm surprised they haven't already," Tammy said.

"It must have just floated in." Meiko looked up at the vultures circling above the small islands.

"But from where?" Tammy asked.

"I don't know. Port of Spain, maybe," Meiko said.

"I don't think so," Julie said. Then she gave it the gas, shooting the dinghy over the waves toward the yacht club.

"They'll never find it, you know," Meiko said over the roar of the outboard.

"Not our problem," Tammy said. That was the last word spoken among the three women until Julie backed off the gas twenty minutes later and they were motoring into the yacht club.

There was a reception committee waiting for them as they approached *Fallen Angel*. Two men, one staring out at them with his hand in front of his face to shield his eyes from the sun. Sweat was beading up on his forehead and Julie wondered why he didn't wipe it off. He stood straight backed and she thought that he probably even starched his tie. When they got closer she saw the sweat ringing his collar. His suit was cold British perfect on this hot Trinidadian day.

The other man wore a rumpled police uniform, and the way he shifted back and forth on his feet and refused to make eye contact told Julie that something was wrong. Both men were dark-skinned African Trinidadians.

"Police," Tammy said. "And they don't look happy." The uniformed officer looked at the ground as they approached. The other man caught Tammy's gaze and held it for a second, then he also turned away.

"How'd they know?" Meiko asked. Julie cut the engine. The still silence, coupled with the downcast eyes of the policemen, gave the morning a funereal atmosphere.

"They don't," Julie said. "It's something else." She coasted the dinghy toward the swim ladder hanging over the starboard side of the boat. Tammy stood in the front with the painter in her hand and grabbed onto the ladder, stopping the forward motion of the dinghy. Then she tied the painter on to the lifelines with a double half hitch, before stepping onto the ladder and climbing up to the deck. Once up she turned to offer Meiko a hand. Julie followed her daughter and together the three of them faced the policemen on the dock.

"What can we do for you boys?" Tammy asked. She lowered her head as she crossed under the boom.

The man in the suit raised his eyes and pretended a smile, showing two gold front teeth that did more to make him look like a rabbit that the tough image he was trying to project. But he didn't speak.

"I don't bite," she said. There was no humor in her voice.

Julie and Meiko crossed under the boom and stood next to Tammy, one on each side, but the sweating policeman had locked onto Tammy's eyes and he couldn't look away until she released him. She smiled and the policeman came to life.

"Can we come aboard, Miss Drake?" the man asked, wiping the backs of his hands off on his pants. He might be used to the hot sun, but he was melting in front of Tammy Drake, Julie thought.

"Mrs. Tanaka is the captain here," Tammy said. "You'll have to ask her." Tammy turned to look at Julie and Julie nodded her head in assent. "She says, yes," Tammy said. The two policemen stepped from the dock to the deck, both keeping a respectable distance from Tammy.

"It's hot. Would you men like something cold to drink?" Julie asked, as she slid open the forward hatch. A slight breeze started to pick up and Julie looked south to the mountains to see if there was going to be any rain.

"I'd like a soda if you have one," the uniformed man said. His voice was squeaky and high.

"Yes a soda would be nice," the policeman in the suit said, "if it's not too much trouble."

"Come on down then," Julie said. She went down the ladder followed by her daughter, Tammy, and the two policemen.

"Hot down here," the uniform said.

"No air-conditioning, sorry," Julie said. She reached overhead and opened a hatch, but the slight breeze above did little to cool the people below.

"I'll get the other two, Mom," Meiko said. She opened two more hatches.

"I've never been on a boat before," the suit said. "Everything is so small."

"Rather large actually," Tammy said, "for a boat."

"Everything's relative," the suit said. Julie decided she didn't like the man.

"Almost time for lunch," the uniform said. The suit shot him a look that could melt steel and Julie knew that something was wrong.

"*Fallen Angel, Fallen Angel,* are you down there, Julie?" The voice carried the ring of a true southern belle.

"Yes, Alice, I'm here," Julie said, and sighed.

"I'm coming right down. It's so sad." Julie and Meiko exchanged glances.

"Mom?" Meiko whispered.

"It's okay, she means well," Julie whispered back.

"How are you bearing up, dear?" Alice Fuller said, coming down the ladder. She had a sixteen-year-old voice inside of a sixty-year-old body. She reached out for Julie with arthritic hands, and when she didn't respond to the hug Alice dropped her arms, turning toward the two policemen. Her misty eyes turned to slits and Julie saw the fury boiling as Alice tightened up her wrinkled face and stuck out her jaw.

"You men get off," she said. She didn't sound sixteen anymore.

"No ma'am not yet. We can't. We have a job to do," the senior officer said. He was sweating through his suit, big wet rings under his arms.

"And when did you plan on doing it? After tea?" The old woman advanced toward the shrinking policeman and fixed him with a stare that caused him to sweat even more.

"Just now, we're doing it just now."

"What is it? Why are you here?" Julie balled her fists and braced herself for the worst.

"I'm sorry to tell you this," the suit said. "There is no easy way." He turned toward his uniformed companion for help, but the other policeman looked away.

"Just tell me," she said. Ice circled and stabbed at her heart.

"The sailing yacht *Stardust* exploded and sank off the California coast five days ago. All hands were lost. I'm sorry."

"Mom!" Meiko clutched Julie's hand.

"Are they sure?" Julie said. Tammy took her other hand.

"I believe so," the suit said.

"Do I have to do anything?" Julie stammered.

"No, ma'am, not for us. Immigration might want you to remove your husband from the crew list, but, as far as we're concerned, our job's finished here. Again, I'm sorry."

"There is something wrong with you two," Alice said. "And if I was a man I'd thrash you." She turned toward Tammy. "They were up in the bar, drinking cold beer and telling anybody and everybody about how Hideo was on that boat that blew up. But somehow when they have to tell his wife they lose not only their courage, but their decency as well."

"Just making a little talk is all," the suit said. "Everybody likes a little talk."

"I think you men can go now," Tammy said.

"Yes, Miss Drake," the suit said. The three younger women stood holding hands as he went up the ladder, followed by the hungry policeman who didn't want to work into his lunch hour. Usually Julie loved the Trinidadians, but sometimes she hated them. This was one of those times.

"We never did get our soda," the uniform said, his voice drifting from down the dock.

"Shut up, they can hear you," the suit answered, and Julie realized that she'd forgotten to tell them about the body.

"Mom," Meiko said, tears streaming down her cheeks. Julie hugged her daughter and bit into her lower lip, but she was unable to hold it back and she wept too. Hideo was older and she'd always known that someday she'd have to go on without him, but she'd expected more time.

"Honey, we're all so sorry," Alice said. "If there's anything you need, you come to us. We're family, all of us. We stick together. Remember that. And remember that we love you."

"Thank you, Alice," Julie said.

"I better go check on Chad. Remember what I said."

"How is he?" Julie said, numb.

"Better today. It was a nasty flu." This time when Alice opened her arms Julie fell into the hug. Then she was up the ladder and gone.

Julie and Meiko sat on the starboard settee, holding hands and sobbing. Tammy sat on the settee opposite and silently waited for the two women to work through their grief, and after awhile the crying eased up.

"What are you going to do now?" Tammy asked. She was shredding a napkin, turning it into paper snowflakes on the floor.

"I don't know," Julie turned to look at her. Julie had thought it was a good thing that Meiko had found a friend in Trinidad when she started hanging around with Tammy, but she was falling under the singer's spell and it worried Julie.

"Are you going to keep the boat?" Tammy asked. Her concern sincere.

Julie shivered. Quiet ruled the salon. The sound of the ocean lapping against the sides of *Fallen Angel* and the creak of the dock lines as the boat swayed dominated the room for a few seconds before she answered.

"I don't know that either," she said. "The boat is really all we have. I think we're about out of money. We were counting on what Hideo was going to make on this delivery just to get through the next couple of months. We were in the boatyards so much and for so long, and it seems like everything they did had to be done over, some things three times. It wound up costing so much more than they said it would."

"But don't they have to stick to what they say?" Meiko said.

"In America they do, but not here." Julie paused, the bitterness evident in her voice. Then she said, "I'm sorry, Tammy, I know Victor's your brother, but Drake's was just as bad as Corbeau's."

"I know you got screwed in the yards, but at least you can understand Victor's phony British accent. I can't tell you how many times Dieter has gone on speaking German in front of me like I'm not even there," Tammy said.

"Maybe it's a mistake," Meiko said. "Maybe he's in a life raft."

"It's no mistake, Honey," Tammy said. "If the boat was lost at sea, maybe, but not off California. They have a real coast guard there. If there was any chance that he'd survived, we'd know it. I'm sorry. I'm just so sorry."

"Hello the boat," a crisp voice called out, followed by a rapping on the hull.

"I'll see who it is," Tammy said. She brushed her bangs out of her eyes, and went up the up the ladder.

"Mrs. Tanaka," the voice hailed. It sounded like it belonged to a friendly man, Julie thought, and it sounded American.

"I'm here," Julie said, and she followed Tammy up.

"Mrs. Tanaka?" the man said. Julie poked her head through the hatch. The first thing she noticed about him was his shaved head. The second, his window-clear blue eyes.

"Yes," Julie squinted against the bright sun.

"Mrs. Hideo Tanaka?"

"Were you expecting someone older, or more Japanese?" She met his cold stare with one of her own.

"I'm sorry," he said, but she knew he wasn't. "I'm Bill Broxton, but you can call me Broxton, everybody does." He handed her a leather wallet, open so that she could see his identification. His smile seemed pasted on, and his good old boy attitude wasn't welcome.

"Drug Enforcement Agency," she said, handing back his wallet.

"Yes, ma'am." He snapped it closed and stuffed it in his hip pocket. There wasn't a drop of sweat on him. He was as cool as his ice-blue eyes.

"Why does the DEA want to talk to me?" She reached out to one of the shrouds and held onto it.

"Could we talk alone?" He nodded toward Tammy.

"Not without me you can't," Meiko said, coming through the hatch. She took her mother's hand.

"And I'd like to hear as well," Tammy said.

"It's about your husband, ma'am."

"I'm sorry, I can't help you. I was just informed that my husband is dead."

"We know that, ma'am. It's something I'd like to talk about, but alone." His good old boy voice turned hard.

"Do you shave your head so you'll look dangerous? Like a tough guy?" Julie said, and for a flash of a second she thought she saw the corners of his lips start to curve upward and his cold stare melt a little, but he checked himself, flattened out what might have been a pleasant smile, and forced the twinkle from his eyes.

"No ma'am." He ran a hand across his head, lingering for a second on a scar above his right ear.

"Then why?"

The DEA man shuffled his feet and didn't answer. Tammy and Meiko stood on deck, watching and listening. Meiko's eyes were tearing up and she was digging the nails of her left hand into the palm to keep from crying. Tammy took the girl's hand in hers and Meiko relaxed the pressure.

"Come on, Honey, let's take a short walk." Tammy led Meiko across the deck. They were standing next to the DEA man and Tammy looked into his hard eyes.

"I'll give you five minutes with my friend," Tammy said, the cold in her eyes every bit a match for his. "You won't come on the boat and I won't let you out of my sight." She led Meiko to a bench on the dock, just out of earshot. The two woman sat facing the sea. Meiko buried her head in Tammy's breasts and softly cried, while Tammy had her head turned, eyes on the DEA man.

"Your friend gives orders like she expects them to be obeyed." Broxton dropped his hands to his sides.

"Tammy would never give an order she couldn't enforce," Julie said.

"And if I come on the boat?"

"How long can you tread water?"

"I don't follow."

"All she has to do is raise her hand and every Trini on the dock will come running and you'll go swimming."

"Then I better stay where I am and not give her a reason to raise that hand." For a second Julie thought Broxton was making fun of her, but there was no twinkle in his hard eyes and she realized that he must know who Tammy was.

"Three bodies washed up on the beach the day the sailing yacht *Stardust* went down. A German national, A Cuban from Miami, known to be working for the Salizar family, a Colombian drug cartel, and your husband."

"And you think my husband had something to do with drug trafficking?"

"No, we think he was just in the wrong place at the wrong time. But there are some questions that have to be asked."

"Mr. Broxton, I was informed less than five minutes ago that my husband is dead and now you come here with this. I think you should leave."

"This is very important, Mrs. Tanaka, or I wouldn't have intruded."

"You'll have to come back later."

"I'm sorry about your husband, but really these questions shouldn't wait."

"Tammy," Julie said, loud enough for her friend to hear, "Mr. Broxton is leaving now."

Tammy started to rise.

"Okay, you win, but I'll be back," Broxton said.

"And I'll be expecting you," Julie said.

CHAPTER TWO

THE ALARM ON JULIE'S WATCH went off at five in the morning and she opened her eyes from a sad sleep. She reached over and nudged her husband in the back. She'd had a horrible dream. Then she realized it was no dream. It wasn't her husband sleeping next to her, but her daughter. Meiko hadn't slept with her since she was ten years old.

She stared through the overhead hatch and studied the heavens. He'd never hold her again, never comfort her. They'd never sail the world together, never explore the South Pacific, never walk together again, never talk again, never make love again.

"Oh, Hideo," she quietly sobbed, "I love you so much." Her alarm had been set to pick him up at the airport, something she wouldn't have to do.

She closed her eyes over the mist and willed herself back to sleep, listening to her own heartbeat. Then she heard a quiet noise. Wood sliding against wood. Her eyes popped open, but she lay still, staring at the heavens. A satellite moved overhead, going from west to east, as bright as any star. She took shallow breaths, and she heard the sound again.

A drawer being eased open. Someone was on the boat. Not on the boat. In the boat.

She stifled an urge to scream out. Guns were illegal in Trinidad, but plenty of people had them. She lay her hand on Meiko's side. She was breathing the steady rhythm of someone deep asleep, but Meiko had always been like that. Any unfamiliar sound, no matter how muffled, could wake Julie. She was a light sleeper, while nothing disturbed Meiko.

She strained her ears, searching for another sound, proof that it wasn't her imagination. She heard another drawer being opened with a quiet burglar's touch. He was in the galley. Looking, robbing, stealing.

She removed her hand from her daughter's side. Meiko's heart was beating along with the ship's clock in the salon, while Julie's was racing, at least two beats for every tick of the clock.

She heard the faint tingle of silverware. A fork or spoon must have been jarred out of place as the drawer moved. She listened for another noise.

Silence.

She didn't move. Didn't dare breathe.

How could he have gotten on the boat without her hearing him? True the back hatch was left open at night, as was the one above her head, so the breeze could pass through and cool the boat, but he'd still have to come down the ladder and across the salon to the galley. It was a boat. The floors creaked. And the hatches in the floor groaned. A cat would be hard pressed to move through the salon silently, and that was no cat out there opening and closing and looking in her drawers.

Looking for what?

She tried to think. She wanted him off the boat. Maybe it was one of the local kids looking for a few bucks, but what if it wasn't? She didn't have much of value on the boat. They had been in the yacht club for over a year and there were no secrets in the small community, not from the yachties and not from the locals. Everyone knew they weren't rich. No expensive cameras, no jewelry, not even a television.

So what was he looking for? It must be a kid. Had to be. For a second she thought about charging out there and grabbing him, but something held her back. What if it wasn't a kid? He was awfully quiet. Could a kid be that quiet? She wanted to slip out of bed and peek out of the cabin and see if she could see who it was, but she knew she couldn't be that quiet.

She closed her eyes and attempted to control her breathing. She mentally counted backwards from ten to one, forcing her mind to clear and it came to her, like lightning from a dark sky. All she had to do was to make a normal, getting up kind of sound and whoever was out there would quietly slip away, just like they quietly slipped in.

She had to pee. She stretched and yawned aloud, hoping it sounded more normal to whoever was out in the galley than it did to her. She didn't hear any movement from the back of the boat as she stepped out of the double berth and went into the head. She turned on the light, dropped her shorts and panties and sat on the toilet.

She took steady, even breaths with closed eyes, but she heard nothing. When she was finished she got off the toilet and pumped some sea water into the bowl, then pumped it dry.

"Want coffee, Meiko?" she said for the benefit of the man in the galley, because she knew Meiko wasn't going to hear her, not the way she slept. Then she ran the water in the sink and washed her hands. She was stalling. She dried them. Still stalling. Time to take the plunge. She bit her lower lip and opened the head door, stepped out and started toward the galley, turning on an overhead light on the way.

There was no one there. Not a sign that anyone had been. Probably just a kid looking for money or something to sell. Or maybe no one at all. She'd been jumpy, she had a shock yesterday, maybe she imagined the whole thing.

Calm, she told herself, and again she counted from ten to one backwards, putting the incident out of her mind. She had much more important things to think about. Like what was she going to do now that Hideo was gone? She didn't have much money, and no way to earn any more. She'd never had a job. Never earned a cent in her life. Hideo had been her life, Hideo and Meiko. She'd have to sell the boat.

The boat had been their dream. To sail the world. She couldn't do it without him, but she didn't want to give it up. The boat had become their home. They had designed the interior from the bottom up. It had taken all of their savings and she knew she could never get out of it what they'd put into it. She'd have to take a huge loss. The dream was going up in smoke, she thought, but then she corrected herself. The dream was dead. It died with Hideo.

She ran her hands along the top of the teak table in the breakfast nook opposite the galley. Hideo had build it with loving hands. She moved her eyes to the teak cabinets in the galley, also built with Hideo's love, like the whole boat, everything in it, built with love. Their love. Hideo's and hers. No, the dream may be dead, and she might not have much money, but she wouldn't sell the boat.

No matter what, she wouldn't sell the boat.

No matter what, she'd keep the boat.

She put on the coffee. She was still wearing the same clothes she'd had on yesterday. She slipped out of them and took a shower while the coffee was brewing, but the enjoyment she usually felt when the hot water cascaded along her body was absent.

She didn't think she'd ever enjoy anything again.

Out of the shower, she slipped on clean shorts and a halter top and went back to the galley for the coffee. She usually drank it with cream, but Hideo drank it black. She decided to have it black today. She sipped the hot liquid and tried to imagine what Hideo would be thinking now, with the strong black coffee in his mouth, while the distinctive aroma assaulted his nostrils. She would never use cream again.

"Are you okay, Mom?" Meiko's dreamy voice drifted out from the forward cabin.

"Yeah, I'm fine," she said, and she sat in the salon and cried. Images attacked her, the sparkle in Hideo's eyes on Christmas morning, his grin as she unwrapped a huge teddy bear on her twentieth birthday so many years ago, his true belly laugh, his hair, too long for his age. She wiped her eyes with the back of her hand. He was so many things to her—husband, father, friend, teacher, lover and protector.

She dozed.

"Mom, are you all right?" Meiko's voice pried her awake.

"What time is it?" she said, rubbing her eyes.

"You've been crying?"

"I guess."

"It's a little after six," Meiko said.

"Why don't you go back to sleep? I'd just like to be alone for a little while."

"No. I won't leave you out here crying in the dark like nobody loves you. I love you and besides, I need you. A bad thing has happened to us and I need you near me."

"Oh, baby come here." She was so overwhelmed by her own grief that she forgot about Meiko. He was her father and they were close. She started adoring him the instant her eyes first opened, and she'd never stopped.

Meiko sat and Julie draped an arm around her shoulder as her daughter snuggled close and together they shivered in the heat. It was going to be another hot and humid equatorial day and both women fell back into the dreamless sleep of the grief stricken.

Julie woke again to the sound of running water. Meiko was taking a shower. She refreshed her coffee and climbed up into the cockpit. She leaned back in the seat and inhaled the sea air. She watched two frigate birds riding the thermals above the swiftly moving clouds.

"It's really something, isn't it? The way the clouds move like that?" Meiko said, coming into the cockpit with her own cup of coffee. Her blue-black hair was glistening, wet from the shower.

"Yes," Julie said.

"It's like film speeded up."

"I guess you're right." Julie took a another sip of her coffee and she noticed that Meiko was drinking it black also. The air was moving overhead, but it was quiet and still below, waiting on the sun to heat the land and start the early morning breeze. The beginning of the day. Julie's favorite time.

"I don't have to leave," Meiko said. "I could stay longer. It wouldn't hurt if I missed a semester."

"Much as I'd like having you, I don't think it's a good idea. I'd never forgive myself if you didn't finish."

"But you need me. You can't sail this big old boat by yourself."

In spite of how she felt, Julie laughed. Ever since she could talk Meiko had been helping out. They were a team, the three of them, broken up only when Meiko had started going to college. As tempting as it was, and it was tempting, Julie knew she had to turn down her daughter's offer.

"I'd really love to have you, but we don't have to think about it for a couple of months," Julie said. She hated the fact that she could never make up her mind. Hideo could make snap decisions. She couldn't. She'd weigh a problem from every angle, then weigh it again, hoping the solution would either present itself or the problem would go away.

The sun started to rise and brought a slight breeze with it.

Something thudded into the side of the boat.

"What was that?" Meiko asked, with a slight shudder.

"Don't know," Julie said. The image of the dead man from yesterday flashed across her mind.

Meiko stepped out of the cockpit and looked over the side. "It's a waterlogged coconut."

"You know what I was thinking?" Julie said as Meiko sat back down beside her.

"Yeah," Meiko said. They had always been close. Like sisters, like twins.

"We should have told the police about the body."

"It didn't seem important after the news about Dad," Meiko said.

"I don't think they'd see it that way," Julie said, and as if on cue they looked up to see two uniformed police officers coming down the dock.

"I didn't think anybody in this country worked before breakfast," Meiko said.

"Especially not anyone who works for the government, and certainly not the police," Julie finished.

"Tammy must have told."

"Yeah."

They watched as the two black officers walked up the main dock and turned left toward *Fallen Angel*. They were walking out of step, taking their time.

"Looks like they're coming here." Meiko took a sip of her coffee.

"Yeah." Julie did the same.

The policemen squinted into the morning sun. Their uniforms pressed and neat, grey shirts with epaulets, black trousers, black belts, black shoes, black hat brims. One wore sergeant's strips, the other had no stripes at all. They were tall, thin, angular men, ambling up the dock, enjoying the day, both smiling.

Their smiles disappeared when they approached the boat and noticed the women watching them. Wiped from their faces and replaced by twin scowls, like children in school, caught sending notes when they were supposed to be studying.

"Mrs. Tanaka?" the one with the stripes said.

"Yes," Julie answered.

"We have some questions."

"Before coffee?"

"We're on important business."

"I have some sweet rolls," Julie added and the younger officer looked at his superior expectantly.

"Another day," the sergeant said, and a frown covered the junior man's face.

"Hello, *Fallen Angel*," a high, squeaky voice interrupted the policeman.

Julie turned toward it and saw a comical looking little white man, sweating already, in a short sleeved, white shirt with a dark blue tie. He wiped some moisture from his bald head and looked up at the two women, like a mongrel dog looking for scraps.

"Excuse me," the sergeant said, "we have business here."

"Julie Tanaka?" The little man ignored the policeman.

Julie nodded.

"There's no nice way to say this. Your boat's been arrested. You have to leave. I'm to see that you take nothing off but personal possessions."

Julie's eyes narrowed as she took in what the man said.

"It's legal," the man said, reaching into a briefcase she hadn't noticed and coming out with a fistful of documents. "You have to surrender the ship's papers to me and leave the boat. You can have a few minutes to gather your things."

"I just found out that my husband is dead and now you come around here sniffing like a weasel trying to steal what he might have left behind."

"Your husband owed money to Corbeau Yacht Services and he's not able to repay it."

"They're vultures, just like their name," Julie said, "and we don't owe them any money."

"It's not our fault if your husband chose to keep you in the dark."

"He didn't keep me in the dark. Our bills are paid."

"It says here they're not."

"How long have you known? How long did it take you to go to court and get your judgment?"

"I wouldn't know."

"Longer than twenty-four hours?"

"I wouldn't know," the little man repeated.

"Get out of here."

"I'm here to see that you leave the boat."

"Get out of here before I scratch your eyes out."

"I'm not leaving."

"Little man, if you don't stop bothering my mother I'll jump down there and kick the shit out of you." Meiko stood up and looked down at him.

"Officer," he said, grabbing the sergeant's arm. The sergeant shrugged him off and the little man stepped in front of the taller man and added, "I demand you put these women off this boat. I've got a court order and it's your duty to uphold it." He punctuated his words with pointed fingers, shaking them in the sergeant's face.

"Is it true? Did this woman's husband just pass?" The sergeant asked.

"It's not relevant." The man poked the sergeant in the chest with the pointed finger.

"It is to me," the sergeant said. He slapped the little man's hand away with a crack that could be heard halfway down the dock.

"You can't."

"Shut up," the sergeant said.

"But—"

"Another word and I'll arrest you and forget where I put you. Do you take my meaning?"

The little man glared at the policeman and nodded his head.

"Go," the policeman said, and the little man went, walking stiff-legged down the dock toward the club house. He moved fast. A pressure cooker ready to blow. The policeman had made an enemy, Julie thought, and so had she.

"Thank you," Julie said. She saw the policeman she had been so prepared to dislike in a new light. For him to strike a white man was a big thing, even if nobody in Trinidad would admit it.

"I am truly sorry," he said. "I didn't know about your husband. I should have shown some respect."

"You couldn't have known," Julie said.

"We have to ask you some questions about yesterday."

"About the dead man?"

"Yes."

"All right," Julie said.

"Why didn't you report it?"

"I was going to, but when we got back to the boat there were two policeman here and they told me about my husband. The dead man just didn't seem important anymore." Julie flicked a few strands of hair from her eyes with the back of her hand. She wished she had her sunglasses on.

"Do you remember anything about the man?"

"Not a thing."

"I do," Meiko said.

"Yes, Miss."

"He was white and he was fat."

"We already know he was white and the corpse was probably bloated."

"I'm premed, in Los Angeles. I've attended my share of autopsies. I've seen floaters before. I know the difference. This man was fat. Fat with small feet and close cropped hair. It looked like he might have had a bald spot on the top of his head, but I couldn't really tell, fish had been at the corpse. If I had to guess I'd say he was between four-six and five feet, a short man."

"Anything else?"

"Yeah, the man had a scar, big, almost like a brand across his chest. It reminded me of a lightning bolt."

"You've done very well. Most people can't give us as good a description of a living person."

"Like I said, I've been trained."

"How come you're not writing it all down?" Julie asked.

"It isn't necessary. From what the young miss has said I know who the man is. All of Trinidad knows who that man is."

"Who is he?" Julie asked.

"Don't you read the papers?"

"Not really. Ever since my husband and I bought this boat it's been all we could do to keep up with it."

"Michael Martel, Martel's Magic Manufacturing. He makes and ships magic tricks all over the world. Very famous, but not because of his magic tricks. He was the witness in the Chandee murder." The policeman shifted his weight from his left foot to his right and fixed Julie with a steady, brown-eyed gaze.

"The attorney general?" she half gasped, meeting his steady eyes. He wasn't the lazy policeman his slow, ambling gate suggested.

"The one and the same."

"I don't understand," Meiko said.

The policeman moved his eyes to Meiko. "The attorney general was murdered six months ago. There was one witness and he's been in protective custody until two weeks ago, when he disappeared. It's been front page news."

"How do you disappear from protective custody?" Julie asked.

"I think we'll have that coffee now," the policeman said. "And my name is Lawless, Sergeant

Leon Lawless. Please don't make fun of the name. I've heard all the jokes. May I come aboard?"

"Certainly," Julie said. "What about your friend?"

"He'll be going to the bar."

"What for?" The second policeman spoke for the first time. His voice was deep, with a touch of gravel.

"To arrest that little white man for assaulting an officer of the law."

"But he didn't."

"You saw him poke me in the chest," Sergeant Lawless said, and a smile lit up the other policeman's face.

"You want me to put him in handcuffs in front of everybody in the yacht club?"

"Yes, in front of everybody in the yacht club. Handcuff him and sit him down in the bar and wait for me. If he utters one word, smack him across the mouth."

"What?" The young officer's eyes widened along with his grin.

"If you want to keep your job, no words will pass that little man's lips, no ears will hear a thing he has to say. Do you understand me?"

"Yes, sir. Yes I do, sir."

"Then do it."

"Yes, sir. Right away, sir." He made a snappy about face and jogged down the dock toward the bar. He also was no longer the image of the slow moving Trinidadian policeman that she'd seen so often in her two years here.

"Seems he's going to enjoy arresting a white man." He swung a lanky leg over the lifelines and stepped on board.

"Seems so," Julie said.

"How do you like your coffee?"

"Black," he said.

"My husband drank it that way," Julie said, under her breath. She went below to get the man his coffee.

"Yes, your husband." Lawless followed her, uninvited, below. Meiko came down after him and they both watched as Julie pulled a cup from the cupboard above the coffee pot and poured Lawless his coffee.

"Have a seat," Julie said. Lawless sat down at the salon table. Julie and Meiko joined him.

"Do you want a sweet roll?" Julie asked.

"No, just coffee."

They sipped their coffee in silence for a few moments, with the ticking of the old brass ship's clock counting off the seconds. The man had something to say and Julie had learned that in Trinidad it's best to have patience, especially when dealing with customs, immigration or the police.

After a long minute the policeman began to talk.

"Four years ago my wife was taken from me. I loved her so much. We have three children, three girls. I thank the lord every day that they are easier to raise than boys." There was the beginning of a tear in the policeman's eye.

"I loved Hideo like that," Julie said, quietly. She reached out and took his hand. He looked her in the eyes and the hard questioner was gone, replaced by a bereaved man, still suffering over a wife he'd lost a long time ago. Would she grieve for Hideo that long? She would, and longer.

"I have a few more questions," Lawless said, easing back his hand.

"How did that witness walk away from protective custody?" Julie asked first.

"He just walked away."

"Didn't anybody try to stop him or follow him?"

"Why should they? It was his right."

"Now he's dead," Julie said.

Then Lawless changed the subject. "Can you sail this boat by yourself?"

"I think so," Julie said.

"Then you should go to Immigration and check out. You should leave Trinidad as soon as possible."

"There's no way I could do it today. I'd have to get Meiko on the crew list. That'll take a least a day. There's no way that obstinate man over in Immigration will do it any quicker. And by then it'll be too late, because that weasel will be back here with his papers and more policemen to throw us off the boat. I guess the only thing I can do is hire a lawyer."

"Justice moves very slow in Trinidad," Lawless said.

"There isn't anything else I can do."

"You should go to Immigration about an hour or so after I leave here and check out. The forms will already be filled out and dated two days ago. You and your daughter will merely have to get your passports stamped. Then come back here straight away and take your boat away from Trinidad."

"You can do this?" Julie said.

"That obstinate man at Immigration is my son from my first marriage. That's how I know girls are easier. He was never anything but trouble. Into everything and anything. Still, he minds his father."

"And your first wife?"

"She died in childbirth."

"I'm so sorry," Julie said, looking deep into his brown eyes.

"It's not your fault," Lawless said. "Others have suffered as well." His words brought back Julie's own pain.

"Why are you doing this?" Julie asked, but she knew the answer even as the words left her lips.

"Because you've lost your husband," he said, "that's enough. I won't let you lose your home as well. Make yourself ready to go. Don't spend the night in Scotland Bay. Get clean out of Trinidad. If possible you should be sailing through the Bocas by noon." Lawless smiled at her as he hefted his lanky frame up from the table.

"What about the man with the papers?" Meiko asked.

"He's going to spend a very unhappy twenty-fours in jail, but he'll be out by tomorrow morning. Out and mad and looking for you and your boat, and when he doesn't find them he'll be after my black skin."

"Will you be okay?" Julie asked.

"He works for a very powerful man."

"Who?"

"Robert LePogue."

"Should that mean something to me?" Julie asked.

"He's the lawyer defending Cliffard Rampersad."

"Let me guess, the man that shot the attorney general?"

"That's what they say."

"I'll be out of Trinidad by noon," Julie said.

"That's best," the policeman said, rising.

Julie and Meiko followed him topside and watched him walk down the dock. Then they started securing the boat for travel.

CHAPTER THREE

BROXTON WALKED ALONG THE SEA WALL, squinting against the morning light. He stopped a hundred yards away from her boat, then turned away from the sun. He fished his sunglasses out of his shirt pocket and slid them on.

Then he ran his hand over his shaved head. Should he be angry or not? She'd made fun of his head and his name and it bothered him, and it bothered him that it bothered him.

Others had made fun of his Kojak look and he always shook it off. His shaved head set him apart, gave him that power look, struck fear in the hearts of petty criminals, drug traffickers, and back stabbing colleagues alike. But for the first time in the ten years that his head had been reflecting the sun's glow, he worried about what a woman might think about it.

Something about her struck a chord where he thought no music would ever play and he knew he would never take a razor to his head again. In the few moments that he'd spent talking to her she'd wormed her way into him, burrowing deep into places that had been long empty. He blinked, remembering the vision of the sun glowing through Julie Tanaka's light brown hair and reflecting off her sparkling green eyes, and he smiled.

Lawless was still on the boat. He'd have to talk to her later. He turned and walked back to the clubhouse. Not with his usual man-with-a-mission stride, but slowly, like a boy being dragged from a big league ball game at the seventh inning stretch, because his mother wants to get out of the parking lot before the traffic jam.

He ordered his eggs over easy in the clubhouse and watched the young policeman put the cuffs on Henry Hackett. There was going to be one pissed off attorney in Trinidad. For a minute it looked like the little man was going to protest, but something about the cop's demeanor held Hackett in check. It was almost like the policeman wanted him to resist.

He was still in the clubhouse, finishing his breakfast, when Lawless came from the jetty, sweeping the young cop and Hackett in his wake. Julie Tanaka was pretty popular with the law lately, he thought. Then he paid his bill and walked over to the yacht club office.

"Anything for me?" he asked the girl behind the desk. She was a scatter brain, but she had an hour glass shape.

"Nothing." She didn't like him. He knew it, but he'd never cared before. Today he cared.

"Here, Lacy, buy yourself something nice," He held out a blue TT hundred dollar bill, the equivalent of eighteen dollars, US.

"Thank you, Mr. Broxton." She took the bill and slipped it into her purse.

He turned to leave.

"You did have a call though."

He stopped, turned back.

"Yeah?"

"He said to call him at home," she said.

"Thanks." He started for the door.

"But he didn't say who it was. He just said, 'Tell Broxton to call me at home.'"

"That's all right," Broxton said. Then he was out the door and back into the bright Caribbean day. He knew who the caller was. There was a reason he received certain faxes and phone calls at the yacht club and not at the embassy.

He stopped at the wall phone outside the office, inserted phone card and dialed direct. Four rings and he hung up and redialed. This time his call was answered at the first ring. "Is it you?" a quiet male voice asked.

"It is."

"The long knives are out."

"Do they want me whole?"

"No. They aim to slice." Whole meant alive and sliced meant dead.

"Why?"

"They found about a half million dollars in your secret bank account."

"What secret account?"

"The one at B of A in San Diego."

"Christ, some secret." He'd been depositing three hundred dollars a month in that account for the last five years. It was automatic. It came out of his check.

"I guess they figure you're stupid."

"I guess," Broxton answered.

"Any idea how it got there?"

"No."

"You must be getting close for them to invest that kind of money."

"But close to what? And to who?"

"For you to find out, my friend, and fast."

"Do I get to plead my case?"

"No," the voice said, but Broxton knew the answer before he asked the question. He'd been branded a turn coat. The only thing worse than a drug lord was a DEA agent that worked for one. They'd shoot first, both his own people and whoever put the half million in his account.

"How bad is it?"

"Your account has been closed, your cards are canceled, your passport number and details are in every airport in South America and the Caribbean. And of course US Customs will arrest you on sight."

"Great," he said, but he'd expected it.

"You gonna be okay?" the voice asked.

"Yeah."

"Good luck."

"Thanks," Broxton said, and hung up. He looked over his shoulder, more out of reflex than worry, and he saw the man crouched under a trailered speedboat. He jumped aside as the man fired the silenced pistol. Broxton felt the speed of the bullet as it tore a neat hole into his Hawaiian shirt and sliced along his side, but he didn't hear the thud it made when it pounded into the brick building behind him, because he was too busy rolling and grabbing for his own gun.

A pair of trash bins stopped his roll and he scooted behind them, holding the gun in his right hand, hoping to get a shot at his assailant before he fired again. He realized he was too late when he heard the sound of a dinghy roaring away from the club. He jumped to his feet and ran to the water.

They were too far away for him to get a good look, but maybe not far enough for him to catch them. They had nowhere to go but the Yachting Association or the Five Islands.

He charged down the dock, leapt over a diesel jug and shoved aside two workmen carrying teak to a boat on the right. He slipped at the sea wall, but caught himself before he went down, and he ran on toward her boat.

"Hey *Fallen Angel*," he yelled.

She must have recognized the urgency in his voice, because she popped out of the hatch right away.

"Need your dinghy," he said, panting.

She saw the blood on his shirt, the gun in his hand and the dinghy fleeing in the distance. "I'm going too."

"No."

"I can't let you take off alone. You're hurt." She turned and shouted down to Meiko below, "Be right back." Then to him she said, "Come." She grabbed onto a spinnaker halyard, lowered herself into the dinghy and pulled the starter cord.

He dropped into the rubber boat after her. She was turning the dinghy before he was even in it and in seconds they were away from *Fallen Angel*, heading out into the gulf. She had the throttle half open as they swung past the breakwater and a breaking wave covered them both with spray.

She straightened out the boat, opened the throttle wide and the dinghy jumped up onto a plane. Broxton held on.

"We're gaining," she yelled to be heard above the engine noise. And Broxton marveled at how quickly she grasped the situation. No questions, just action.

"We'll never catch them," he yelled back.

"We will. Yachting is over two miles away. We'll be on them way before they get there." And to Broxton's amazement they were closing. She was right, they were going to catch them. She had a faster boat.

There were two of them in the dinghy ahead, the one at the engine was keeping himself low, and the one in front was keeping an eye on their pursuers and urging his companion to speed up.

Then without warning the dinghy ahead spun around and was coming at them head on. The hunted intended on becoming the hunter, but Broxton was having none of it. He held onto the dinghy painter and stood, offering them a perfect target. The rider with the gun took aim, but Broxton fired first and the man flew out of the dinghy in front. Broxton didn't see him hit the water, because a loud whoosh of escaping air whistled below him and he went over the side, too.

He lost the gun and the sun glasses when he hit the water and shock waves of pain radiated from his side. He struggled to the surface, treading water, and saw the dinghy ahead screaming away from them, headed for the Yachting Association.

Julie maneuvered the dinghy over to him and cut the engine.

"Are you okay?" she asked.

"Yeah." He tried to pull himself up into the dinghy, but the weight of his wet clothes was against him and he fell back into the water. The second time he tried she reached out and grabbed him by the back of his shirt and jerked him into the boat.

"Thanks," he said.

"Just trying to help."

He pulled himself up next to her. "Flat," he said.

"Yup, flat," she answered. They were sitting on the left pontoon, the right pontoon was flat, causing them to lean to starboard.

"I don't get it."

"Three independent tubes, front and two sides. In case someone shoots at you, you don't sink."

"He's getting away." They both had their eyes on the escaping man, and they watched, until he passed several boats at anchor at the Yachting Association and moved out of sight.

"But he didn't," she said, indicating the floating body with a turn of her head.

"No, he didn't."

"What'd he do?"

"He tried to kill me. I don't know why."

"Well, he won't try again."

"No, I guess he won't," he said. Then he asked, "Can you get us back?"

"I think so," she said. She pulled the starter cord and after a few seconds of moving the dinghy back and forth with a gentle throttle she said, "Yeah, I can get us back, but it will take forever against this current, better if we go on to Yachting."

"You're the captain." He looked at the body as it floated away.

"I've got a lot of problems hanging over me right now," she said, "and I have to leave Trinidad this afternoon. If we bring that back I'll never get out of here."

"I don't need a body in my life right now either," he said. "Let's go."

"He's fish food now." Julie pointed the wounded boat toward the Yachting Association and increased the gas slightly.

He nodded, and winced. The salt water was stinging his wound.

"Thanks for helping me," he said.

"You know, the day before yesterday I'd have been horrified, but my husband's death has overwhelmed me. I'm sort of running on autopilot."

He looked at her as she attempted a smile and his heart went out to her. She'd known about her husband's death for less than a day and here she was, driving the dinghy to beat hell, trying to catch someone that tried to kill a man she hardly knew.

"I'm sorry about your husband," he said.

"It's not your fault." The sadness in her voice almost brought tears to his eyes.

"Maybe it was." He hated himself for saying it, but couldn't hide anything from this woman.

"What do you mean?"

"*Stardust* was carrying drugs. I knew it, but I couldn't prove it."

"Why didn't you stop it?"

"Trinidad's not America. Besides, I boarded her one night and searched, and I didn't find anything, but they were there. I could feel it."

"You should have told the coast guard." She brushed the hair out of her eyes, but she kept her cold gaze on him.

"I didn't find anything, so how was I going to call the coast guard? What could I have said?"

"Then it wasn't your fault," she said, and her eyes softened. "It was just bad luck."

He heaved a sigh of relief, deeply glad that she didn't blame him.

"Why are you leaving Trinidad today? It seems kind of soon." he asked after a few minutes silence.

And she told him.

"That policeman is taking a hell of a chance, he must be a good man."

"He is," she said.

The sea turned a little choppy and they were taking some spray over the side, but she couldn't add power, so they sat quietly and slogged toward the Yachting Association.

"The dead man," she said, breaking the silence as they approached the small bay, "do you do that kind of thing often?"

"First time."

"Serious?" she said.

"Serious," he answered.

"Were you scared?"

"I've been trained. I always knew I might have to shoot someone someday."

"You didn't answer my question, Broxton. We're you scared?"

"I was afraid you might get hurt," he said.

"Really?"

"Yes, and it bothered me."

"Why?"

"Because I've always been a number one kind of guy."

"Are you married, Broxton?"

"I was."

"What happened?"

"We got a divorce."

"Why?"

"I'd rather not talk about it," he said.

"Why?" she repeated.

"She was having an affair."

"I'm sorry."

"The man was her boss. They'd been having an affair for over a year and I didn't know it. Didn't know till his wife told me at their annual Christmas Eve party."

"Did you love her?"

"That's the hardest part. I didn't, I never did and I don't think she ever really loved me."

"Then why'd you get married?"

"That's what good Catholics do when the girl gets pregnant."

"And the baby?"

"She lost it nine days after the wedding."

"And you stayed married?"

"For five years."

"Hideo and I were in love for every minute of every day. I think we were in love even before we met, and if it wasn't for our daughter I think I'd take my own life so that I could be with him now." Her words sent shivers through him. She seemed to sense it, and she said, "But don't worry, I won't."

Then they were in the shelter of the bay and motoring past the boats at anchor.

"Hey, Julie, flat tire?" The British accent belonged to Howard Hawes. He gave the weather on the morning radio net.

"Yeah, Howard, can you help me out?"

"Motor over and we'll patch it." He was a blustery single hander who'd been most places in the world, and he'd give you the shirt off his back if he liked you. He'd always liked Hideo and Julie. He had the dinghy patched and pumped up in no time. They didn't bring up Hideo, but she knew he was overcome. There were no secrets in the small boating community.

Thirty minutes later they were past the breakwater, motoring into the yacht club.

"I'm going to drop you at the dinghy dock, by the bar. That way you won't have to walk through the whole club looking like a drowned rat."

"About the dead man," he said. "It never happened."

"It never happened," she said, then added, "Shake on it." She held out her right hand and he shook it, wondering why he didn't want to let it go. But he did. Then he raised his hand and snapped his fingers in front of her eyes. She gasped as he opened his palm. There was a card in it, face down.

"How'd you do that?" she asked.

"Magic," he said, continuing to hold his palm out. She took the card from him and turned it over.

"Don't tell me." She smiled. "You've given me your heart."

And he climbed out of the dinghy and walked away from her without looking back. For years he'd wondered why he'd always used the Ace of Hearts for that trick. Most magicians had a dark side and turned over the Ace of Spades.

The outside bar was empty, except for two young Trini bartenders so busy talking to each other they didn't notice him as he passed through. He made it to his car without incident and was out on the two lane highway, headed for Port of Spain, before he realized that he couldn't go to the embassy. And he probably couldn't go to his apartment either.

He swerved to avoid a maxi-taxi full of laughing Trinis and smiled to himself. Others thought the Trinidadians drove like madcap crazies, but he preferred calling them flamboyant. Any car in front of any Trini was a challenge and they tried to pass it even as the car tried not to be passed. He glanced in the rear view and forced back a laugh. A yellow Mini was hot on his tail, less than a foot from his bumper.

Then a bullet punched through the back window, tore thought the passenger head rest and smashed into the dash above the glovebox. He grabbed a second look in the rear view. The passenger in the car behind was hanging out the window and he was holding a pistol.

Broxton braced himself, stomped on the brakes, locking the back wheels, and the Mini collided into his rear. He stiffened his arms, clenched the wheel, stole a glance in the side mirror and saw the shooter's neck snap back and slam into the door post with the whiplash. The pistol went flying across the road.

He kept his foot on the brakes and cranked the wheel to the left, causing the small car behind to carom off his rear, going right and onto the other side of the road. Then he spun the wheel back to the right and shoved in the throttle, bringing himself back to the center of the road and up with the flow of traffic.

He looked right in time to see the Mini collide head on with a Nestles milk tanker. The tanker rolled over the Mini like it was made of paper and then Broxton was past West Mall and on the road to Diego Martin, without ever hearing the screeching of the tanker's brakes or the screaming of the school children on the sidewalk who saw the whole thing.

He drove off the road and into the Starlight Plaza parking lot. There had been two attempts on his life and according to the sun it was only noon. Somebody knew where he would be this morning and they knew what his car looked like. A killer was waiting for him in the yacht club and another was waiting for him outside in case the first one failed. Somebody wanted him dead.

He pulled into a parking spot in front of the Republic Bank and killed the engine. The lunchtime crowd was filing into Joe's Pizza and he grinned at a young woman coming out of the bank. She noticed the state of his car and frowned back.

Only embassy personnel knew where he was going to be this morning and he knew them all well enough to know that none of them were involved in drugs or would be involved with murder, but if asked by the powers that be they would have given up his whereabouts in a heartbeat.

He sighed, left the keys in the ignition and got out of the car. He walked away without locking it or without looking back. It would be gone within the hour and in the morning it would be sold for parts in the Bamboo. Some things in Trinidad were very predictable.

He took his wallet and passport out of his hip pocket and headed toward the trash can in front of Joe's. He opened the wallet, took out the bills and put them in his shirt pocket, dropping the wallet and passport in the can as he walked by. Now he had only three hundred US and six hundred and eighty TT, and no passport.

He felt his side, where the bullet grazed him. It was already starting to clot. Barely a scratch, but it stung. He noticed people looking at him. He was still a little damp. Clothes dried quickly in a hundred degree heat, but the bloody shirt was grabbing attention he couldn't afford.

He went into the men's store two doors down from Joe's and bought a blue batik print shirt. He wore it out, leaving his bloody Hawaiian in a waist basket by the dressing room.

Now he needed a place to stay and he remembered when he took that Jazz singer to the Normandy Hotel. They hadn't asked for identification. He walked down to Western Main Road and stopped the first maxi-taxi that came along.

"Going to the Savannah?" he asked the driver.

"Going to Green Corner, downtown, you can walk up from there," the driver said.

"Fine," Broxton said, and he climbed in and sat next to an old man. He sat back and closed his eyes while the driver sped along the highway. The other passengers apparently all knew each other, because they were carrying on a running debate about rising food prices, the homeless sleeping in the streets, aids and a host of other social ills that Broxton wanted to block out.

The Normandy was just off the Savannah, a ten minute walk to the Hilton. Not as grand, but it was quainter and quieter and a quarter the price. Smaller and safer.

A young Indian Trinidadian came out of the office. "Can I help you?"

"How much for one night?"

"No baggage?"

"It's coming later," Broxton lied, forty-five dollars later, he had a room key in his hand. A safe haven for a day. But before going to the room he decided to go to the hotel restaurant and have something to eat. He entered and took a table by the door.

"Hey, it's been a long time," a slim waitress said.

"Six months or so, Jenna," Broxton said, reading her name off her name tag. "Do you remember all your customers?"

"No, just the special ones." She winked.

"What was special about me?"

"You gave me a blue one for a tip," she said, but Broxton didn't think the hundred TT tip was enough for her to remember him.

"You're a great waitress and this is an international hotel. You must get a lot of good tips."

"You shave your head," she said, "and you were with that nice coffee-colored girl. She was very pretty. Pretty like me." And Broxton studied her face, her curved up lips, her smiling eyes, her perfect skin and he smiled himself, because he saw the resemblance.

"She was your sister?"

"Right and you're the drug agent man."

"Not any more."

"You get fired?"

"Sort of."

"Didn't catch enough bad guys?"

"More like they caught me."

She saw a customer holding up an empty glass three tables south. "Hold that thought," she said. "I'll be right back."

He watched her go to the bar and order the drink and saw her write something on a notepad while the bartender did his work.

He took in the restaurant and concluded that it must be crowded every night. He wasn't surprised. The food was good, the service excellent, and the prices fair. He picked up the menu, but was sidetracked from it by the conversation at the table behind. The man was obviously out with a colleague's wife and the woman was pressuring him to make a commitment. She wanted to leave her husband and move in with her lover. He was having none of it and Broxton thought that the restaurant was the perfect place for this kind of conversation. It civilized the talk. Prevented the yelling.

And he remembered a similar conversation in another restaurant, not so long ago. He was the man. Marietta the woman and Bob Prichard, his friend, the husband. She wanted to run away, go back to the States with him and leave Bob. Like this restaurant, that restaurant too, prevented the yelling. They were civilized, but their affair was over that night, and when they spoke at the embassy it was strictly business.

And he was going to have to call her tonight.

"Penny for your thoughts?" Jenna said. He took his eyes from the menu he hadn't been reading and let it fall. She had a smile in her voice and a melody in her eyes.

"If they were worth that much I'd tell you," he said.

"You might be surprised at what they're worth."

"You don't want my troubles."

"I'm good with other folks' problems."

"Not mine."

"I'm working a double shift today. I get off at midnight. We could have a drink. The bar stays open late."

"Any other time," he said.

"If you change your mind, I'll be here, I'll wait till closing. Whoops, gotta please another customer," and she was off to take an order from a touristy looking couple on the other side of the dining room. When she had her back to him, he got up and slipped out of the restaurant. She was attractive, and under other circumstances he would have been interested, but he knew he wouldn't be coming back at midnight.

He decided to buy a newspaper, then go to his room and make the call he was dreading. He headed for the rack in the lobby, catching the desk clerk on the phone with a surprised look on his face, and he knew instinctively who he was talking to, and what he was talking about.

"I'll pay for it when I check out," he said, holding up a newspaper.

The clerk nodded, and with the phone still at his ear, he turned away from him.

Broxton walked out the door and stepped into the front seat of a waiting cab.

"Cab's taken," the driver said.

"Thought you were waiting for me." Broxton handed the driver a blue hundred, as he heard the sirens off in the distance.

"Where you wanna go?" the driver asked, shoving the bill in a shirt pocket.

CHAPTER FOUR

"I'M BAKING AND IT'S ONLY TEN O'CLOCK," Meiko said.

"Me too," Julie said, as she stepped onto the boat. Her head was still spinning from the royal treatment she'd received from the immigration officer. True to his word Lawless had arranged it so that she was checked out in record time. Both the forms and the stamp in her passport were dated a week ago.

The government of Trinidad and Tobago had no authority to seize a boat that was outside their waters. The backdates on the clearance forms made the little man's papers worthless, unless, of course, he showed up again before she managed to get *Fallen Angel* out of Trinidad, but that wouldn't happen. Lawless had said that he'd hold the man until tomorrow.

Julie started toward the swim ladder on the starboard side.

"Are we gonna bring up the dinghy now?" Meiko asked.

"No, we're going for a ride back out to the Five Islands."

"That's stupid. What could be more important that leaving? That policeman said we should get out of Trinidad. I thought that's what we were going to do."

"We are, but I saw something out there."

"What?"

"It looked like a small boat pulled up into the foliage, like someone wanted to hide it. That's why I almost lost control of the dinghy yesterday, I was trying to make out what it was." Julie stepped into the dinghy and started squeezing the priming bulge in the fuel hose.

"We're going back out there?" Meiko said.

"The water's flat calm. Not a ripple. We can be there and back in less than an hour," Julie said. Meiko nodded, as she stepped over the lifelines and climbed down. She was her mother's daughter and carried the same reckless streak of curiosity.

"Think it might be connected with the dead man?" Meiko stepped into the rubber boat.

"How could a man be dead in that water for two weeks?"

"I don't know."

"It's not possible. The current would take the body out through the Bocas and into the open sea in a matter of hours."

"What are you saying?"

"I want to know why it didn't," she said. She jerked on the starter cord. The engine roared to life and Julie backed off the gas.

With flat seas the fifteen horsepower Evinrude had the ten foot dinghy up on a plane, sizzling over the ocean, like a magic carpet flying over Arabia.

"See over there," Julie said, fifteen minutes later. They were closing on the largest of the islands. It was big enough to carry two abandoned buildings and a water tank, now all covered with tropical growth. There was a land bridge to the smallest island, fifteen or twenty feet long. You had to know it was there, because at high tide it was under water.

Julie cut the engine as they approached a brick dinghy dock that hadn't been used in years. It was covered in tropical green and easily missed. The rubber boat brushed the dock and Julie jumped out with the painter in hand. She tied it to a low hanging branch, then extended her arm to her daughter.

Meiko grabbed her mother's arm in a Viking grip, wrist to wrist, and Julie pulled her out of the boat. She could have jumped out herself and Julie knew it, but her eyes told Julie that she appreciated her mother's help.

"This way." Julie led Meiko through the brush. Julie was following an overgrown path, pushing bush and branch aside, clearing the way for her daughter.

The corbeau birds took to the air without protest as the women moved up the hill, letting the thermals carry them skyward until most were dots circling below the huge, fast moving clouds. Julie looked up at the vultures, so beautiful and graceful in flight and so awkward and ugly on foot.

They reached the top of the hill and passed the first abandoned house. Julie stopped to catch her breath and Meiko walked over to the building that had been beaten down by years of neglect, wind and rain.

"Careful," Julie said, as Meiko stepped up on the concrete porch.

"I'm just going to look inside," she said. Then she screamed and jumped back as several bats flew out of the dark living room, most of them missing her face by inches.

"You can go in now," Julie said, fighting back a laugh.

"No, I won't," Meiko said.

"You've scared them all away."

"How do you know?"

"They're more afraid of you, than you are of them."

"How can you say that, Mom?"

"You're still here. They're gone," Julie said.

"I'm still not going in."

"We don't have time anyway, we have to go. We're in a hurry, remember?"

"Yeah," Meiko said.

Julie turned away from the abandoned house, glanced at the water tank, cracked and overgrown, and the other house, then started down the hill, making her way on the path to a tiny beach below. The beach was only ten feet wide, but it would have been an excellent place for children to play, and when they tired of the water they could scamper across the land bridge and have the small island to themselves. It must have been a wonderful place once.

"Move over, slowpoke." Meiko scooted by Julie, moving so fast she tripped and slid part way down the hill before she caught herself, laughing. Then she stopped. "It seems wrong," she said, getting her footing and getting back on her feet, "laughing so soon after Daddy..." She let the sentence dangle.

"It's okay, darling," Julie said. "He wouldn't have minded. He'd want you to keep on laughing."

"Mom, look." Meiko bent over.

"What is it?"

"I don't know," Meiko said, straightening up. "It must have gotten tangled up in my shoe as I slid down the hill." Meiko studied her treasure. "It's an American half dollar on a silver chain."

"Can I see it?"

"Sure." Meiko handed over the necklace.

"It's a silver Kennedy half dollar. Kinda rare, because they only made them in the early part of 1964, then they switched to the copper-silver sandwich. Your father used to carry one of these, but he lost it on a stupid bet."

"What was the bet?" Meiko asked.

"He bet on Mondale over Reagan," Julie said.

"That was a stupid bet," Meiko said, laughing.

Julie looked at the coin and lost her smile. "The date's wrong," she said.

"Come again."

"Remember I said 1964 was the only year they made silver Kennedy halves?"

"Yeah."

"Look at the date," Julie said, and she passed the necklace back to her daughter as a slight shudder ran through her.

Meiko noticed the shudder and felt it herself as she stared at the coin. She handed it back to her mother and the electricity between their fingers as they touched sent tingles running down both their spines.

"I feel like I'm walking in the Twilight Zone," Meiko said.

"2124," Julie said. "I'll lay you any odds you want that it's not a minting error."

"What's it mean?" Meiko said.

"Someone had it made up special. I wonder why?"

"Or it accidentally dropped out of someone's pocket as he climbed back into his time machine."

Julie slipped the necklace over her neck and shuddered anew as the half dollar slid under her halter top and slipped between her breasts.

"Kinda feels like someone's walking over your grave, doesn't it?" Meiko said.

"Yeah," Julie answered, "just like that." She started down the hill, heading toward the small beach. She wiped sweat off her forehead and hair out of her eyes. Then she saw the overturned boat hidden under the foliage that overgrew the island.

Meiko came up behind her and both women stared at the boat. Meiko spoke first. "If he was too hurt to crawl up the hill to the shelter of those houses, he might've crawled under the boat for shelter, and maybe died there."

"And with the rise and fall of the tides the body gradually worked its way out from under the boat just as we happened to be motoring by."

"Something like that."

"That would explain why the current didn't take it out to the open sea two weeks ago, and it would also explain why the vultures hadn't eaten it."

"But if he was too weak to crawl up the hill, how'd he turn the boat over and why would he pull it under those low branches to hide it?"

"Exactly."

"Someone else turned the boat over, dragged it under the bushes and stuffed him under there."

"I think so," Julie said.

"You're saying you think someone killed him? That it was murder?"

"Yes," Julie said, fingering the half dollar through her halter top.

Meiko studied the overturned boat, then looked back up the path they'd come down. "Is that why you docked on the far side of the island?"

"I don't know why I didn't come round to the beach. Maybe it was because I was afraid of what we'd find, or maybe it was because of that," Julie said, turning and cocking her head.

"What? What do you hear?"

"Dinghy coming," Julie said.

Meiko started down the small beach.

"Stop," Julie called out.

Meiko stopped. "Why? I just want to see who it is."

"We might not want them to see us."

"Oh."

"Hurry. Quick. And keep down." Julie bent low and started back up the hill, moving fast, like a soldier in combat. Meiko scurried after her keeping as low as her mother. They were in the foliage and closing on the two abandoned houses when the dinghy rounded the bend.

"What are we gonna do?" Meiko asked, panting.

"Don't know. Let's wait and see." They moved behind the house closest to the beach and waited as the sound of the dinghy grew louder, till the chugging motor seemed like a jackhammer thundering along Julie's spine. She wiped sweat from her forehead, but could do nothing about the moisture forming under her arms and between her legs.

They huddled out of sight as the motor slowed, then went into neutral and finally died when its operator hit the kill switch.

"They're at the beach," Meiko whispered.

"I know," Julie said, and they both listened to the sounds of two men grunting as they pulled their dinghy up onto the sand.

"I still say this is a waste of time." The thickly accented voice traveled well in the still morning air.

"Kurt," Julie whispered.

"Yeah," Meiko whispered back.

"It's gotta be here somewhere." The second voice also carried a German accent up the hill.

"Dieter," Julie whispered, quieter than before. Julie knew both the voices from the three months they'd spent in Trinidad Yacht Services, Dieter's shipyard.

"There's the boat." Kurt said. "How do you suppose he got it here and how do you think he managed to turn it over?"

"He was a pretty plucky man," Dieter's more refined voice said.

"He was a fat slob."

"He had a lot of guts."

"If it's here, we're never going to find it."

"Not if we don't start looking," Dieter said.

"He was wearing it."

"If that's the case then we might as well give up, and I didn't get where I am by quitting."

"We can't comb the entire island for a key," Kurt said, "and even if we find it, we'll still need the number."

"I have a feeling if we find the key we'll find the number. Our fat friend had courage, but he wasn't ever accused of being too bright. There's a reason why he had his wife's name tattooed on his arm."

Julie strained her ears, but for the next few minutes all she heard was the rustle of the wind through the trees and she imagined that the two men were looking for their key. Again she fingered the half dollar hanging between her breasts and she wondered if it had anything to do with what they were hunting. And she wondered why they were speaking English when Kurt would obviously be more comfortable with German.

"How about up there?" Dieter's voice rose up from below.

"No way he could have made it up there," Kurt answered, and Julie clenched Meiko's hand and tried to wipe the picture of Kurt's face from her mind. Most of it vanished, but the picture of the jagged scar on his right cheek remained.

"We'll look anyway," Dieter commanded.

Still holding Meiko's hand, Julie led her into the first of the abandoned houses, the one Meiko had almost entered earlier.

"Mom," Meiko whispered, resisting, but Julie's tug was urgent and Meiko followed. They went into the musty darkness, through a small living room still full of worn and decaying furniture, into a dark windowless hall and on into a bedroom with boarded windows. The bedroom was almost as dark as the hallway, but a few faint slivers of light creaked in through the cracks in the boards.

Meiko pointed up and Julie followed her finger with her eyes and saw that a part of the ceiling across the room had fallen down over the years. Light peeked in through the cracks in the roof and she heard the rustling sound of small animals in the rafters above. Meiko tugged on her shoulder and pointed to the floor on the other side of the room. It was covered in guano.

"Bats," she whispered.

"Quiet."

"I don't like bats."

"They'll hear you."

"The bats or the men?"

"Both."

Meiko took her mother's hand again and squeezed it as they heard the two men outside. Julie squeezed back and bit her lip as one of the bats dropped from the ceiling and fluttered toward the door. Another, then another dropped and followed the first toward the light.

"Shit," she heard Kurt scream. He had been as startled by the bats as Meiko had been earlier.

"Just bats. Harmless," Dieter said.

"I'm not going in there. I'll stay till dark and search this bloody island, but I'm not going in there."

"Right, I'll go." Dieter said, and Julie and Meiko held their breath as Dieter entered. "We should have brought a flashlight," he said.

"I'll pull the boards off the windows," Kurt said. Julie heard him move around to the side of the house and then had to fight a scream as Kurt wrenched a board from a window only inches from where she was standing. Light flooded into the room.

"Can't see anything," Kurt said.

"Shit! Mother fuck!" Dieter yelled, then there was a crash as his huge form collided with the floor. "Come round, quick." Dieter howled and the women heard Kurt scramble around to the front of the house.

"What happened?"

"Stepped on a broken bottle."

"Should have worn shoes."

"Shut up."

"Can you get up?"

"Not without help."

"It's just a cut. It doesn't look that bad."

"You're going to have to help me out of here."

"What about the key?" Kurt asked.

Then Dieter let out a scream that pierced the air. Julie almost rushed out to help him, but Meiko clenched her hand tightly and Julie knew that she was right. Better to keep quiet and unobserved.

"Careful, you son of a bitch!" Dieter yelled. "It really fucking hurts." And Julie wondered once again why they weren't speaking German between themselves. And where had Dieter's accent gone?

"What do you want me to do?" Kurt asked.

"Just get me out of here and into the open air. Then you're gonna have to go for help."

"You can't get into the dinghy?"

"Not with just you to help. I'm gonna have to be carried."

What a wuss, Julie thought. She'd fractured two ribs and broken her right femur in an auto accident ten years ago. It hurt, plenty, but she didn't simper and sob and she didn't scream in agony. Her only concern had been for Hideo who'd been knocked unconscious by the speeding drunk driver. All Dieter had was a cut on his foot and he was whining like a little boy.

He screamed again and she used the cover of his sound to cross the room. She was still holding Meiko's hand and her daughter followed. Julie decided to risk a peek around the door and had to fight back a sneeze when the side of her face came in contact with the dusty door jamb.

Meiko tried to hold her mother back, but relented when she saw that Julie was determined. Julie slid her face around the door jamb in time to see Kurt helping Dieter hobble out of the house. She thought that he looked every bit as pathetic as he sounded.

"I want you to bring as many people from the yard as you can, we're going to go over every inch of this island. If it's here, we're going to find it, period. And bring that fucking doctor from Glencoe. I'm not moving one inch off this island without a doctor." Dieter spat the words with such venom that both women shivered. He was not the courteous businessman that ran TYS now.

"Yes, sir," Kurt said, and from the timbre of his voice Julie knew that he was afraid of him. She wondered about Dieter, so smooth and suave and macho. She saw two new sides to him this morning, first a whiner, then a tyrant. She hadn't found much to like about him before, now she found much to dislike and she was more convinced than ever to remain hidden. It would not be a good thing for Dieter to find them here.

"Get me down to the beach. I'll wait for you there. And don't keep me waiting all fucking afternoon, you understand me?"

"Yes, sir," Kurt answered, still the frightened servant, and Julie wondered what could ever frighten Kurt.

They watched from inside the abandoned house. Kurt helped his boss down to the beach. Then he started to pull the dinghy back into the water.

"Wait."

"Sir," Kurt said. The word was clipped short, like a German soldier being upbraided in ranks.

"I forgot the fucking phone." Julie had known Dieter on both business and a social level for the last two years and she'd never heard him swear. Now it seemed like every other word out of his mouth was an obscenity.

Kurt stood with water up to his knees as Dieter pulled the small phone out of his shirt pocket and punched the buttons. Both Julie and Meiko were watching and listening from the house above.

"Fritz, it's me. I'm out on the little beach on the nearest of the Five Islands. Get out here and bring about five of the boys with you. If you're here in less than twenty minutes you get a five hundred dollar bonus. If it takes you longer than thirty, you're fired." He slapped the pocket phone closed. "Now we wait and see if that bastard keeps his job."

"You forgot about the doctor."

"Shit," Dieter said.

Kurt turned away from his boss and started to haul the dinghy back out of the water.

"Now," Julie whispered, pulling Meiko out of the house. They made their way down the other side of the hill as quietly and quickly as they could, to where their own dinghy was waiting.

Julie, still in the lead, pushed the overgrowth aside and clambered over the dinghy dock. She hopped in the boat. Meiko jumped in after her and landed badly. She slipped and started to go down, but Julie caught her.

"Easy," she said, voice barely above a whisper.

"Thanks." Meiko sat down on the right tube. "What's this?" she said, noticing the new patch for the first time.

"I patched a leak this morning," Julie said. Then she grabbed the starter cord and was about to pull it when Meiko's hand closed over hers.

"What?" Julie said.

"They'll hear."

"Forgot. I was in such a hurry to get out of here that I wasn't thinking." She sat silent for a few seconds. "We'll have to row."

"Back to the yacht club?"

"No, Dieter's Germans would see us way before we got back, besides the tide is going out and I don't think we're strong enough to row against the current."

"What are we going to do? They'll find us when they get back, for sure."

"We'll row to the next island. It's not too far. We'll be able to make it way before Fritz gets here."

Meiko scooted toward the front of the dinghy, untied the painter and pushed off. They each grabbed an oar and started to row toward the island.

Off in the distance they heard the buzz of two or more outboards and they put more muscle into the oars. There was hardly any distance between the first and second island, but it seemed like the end of the world to Julie as they rowed against the current. She was afraid they wouldn't make it before Dieter's Germans came into view. She hoped they'd head toward the beach side of the island, so intent on getting to their boss on time that they wouldn't notice them.

"What will they do if they catch us?" Meiko asked.

"They won't."

"But if they do?"

"I don't want to think about it," Julie said, rowing even harder. Meiko matched each stroke. It was getting close to noon and the sun was straight overhead. The gray, rubber tubes of the dinghy were hot to the touch and Julie took a flash of a second to wipe the sweat from her brow. Meiko did the same.

The buzzing outboards sounded like an angry hive of bees swarming above their heads and Julie imagined them up there, with thousands of stingers, ready to attack any second.

"Harder," Julie said, and both women pulled with a dogged determination. Julie felt the sweat pouring off her forehead and she could taste the salt of it as it ran into her mouth from her upper lip, but she couldn't take her hand from the oar to wipe it off now, she needed every ounce of her strength to move the boat.

And the buzzing got closer.

"We're close," Meiko said, "but we're not gonna make it. They're gonna be around the island any second and they'll see us."

And the buzzing got louder.

"No," Julie said, and she pulled her oar out of the water and threw it into the bottom of the boat.

"Mom!" Meiko said, but Julie pulled the starter cord.

"Get the oar in," Julie said. Meiko obeyed as the motor roared to life and Julie gave it the gas.

And they couldn't hear the buzzing any more. They rounded the back side of the second island scant seconds before the two dinghies from TYS would have come into view. Julie cut the motor as soon as they were safely out of sight.

"That was close," Meiko said. "Do you think they heard?"

"I don't think so. I think the sound of the big motors on the TYS boats drowned out ours." A shudder ran through her. A man was dead, most likely murdered, a witness in an assassination, and it looked like Dieter had something to do with it, or at the very least, knew something about it. What kind of man was he? What kind of man had the yachties been doing business with? What kind of man had Hideo invited to their table on numerous occasions?

"Dad was wrong about him," Meiko said.

"He sure was."

"What are we going to do now?" Meiko wiped sweat off her brow with the back of her hand.

"We're going to wait till they leave, then we're getting out of Trinidad."

"We should've left right away."

"You're probably right, but then we wouldn't have known about Dieter."

"Maybe we'd be better off."

"Maybe, but we're in it now."

"How do you figure?"

"We have to tell the police."

"Excuse me, Mom, but you're crazy. We're going to forget this ever happened. When they leave, we leave. We get on *Fallen Angel* and we sail out of Trinidad and we don't come back. And we don't ever, ever, ever tell a soul." The fierce look in Meiko's brown eyes startled Julie and it reminded her of the agreement she'd so recently made with Bill Broxton.

"What about responsibility? You've always raged against women that refuse to testify in their own rape trials." But she knew, even as the words left her lips, how hollow they sounded.

"This is different. Trinidad is a major transshipment point for the Colombian drug cartels."

"How do you know that?"

"Come on. They talk about it in the *Guardian* and the *Express* all the time. Don't you read the local papers?"

"No, sorry."

"Like I was saying, Trinidad is a big deal for the Colombians. The attorney general was murdered. I'll bet dollars to donuts that it was a drug deal. Those kind of people don't forget. You go to the police, they'll be after you for the rest of your life. Heck, I'll bet if they even knew we were here our lives wouldn't be worth zip."

"If everybody felt like that then the criminals would rule the world."

"Wake up, Mom. They do."

"That's not a very pretty picture you're painting."

"How come you and Dad bought a boat? I thought it was to get away from all of that."

"It was, but—"

"No buts," Meiko said. "And think about this, if you go to the police you'll never get *Fallen Angel* out of Trinidad. They'll make you stay here and you'll lose the boat."

"All right, you win, no police. But I'll make an anonymous phone call as soon as we get to Grenada."

"And how long do you think it'll take the bad guys to figure out it was you? No. No phone calls. We mind our business and we let the police do their job."

Julie didn't like it, but she had to admit that Meiko made sense. But maybe in a couple of days she'd call Broxton, the bald headed DEA man.

CHAPTER FIVE

THE CAB DROPPED HIM in front of McDonald's busy fast food restaurant on Independence Square. He stepped out into the noonday sun and tasted the exhaust fumes. He moved through the throng and into the restaurant. The line was long. McDonald's had been in Port of Spain for only a few months and the locals were still fascinated with fast food that was actually fast.

He ate and watched the world go by from a window seat. Port of Spain was built by the British and had a distinctively European flavor. Independence Square reminded him of the Ramblas in Barcelona, a large walkway in the center of the street. Many benches, shady trees, old men playing chess, street vendors plying their wares, shoppers, businessmen, workmen, but homeless begging instead of children playing.

Trinidad hadn't been independent long enough to deal with its social problems, so the citizens barred their windows, bought big dogs, built tall fences, and kept their children at home. Across the room an armed security guard watched the patrons eat. Guards were supposed to make the voters feel secure, but they never did. The government had a lot to learn.

He was halfway through the hamburger and still watching, when he saw two policemen moving through the crowded square. Port of Spain was a bustling city, but everybody downtown was black. He stood out like a carrot in a cabbage patch. As inept as the local police were, they'd find him soon enough if he didn't act quickly.

He wolfed the rest of the burger, left the fries and went to the card phone by the restrooms to make his call. She answered on the second ring.

"Yes."

He recognized her sultry voice immediately. "It's me."

"I should hang up on you,"

But he knew she wouldn't. "I'm in trouble."

"Don't I know it."

"What are they saying?"

"I can't talk to you," she said, not answering his question.

"Marietta, I need help."

"And what can I possibly do for you? You don't need anyone. Remember?" Even though she was across town her words made him flinch. He deserved the rebuke, but she shared some of the blame as well. He'd never made any promises.

"I need a passport."

"It'll be a Z." He heard the snap in her voice. She didn't sound sultry now, and that should have warned him.

"I don't understand," he said. At least she hadn't rejected him outright.

"Passport number starts with the letter Z. Means it was issued outside of the United States."

"How will I get you a picture?"

"Don't come here," she said.

"I hadn't planned on it."

"I'll meet you at Rafter's after work. Five-thirty. Give me the photo then. You'll get your passport tomorrow, same place, during lunch."

"Thanks Marietta. I know you're taking a hell of a chance."

"For old times," she said, and the sweet sultry was all back in her voice. Doubly warned.

He hung up and looked at his watch. He had four hours to get a reasonable looking wig and a passport photo. There was a full service hair and body salon on the third floor of the Long Circular Mall.

An hour and a half later he left the salon and took the stairs down to the first floor. It was a small mall by American standards, but it was full of people, women hustling from store to store, teenagers lounging and talking, children busy blasting space ships to dust in the video arcade and a food court full of late lunchers. He wondered how they kept the riffraff out of the mall, then stopped wondering as two guards passed by. Both big, both carrying heavy nightsticks.

Why hadn't he ever noticed the security guards before? Now that he thought about it he realized that they were everywhere, the bakery, the supermarket, the hardware store, there was even one in front of the video store where he rented his movies. He had been wrapped up in his job while the real world moved along without him. Well, he was caught up in the real world now.

He had a passport photo taken at Photo Place on the first floor. The flash put stars in front of his eyes and the young woman smiled when she handed him the photo. The kind of smile he wasn't used to getting. He paid the cashier and was rewarded with another smile. He smiled back and then he caught his reflection in the glass camera case behind her and he understood. He hadn't realized it in the salon, but out in public, reflecting back at him, he saw it. A softer, gentler version of himself. The girl in the salon had done an excellent job, taking a woman's wig and cutting it down. He looked like he was in his mid-twenties, a youth with moderately long hair. Gone was the tough guy, macho look.

And he felt different. More human.

A young couple passed by holding hands. The man, tall and neatly dressed with a Rasta hair style, the woman almost as tall, pretty, with close cropped hair. Both thin, both smiling, both with the rest of their lives ahead of them. He followed them with his eyes as they walked into a jewelry store.

Engagement rings.

He watched them through the glass for a few minutes before he realized that he couldn't stand in the middle of the mall till five. Then he remembered the snap in Marietta's voice. And he remembered that there was a roti place directly across from Rafter's. He hadn't had a roti in months.

He caught another cab.

He liked his roties without the bones and he liked to eat them with a knife and fork, but Trinis ate rotis, thick crepes wrapped, burrito like, around beef, chicken, potatoes, or a combination of all three, with the bones and without the cutlery. He'd be eating carefully, and with his hands, but he had plenty of time to weed out the chicken bones. He took a window seat that afforded a perfect view of Rafter's across the street.

He was nursing his second Carib. He didn't like drinking in the afternoon, but he wasn't in the mood for a sweet soda.

"Next beer?" the man behind the counter asked.

"Sure, but cut me off after this one. Anything over three beers and I tend to fall asleep." Broxton was the only late afternoon customer, so it was just him and the Indian Trinidadian serving him.

A police car pulled up across the street, blue lights flashing.

"Do you have a back way out of here?" he asked, mentally kicking himself for not thinking about an escape route earlier.

"Yes," the counterman said.

"Show me."

"Big troubles?" the man asked, and Broxton studied his aging features. Sagging mustache, hair growing from his ears, cracked skin, but sweet and clear eyes, noticing everything.

"Yes, sir, but I didn't do it."

"What?"

"I don't know, but whatever they say, it's a lie."

"Through the kitchen there's a door opening to the alley behind. Go left to the first street, then right, there's a blue Hyundai, new, parked by the corner. Leave it in the West Mall parking lot," he said, putting the keys in Broxton's hand. Out the window they both saw two uniformed policeman get out and head toward the roti shop.

"Why?" Broxton asked.

"I have met the police, and they have met me. It was not a very pleasing experience. Go now." The Indian offered his hand and Broxton shook it. "Quickly. I will talk to these two policemen till they are very tired of hearing my voice." Broxton turned and made his way through the kitchen. People never ceased to amaze him.

Out the back door, he went left as instructed, but stopped when he saw a police car drive by at the end of the alley. Five thousand policeman in Trinidad and only a hundred police cars. It was rare seeing two in one day, much less two in under a minute. Whoever had the knives out for him had painted quite a story for the locals. Getting caught by them would be a bad thing.

And any second he expected them to come blasting down the alley, speeding, laughing, smiling, looking for him. The alley was a trap, and the only way out was through the back door of one of the businesses. The shops on the left opened on the street where the police were, the right side of the alley was fenced off. The high back fences of private homes. That meant big dogs, trained dogs, Rottweilers mostly. He hated guard dogs. He'd have to try his luck on the left.

He wiped sweat from the back of his neck with his left hand, and tried the back door of an auto parts store, two buildings away from the roti shop, with his right. Locked. He wasn't surprised. Sweat trickled down his back. His underarms itched. He closed his hands into tight fists, attempting to squeeze out the tension. An old trick that sometimes worked. This time it didn't.

He struggled to remain calm and tried the next door. Locked. The next building had an open barred door that closed over a wooden one, sort of like a super secure screen door, Broxton thought. Maybe the proprietor was expecting a delivery. He tried the wooden door and sighed with relief when it opened. He slipped in and shuddered with the loud sound the door made when it latched closed, but Rod Stewart was singing loudly, out of large speakers, about a big bosomed girl with a Dutch accent, and Broxton doubted that whoever was out front had heard him come in.

He locked the door.

The window in the top part of the door was covered by a blackout shade, the kind his parents had in their bedroom all those years ago, because his father liked to sleep late on weekends. He pulled the shade aside and peeked out in time to see a police car race down the alley from the right. A third police car. If he was caught, he was in trouble.

Letting the shade fall he looked around the room. He was in the back of a fabric shop and the room was cluttered with cloth. Colors of all kinds splashed against his eyes. Piles of cotton batiks were heaped along the walls in no particular order. Bolts of solids, checks, and florals were stacked in the center of the room. There was a small bathroom by the back door, a desk by the bathroom. It too, was covered in color. And the room was cold. The air conditioning was on high. Like most people who lived in the tropics, Trinidadians liked the inside of their homes and stores to resemble the North Pole.

The music stopped and the silence was loud. Instinct said hide. He turned to the bathroom. Then stopped. It would be the first place they looked, if they looked.

He heard muffled voices from the store out front. If they were the police he had only seconds. He clenched his fists again in quick desperation. The sweat on the back of his neck and under his arms felt like ice in the air conditioned room, mixing cold chills with nervous chills.

Time to act, and like a mole, he burrowed into a pile of batik, making sure his legs and feet were fully covered.

"I'm telling you there's no one back here." The accent was white Trini, the voice was young and female.

"He's a dangerous man. We're checking all the stores in the area." African Trini. Normal. Most police were Africans.

"A murderer?" The female voice.

"That's what we said." The speaker was standing close enough to touch.

"She was right. The door's locked." A second male voice. A second policeman.

"Told you," the girl said.

"Okay, let's go," first male voice said, and Broxton sighed to himself. If he hadn't locked the door the police would have searched the room and it would be all over. He took deep breaths and gradually slowed his pulse and allowed himself to think clearly. Marietta had called the police. He didn't think she would, she must really hate him.

He wasn't expected across the street for an hour yet, so they were just checking out the area to see if he was around, hiding, watching. They weren't going anywhere for a while, which meant that he wasn't going anywhere either.

He fingered the keys in his pocket and wondered what the roti man would think when he discovered the car hadn't been used. Maybe the roti store stayed open late. Maybe the man didn't have a second set of keys, but of course he did or he would have told him to leave the car unlocked when he left it. But maybe the second set was at home. Maybe, if he was lucky, the car would still be there after the police left.

In only a few hours he'd been transformed from policeman to criminal. Somebody very important, able to pull many strings, wanted him stopped. But stopped from doing what? Things had been slow. He hadn't done anything to ruffle any feathers. All his cases were wrapped up nicely, no loose ends. No wild speculations, that wasn't his style, he played his hunches close.

Except for that thing in California. He'd shot his mouth off about *Stardust*. He'd had a tip. He'd believed it, but it went nowhere. Until the schooner sank. Then they had to admit he was right. Whose feet had he crunched with that one?

He gave it some more thought and concluded that it didn't make any difference. *Stardust* was gone. No one was going to invest half a million, US, and hire a team of killers because he was right about a load of drugs that had already been destroyed. No, it was something else, but what?

Then it clicked. After word about *Stardust* reached the embassy he'd wondered aloud during a working lunch if *Fallen Angel* was dirty as well. And he'd believed it, till he met Julie Tanaka. He refused to believe that any husband of hers had anything to do with cocaine. But maybe *Fallen Angel* was carrying drugs and she didn't know.

But how? It made no sense.

His thoughts were interrupted by Rod Stewart's gravelly voice drifting large into the back room and assaulting him through the pile of sound absorbing cloth. She was cranking it up loud. The cops must be gone. But they'd still be across the street and they'd still be patrolling the neighborhood. For the time being he was trapped. But he was better off than he'd been just a short while ago. The two beers were having their way and he fell asleep while Rod was singing about broken hearts.

He woke out of a falling dream with a start and a shiver. He hated those. In seconds he remembered where he was and he wondered if he'd cried out. It took him an instant to see that even if he'd yelled his head off it would have been all right, because even buried under four or five layers of cloth, he saw that it was dark.

Stretching, he pushed the fabric away and sat up, then stood and stepped out of his bed of batik. In a few seconds his eyes were accustomed to the dark. He checked his watch, seven-thirty. A cool Saturday evening and he had no place to go, but one thing was for certain, he couldn't stay where he was.

It took him less than a minute to realize that he was locked in.

The windows were barred. The back door was latched and the barred door was closed behind it. He went out into the front of the shop. Same thing. Barred door, barred windows.

He looked up in time to see a shooting star though the skylight and he thought of Julie Tanaka, her fierce beauty burning bright as any meteor. And he saw his way out. No bars above.

Then he saw the phone. It was time to come in out of the cold. He picked up the receiver and dialed, let it ring four times, hung up and dialed again.

"That you, Broxton?" An unfamiliar voice.

"Where's the man?" Broxton said.

"Dead, like you."

Broxton didn't say anything.

"Oh, yes, you are as good as dead. You will never leave Trinidad alive. We are everywhere and we are efficient." The voice had a thick German accent coupled with a high, almost girlish sound. Broxton would know it when he heard it again.

"My mother was a Jew," Broxton said. "Just something I want you to think about while you're waiting."

"Waiting?" the voice said.

"I'll be coming for you, but when I light the fire that roasts you alive I'll be doing it for her, because of what you people did to her family." The man was screaming into the phone when Broxton hung it up.

Then he turned toward the small refrigerator behind the cash register. He was hungry, his mouth was dry, almost raw. Inside he found half a sandwich and three cokes. He ate the sandwich and drank the cokes letting the caffeine jolt through him.

Then he eyed the skylight. When he was younger it would have been easy, but he wasn't younger and it was going to be hard. The cash register would have to go. He unplugged it and set it on the floor. For a brief instant he thought about checking it for money, but he wasn't a thief.

Then he pulled the counter under the skylight. Standing on it, he could reach the ceiling and he wondered if he still had enough power in his arms to pull himself out. But before finding out he'd have to break the glass. He picked up a five foot bolt of floral cotton, climbed up on the counter, squeezed his eyes shut and jammed the bolt up through the skylight.

The glass shattered and rained down on him, but he was more concerned with the wailing burglar alarm.

He tore a large piece of cloth off the bolt, then tossed the roll of cloth aside. The high pitched siren urged him on. He bunched the cloth into a bundle and used it to wipe the glass from around the edges of the skylight. When the sides were free of glass shards he dropped the cloth, took a deep breath, held it, thrust his hands through the skylight, jumped, and pulled himself through and onto the roof.

Blue lights flashing in the distance cut into the hot Caribbean night and he wondered who was pushing the locals. They were operating well above their usual efficiency level. He started to move away from the approaching police cars. The asphalt tiled roof was hot with the leftover heat from the day and it warmed his feet through his loafers as he made his way to the back of the building.

He looked for a ladder or drain pipe, and finding none, he dropped to his knees, lowered himself over the side and dropped to the alley below. He hit the ground running, charging toward the end of the alley, determined to make it before the police.

He didn't.

The siren pierced him before he saw the car and he dove behind a row of garbage cans as the police car rounded into the alley, lighting up the night like a strobe light on a dark dance floor.

A second car followed the first and he heard two or more sirens on the street beyond, in front of the fabric shop. They were out in force. The man with the thick German accent had a lot of clout.

The two police cars braked behind the fabric shop and four cops piled out of four doors, all with guns drawn. Broxton shivered. The largest of the bunch started shouting into the store and two others began clawing at the barred door.

The barred door had the full attention of the four policeman and Broxton stood and eased his way out from behind the trash cans. The moon was almost full, casting ghostly shadows across the alley and affording him a perfect view of the policeman banging on the door. If one of them turned he'd be seen, cast in moonlight, an easy target.

He backed away from the cans and out of the alley, afraid to turn his back on the policemen. He crossed his fingers and said a mental Hail Mary, something he hadn't done since he was fifteen, praying that the car would still be there.

It wasn't.

He stared at the spot where it was supposed to be and clenched his fists. The roti man couldn't have known it would take him hours, rather than seconds, to get to the end of the alley. It wasn't his fault.

And Broxton couldn't stand still all night. Any minute the police would break into the fabric shop. When they found it empty they'd come looking. He started toward Green Corner and the maxi taxi stand at a brisk walk.

It was a hot night. People were out on their porches. Some said hello, others nodded their heads when he walked by. All would remember him. He was white, out after dark, downtown.

He glanced at the sun-faded movie posters as he passed behind the Strand movie theater. A James Bond movie was playing. He hadn't been to a movie in over a year.

Around front two young boys were buying tickets at the box office and blue lights were coming down the street. Broxton groped in his pocket and pulled out some money. He bought a ticket and stepped into the theater as another police car whizzed by.

The lobby was crowded and he felt the press of people as he moved toward the ticket taker. Inside the theater he fumbled forward waiting for his eyes to adjust to the dark, finding a seat seconds before the screen was hit with bright words on a black backdrop.

PLEASE DON'T SMOKE MARIJUANA
IN THE THEATRE AUDITORIUM.

And most of the first row lit up. Then others amid laughing giggles followed suit. Not everyone, but at least two or three in every row. Broxton tasted the pungent smoke as it wafted through the theater and repressed a laugh. The Rasta man next to him lit up a cigar sized joint and a young woman a few seats down was taking a small, tightly rolled one out of her purse. She couldn't be more than sixteen or seventeen, he thought, as she put the joint to her lips and lit it with the flick of a Bic.

Then he did laugh.

This is what he'd been fighting against. What he'd spent his life trying to stop. He glanced around the theater. No violence here. Just a theater full of people having a good time on a Saturday night.

He shook his head in wry humor. Only last week the United States Marine Corps had been sweeping over the country in their fast helicopters, seeking out the marijuana fields. After two weeks of gathering up and burning the weed the new Prime Minister thanked them and accepted a gift of five speed boats to further the fight against drugs.

Did the Prime Minister ever go to the movies, his cabinet, the senators, the police? Did any of them ever go to the movies?

He laughed louder.

"Hey man," the Rasta man said, smiling. He was holding the cigar between his fingers, offering it.

"Why not," Broxton said.

CHAPTER SIX

THE SKY WAS STILL, clear and blue, and the tropical sun was torture. She felt the heat prickle her skin and she envied Meiko's tan. Sweat rippled her brow and her mouth was dry.

"Don't think about it, Mom," Meiko whispered, but it was hard to think about anything else. The Germans had been searching the island for over three hours. She was roasting, she was thirsty, and her stomach was aching the way it always did when she missed breakfast. But at least for the moment, she wasn't grieving.

She fingered the coin. It had to be what they were searching for. The strange date on it had to have some significance or they would have given up the search long ago.

"I'm going to slip in the water and cool off," Julie said, and she wondered why she didn't think of it sooner. For the last three hours they'd been sitting in the dinghy, taking turns holding on to a scrub of a branch to keep the rubber boat from floating out to sea.

And for the last three hours Julie had been worried about the tide going out. If the Germans saw the land bridge, they might cross it and search the smaller island as well, and then they would find them. For the first time since she'd been in Trinidad, Julie was glad that the water in the gulf was dark and murky and not crystal clean and clear like the rest of the Caribbean. The murky water hid the bridge.

She raised her leg up and over the rubber tube and silently slipped over the side. The water cooled her hot skin.

"This is a lot better," she whispered up to Meiko. She had the dinghy between herself and the sun and she loosened her tense muscles as she hung in the water. Her left leg started to cramp up from being scrunched under her bottom for so long in the boat. She was reaching under the water to massage it when she heard the sound of the outboards starting. By the time the cramp was gone, the Germans were, too, their powerful outboards roaring and fading off in the distance, as they headed for the shipyard in Chaguaramas Bay.

Julie climbed back into the boat, cool, but still thirsty.

"We can go now. Right?" Meiko said.

"Right," Julie answered.

"I don't mean just back to the yacht club. I mean out of Trinidad."

"That's a problem. We can't sail at night, so we'll have to wait till morning."

"What do you mean?"

"I didn't want to worry you, but I don't know how to sail all that well."

"I know that, Mom."

"Hardly at all."

"What?"

"Your father and I have only sailed the boat with the guys from the yards. We've never been out by ourselves before, and we've never sailed at night."

"In three years?"

"The boat was in such a mess when we bought it. It took all that time just to get it ready."

"What are we going to do? If we stay in the yacht club that man will come back and take the boat."

"We'll have to hide out for a day," Julie said. " We can do that."

"Where?"

"There's an Island between Trinidad and Venezuela. It used to be a leper colony. Nobody goes there anymore. It's got a nice bay. We can go there for the night and leave for Grenada in the morning."

Four hours later Julie was watching the setting sun as it painted the sky orange behind the deserted leper colony on Chacachacare Island. She spent a minute worrying and wondering about the wretched lives the lepers must have lived, so far from family and friends, and yet so close. They were like her, alone, but not alone. They had each other as she had Meiko.

"It's like a little city," Meiko said. She was sitting opposite Julie in the cockpit and her words broke a five minute silence.

"It was abandoned right after they found the cure."

"Anybody live here now?"

"No. One time your father and I came out here and the army was doing some kind of exercises on the island. Another time some fishermen had a campfire going, but usually it's deserted."

"Can you go ashore?"

"Sure."

"Have you been?"

"Yes. Your father used to like this place. The dormitory where they lived still has all the beds, but they're all rusted out now. You should see the hospital. High ceiling, stained glass windows, it must have been very nice."

Meiko studied the hospital in the fading light and Julie saw her quiver. Three two-story buildings made their way up the hill. They were painted a sort of beige-brown and the roofs were made of corrugated tin, now turning to rust. Trees surrounded the hospital buildings. The patients would have had a perfect view of the bay. It was a hospital, but it was a prison, too.

"Pretty buildings for not so pretty people."

"Something like that, but they took good care of them. They had a church and a cinema and the ones that weren't too sick had their own little houses. Look." Julie pointed. "Can you see where the old road winds around the island from the doctor's houses to the hospital?"

"It's all crumbling back into the ocean. It's a shame."

"I think everybody just wanted to get away from here."

They listened to the quiet sounds of the evening breeze and the gentle lapping of the small waves as they splashed against the dinghy trailing behind the boat. In the advancing shadows the hospital across the bay looked peaceful and inviting.

Julie clasped the coin and bit into her lower lip as her mind raced over everything that had happened in the last day and a half. Finding the bloated body, her husband's death, the lien on *Fallen Angel*, the friendly policeman, the curious and kind of swashbuckling DEA man, and lastly, hiding from the Germans out at the Five Islands.

Staring across the bay, she was filled with a sense of wonder tinged by cold fear. She'd never sailed the boat by herself. Hideo had always had a couple of real sailors on board when they went sailing in the gulf. She'd never done anything on those trips except watch and worry about whether the two of them would ever be able to manage such a large boat.

But she'd done it. She got them to Chacachacare. And tomorrow she was going to get them to Grenada. She didn't know how to navigate, but they had a GPS on board and it would tell them if they strayed of course, if she could figure how to program the position into it. Before she could do that she was going to have to figure out what the position was. There were charts down below and a book on navigation. She'd have to study those just as soon as Meiko fell asleep. She didn't want to admit to her daughter that she'd been living on a boat for three years and didn't know how to find an island the size of Grenada.

A shooting star bolted across the sky and Julie thought of Broxton, the DEA man, standing in the front of the dinghy and blazing away with his pistol, like some kind of cowboy hero. She wanted to tell Meiko about the incident, but she'd promised to keep the dead man a secret and she kept her word. Instead she'd told her daughter that Broxton was in a hurry to meet somebody at the Yachting Association and that she'd given him a ride.

"Do you hear that?" Meiko said, breaking Julie's reverie.

"Yes, and it's getting closer," Julie said. She recognized the sound of a powerful boat moving fast across the water and in less then a minute a speed boat roared into the darkening bay.

"Speed Demon," Julie said, "Victor Drake's boat."

"I like him. Tammy thinks I'm nuts," Meiko said.

"He's her brother. She should know."

"He's all right, Mom."

"Come on," Julie said, "let's put some fenders out."

Julie went to the forepeak, opened the hatch, reached in and withdrew two rubber fenders and handed one to her daughter. Meiko watched as Julie hung the first one over the side, securing it to the lifelines. She copied her mother.

"When did you learn how to tie a double half hitch?"

"Just now. I watched you. I'm a fast learner."

"Are you guys okay?" Victor yelled above the sound of his engine. Julie thought his cultivated English accent made him sound a little gay.

"Cut your engine and come aboard," Julie yelled back.

"What?" Victor yelled, louder than before.

Julie ran a finger in front of her neck, mimicking cutting her throat. Victor got the message and shut off his engine.

"Are you guys okay?" he said, again.

"We're fine, Victor." Julie tossed him a line, then she tied it off on a cleat. Victor secured the line to the bow of the speedboat. When he finished Julie tossed him a second line, which he tied to the stern. Then, with the small speedboat safely rafted up to the larger sailboat, he grabbed onto the port shrouds and pulled himself up and over the lifelines with the ease of an athlete. Julie didn't like him.

"I came by the yacht club as soon as I heard, and your boat was gone. I got worried and came looking. Are you all right?"

"You came awful fast," Julie nodded her head toward the speedboat.

"I was worried," he said. "I thought something might have happened to you."

"No." She decided not to question him further. "We just wanted to be alone for a few days. We'll be back in the yacht club by day after tomorrow," she lied.

"I'm really sorry about what happened." He sounded pure Trini now and she had a feeling that by dropping the false accent he was reveling a part of his true self.

"Are you all right?" she asked.

"I'm fine."

"You look…" She paused for a second, searching for the right word. "Devastated."

"It's how I feel. We all loved you guys. Your loss is our loss." He seemed so sincere, but Julie thought the only love he had for Hideo and her was their money.

"It's hard to accept," Julie said, starting to revise her opinion about him. Victor was shaking and she sensed that he was about to come apart.

"In the five years that I've been in business I've never made friends with a customer, not till Hideo. I loved that man like my father."

Julie thought of the long arguments the two of them got into almost every night. She knew that both men enjoyed the verbal fencing or they wouldn't have kept it up for the last three years. They disagreed about everything. Politics, religion, technology and most of all the price of yacht repairs at Drake's. That was why TYS got half their business, and that was the source of some of their most heated arguments.

A light wave rocked the boat. He steadied himself by holding on to a shroud. Then he said, "You're going away, aren't you?"

"Yes," Julie said.

"You don't have to go."

"Yes we do. If we stay we lose the boat. TYS has a lean against it. Apparently Hideo owed Dieter money that I didn't know about."

"Maybe he didn't. It would be just like him to phony something up, it wouldn't be the first time he took advantage of a situation. You should stay and fight. I'll help."

"You know how it works. They'll impound the boat. Justice is slow here. The boat could be on the hard for over a year, maybe two. I can't take the chance."

"Can the two of you sail it? I could at least help you with that."

"It's wonderful of you to offer, but it's something we have to do by ourselves."

"It is not," he said, and Julie heard a spark in his voice that she'd never heard before. "You aren't very experienced and I happen to know that Meiko has never sailed a day in her life."

"We got the boat here," she said, her eyebrows arching. The wind started to pick up.

"It's one thing to motor ten miles and set anchor and quite another to sail all night to Grenada. The two of you will never make it, not with this boat, so let me help."

"What's wrong with this boat?" Julie had to fight to keep from stamping her foot.

"Not a damn thing, but it's too big for someone who's as inexperienced as you. Look, let me help. I'll not only see that you get to Grenada safely, I'll show you guys how to sail this thing in the process. You need my help and I'm offering, so take it."

"We accept," Meiko said.

Julie slapped her with a look, but Meiko ignored her and she finally surrendered, "Okay, you win. And thanks." Now that it was decided she was secretly grateful for his help.

"When were you planning on leaving?" he asked.

"We've already checked out. We were going to leave at first light."

"I'll tie *Speed Demon* to the old pier. We'll leave right away."

"Aren't you afraid someone might steal it?" Meiko asked.

"Steal from me? Nobody would dare." Julie was again struck by the contradictions in the man. So nice and so arrogant, like his sister.

"I'll follow you to the pier," Julie said.

"I can do it," Meiko said.

Julie looked at her daughter and caught the small smile and the slight way she was shifting back and forth.

"Okay, darling," she said, and she watched as Victor climbed back into his boat, and Meiko slipped over the side and into the dinghy. The rumbling of *Speed Demon's* inboard covered the sound of the dinghy's small outboard, but it didn't cover the way Meiko stared at Victor. She was in love, Julie knew it and she wondered how long it would take Meiko to figure it out, and what Victor would do about it.

Back on the boat, Victor was a whirlwind. He laid the chart out on the nav table and spent a few minutes explaining how to chart your position using lines of longitude and latitude. He showed them how the GPS worked, a wonderful instrument that used satellite information to tell them not only where they where, but what course to steer to get where they were going, and how far away their destination was.

"But then you don't need a compass," Meiko said.

"What if the GPS fails? You should still know how to navigate by the stars, with a sextant, and of course you should always be able to find your way around with a compass." His British accent was back, and he was being condescending, but Julie just nodded her head along with her daughter.

An hour later they hauled anchor by moonlight and Victor steered the boat out through Boca Grande and into the churning sea. "It'll be a little rough for the first fifteen minutes or so," he said, "but after we're away from the land it should calm down."

Julie thought she was going to be sick. The boat was rocking and jumping as Victor raised the main, and it heeled over to port when he unfurled the jib. The sounds of the wind in the flogging sails, the big American flag flapping overhead, the waves slapping the boat, the banging halyards all combined to terrify her. Her queasy stomach was about to give up her late lunch when the sea calmed as Victor promised it would. The halyards stopped clanging and the wind magically filled the sails and the boat slid through the water the way an ice dancer glides over the ice.

"It's wonderful," Meiko said.

But Julie still felt ill. The best thing to do would be to throw up over the side, but she didn't want Victor to see her being sick.

"I have to go to the bathroom," she said, and she started to go below.

"Be careful," Victor said as Julie went down the hatch. It was a challenge with the boat heeled over and she found that being below was worse then being on deck. Her eyes told her the floor was down but the her mind and body told her differently. Up and down were out of kilter. She grabbed onto the salon table to make her way to the bathroom, when she noticed both bilge pump lights glaring at her from the electrical panel.

They only glowed red when they were pumping water, and they only pumped water when there was a leak.

"Help!" she yelled, still holding on to the salon table for support, all traces of her seasickness gone.

"What?" Meiko stuck her head down the hatch.

"Get Victor."

A few seconds later Victor came below. He saw the lights on the panel straightaway. "We have to find the leak," he said, and he started pulling up the floor hatches in the salon. Water was rushing under them, coming from the stern and flowing down into the deepest part of the engine bilge, where the two pumps were pumping it back out into the ocean.

"It's too much water," he said, "we have to stop it." He opened the door to the aft generator compartment and crawled in under the cockpit. "Hand me a torch," he called out and Julie got the flashlight and passed it back to him.

"How bad is it?" she asked.

"Water is pouring in all around the rudder post. We can't stop it from above," he said.

"Does that mean we're going to sink?" she asked, as he crawled back out.

"If we don't stop the leak."

"How can we do that?"

"Do you have any packing material?"

"I don't even know what it is."

"Then you probably don't. We can probably use rags instead. The rudder post is in a tube that comes up through the boat. The tube is welded onto an aluminum plate that's bolted to the fiberglass hull. Someone has drilled through the plate and water's leaking in. We can cram rags up the tube and slow down or temporarily stop the leak, but first we have to stop the boat."

"Someone did this on purpose?" Julie asked.

"Let's stop the boat first, then we'll talk about it."

"Okay," Julie said.

"What we're going to do," he told the two women, "is called heaving-to. We're going to sheet in the main as tightly as possible and then we're going to backwind the jib."

"Won't that make the boat heel over in the opposite direction and push us around in a circle?" Meiko asked.

"Not really," Victor answered. "The sheeted in main and the keel will try to force the boat to go one way, the backwinded jib will try to force it to go in the opposite direction. The result will be that we won't go anywhere at all. We'll just sit here." And in five minutes time they were sitting calmly, bobbing along in the four foot seas.

"Wow, this is great," Meiko said. The boat was perfectly balanced and there wasn't a cloud in the star-filled sky.

"Yes, it's nice," Julie said. "Now what do we do about the leak?" She wanted to ask who would do such a thing, but Victor wouldn't know any more then she would, and besides, stopping the flow of water was the most important thing right now.

"Let's go below and check," Victor said. They followed him below and once again he took the flashlight and crawled into the generator room under the cockpit.

"Is it still leaking?" Julie called in after him.

"A little," he said, "but not as bad as when we were sailing, We have to stop it and I can't do it from in here." He came back out. "If we were at the dock it would be simple, but we're not. Someone has to go down there and jam some rags up that tube."

"You're not serious?" Meiko said. "We're in the middle of the ocean."

"We'll lose the boat otherwise."

"We'll lose more than the boat," Julie said.

"No," Victor said. "We can call for help on the SSB. We're only an hour out of Trinidad. We're pleasantly hove-to, all we have to do is sit here and wait for help to arrive."

"SSB?" Meiko said.

"Single sideband radio," Victor said.

"Not so simple," Julie said. "We don't have an SSB."

"Sure you do, just above the VHF, in the nav station."

"No SSB," Julie said.

"I'm seeing it from here." The British accent was gone. Victor was pure Trini now.

"That's the control head, it connects to the radio via a fiber optic cable."

"So?" Victor said. The muscles on his neck started bulging and his Adam's apple started bobbing.

"The radio was damaged during shipping. We didn't find out till after it was installed. Hideo sent it back just before he left. We should be getting a new one any day now," Julie said.

"That's not going to do us any good," Victor said.

"But the radio works, Mom. I've seen you talking on it," Meiko said.

"That's the VHF, it's used for short distances. For long range you need an SSB."

"Oh," Meiko said.

"Which means that we are in deep trouble," Victor said. "We should think about getting out the life raft."

"You can't be serious?" Julie said.

"If we don't get help in the next couple of hours the boat's going to sink. Those bilge pumps are handling the water now, but if we try to sail the extra pressure will overpower them. We're stuck, the life raft is our only way."

"The current will take us half way into the Atlantic before anyone even knows we're missing," Julie said.

"Do you have any better ideas?" Victor asked.

"We could just wait here. You said if we don't sail the pumps will keep the water out. We're in a major shipping channel. Someone will see us in the morning and we can call them on the VHF."

"That same current that would take the life raft out into the Atlantic will take *Fallen Angel* as well," Victor said. He seemed to be a little more together than he'd been in the last few minutes. For a second or two Julie thought that he might be afraid, but that didn't make sense, not Victor Drake.

"Every half hour or so we could turn the engines on and motor against the current. That would keep us in the shipping lanes, wouldn't it?"

"Yeah, that would work," Victor said.

"Won't they tow us back to Trinidad?" Meiko asked. "You'd lose the boat anyway."

"But we won't lose our lives," Victor said.

"We're not going to lose the boat either," Julie said, "There is no way we're going to let some creep sink us." And for a second she thought about the intruder, then she said, "We'll just have to fix the leak and get on to Grenada."

"We can't go down there," Victor said.

"We sure can. We have scuba gear on board and full tanks. You could go down and plug the leak."

"Not me," Victor said. "I don't dive. Never have."

"Then I'll do it," Julie said.

"Mom, I can do it. I'm the swimmer."

"Have you ever done scuba?"

"No, but I snorkel."

"It's settled," Julie said, "I go. Meiko, you and Victor can cut up a towel in thin strips while I get the gear. And soak them in Vaseline, that should help bind them together and help keep the water out."

Fifteen minutes later Julie tied a line around her waist. Meiko held the other end. Victor stood aside, watching.

"All right, I'm ready," Julie said, and they followed her to the swim ladder. Getting over the life lines was awkward. She'd never gone down the swim ladder with a tank on her back, and she'd never done it at night, and never in the open sea with the boat rocking with the waves.

But she made it without stumbling or slipping. She shivered when her foot touched the water. She had the rags in a pouch tied to the weight belt. She checked to make sure they were secure.

"Good luck, Mom," Meiko said.

"Back in a flash," Julie said, with more bravado than she felt. Then she slipped into the black water. She shivered again, but this time not from the cold. She sucked on the regulator, and drew a deep breath and held it, then she exhaled and dropped below the boat, into the dark.

CHAPTER SEVEN

BROXTON FELT FUZZY HEADED. The movie flew by in a haze of cheers and boos. When Trinis went to see a film they were absorbed by it and Broxton was caught up along with them, shouting encouragement to the good guys, cat calling during the love scenes and hissing the villains. And before he knew it the movie was over and he was on the street again.

He wandered up toward the Savannah, following a group of young people, two boys and two girls. The teenagers were still talking about the movie, imitating the characters, rehashing the lines, reliving the climax. They'd had a good time at the show and they were still sharing it.

And Broxton felt the afterglow. He'd smoked marijuana a few times in college, but he'd never enjoyed it, preferring Jack Daniels and water instead. Tonight, despite the mess he was in, he'd had fun. He'd been carried away by the film and for a few hours all of his cares were gone. It was easy to see why a man with a low paying job, several kids, piles of bills and a dead end future would go to the movies and smoke a joint on the weekend.

He stopped and looked at the sky, taking in the stars, like a child seeing the heavens for the first time. The teenagers kept walking and talking away. Their happy voices carried to him on the cool night breeze.

"Can you help us out here," said a not so happy voice. Broxton was jolted out of his reverie and his attention was riveted on the scene ahead. Two men were confronting the kids, asking for money. The one speaking was spitting his words through a filthy beard and matted dreadlocks.

"We don't got nothing," one of the young boys said.

"Bet you do," Dreadlocks said.

"Honest," the young boy said.

"You got some money for us or you gonna be fucking sorry," Dreadlocks said, and Broxton had the picture. Two men. Late twenties or early thirties. Unkempt. Street people. He moved closer. The men had their backs to him. The children were too frightened to notice.

"All we had was enough to go to the movies," the boy said, and Dreadlocks grabbed one of the girls by the arm, to keep them from running away, Broxton thought. The girl was too frightened to scream, but her wide eyes caught Broxton as he moved up behind the men.

"Listen, boy, you give over what you got or you be sorry." Crackheads, Broxton thought. The underbelly of the snake, the reason why he went to work everyday.

"Let the girl go," Broxton said.

Dreadlocks stiffened, but the other man spun around to face Broxton. He had a knife in his right hand and a glint in his bloodshot eyes. He was tall, six-six, half a foot taller than Broxton, but he was crack thin. Crack thin and crack crazy.

"You wanna mind your own business?" the man with the knife said.

"No," Broxton answered.

"You gonna pay you don't," Knifeman said. Brave words, but the knife was shaking in the man's bony hand.

"One way or another, everybody has to pay," Broxton said, moving closer, keeping his eyes on the blade. Instinctively he lowered himself into a crouch, turning sideways to the man, making himself a smaller target. He wasn't a natural like others he'd known, but he knew how to fight. Everybody did in the barrio, and if you were one of the few Anglo kids and your father was a cop, you had to fight just to keep your place in line at the school cafeteria, and Broxton liked to eat.

Knifeman came in quick, leading with the blade, holding it like a sword. The shakes were cocaine induced, like his courage. Broxton stepped aside, but the man was faster than he anticipated and Broxton felt the cold tip of hot steel slice across his stomach as he brought the back of his right hand down on the man's wrist.

First, the snapping sound of breaking bone.

Second, the clattering of the knife on the sidewalk.

Third, the scream.

Broxton hit him in the mouth, cutting off the scream and cutting his fist on breaking teeth. Knifeman left the ground, arms flaying, bleeding, and landed on his back, his head making a sickening thud when it hit the concrete.

"You can't do that," Dreadlocks said.

"Let the girl go," Broxton said.

"I don't think so."

"Let her go and you can walk away."

Dreadlocks was silent for a few seconds, weighing Broxton's words. The girl looked frightened, but she wasn't struggling and the other three teenagers, to their credit, hadn't run off. The four kids all looked to Broxton with hope in their eyes.

"You a bad ass?" Dreadlocks asked.

Broxton kept his eyes locked on him, but ignored the question as he ran his hand through the slice in his shirt and touched tender skin. He studied the blood on his hand and winced. The cut was starting to hurt.

"I axed you a question."

Broxton bent and picked up the knife.

"I axed you a question."

"Yeah, you axed me a question." Broxton deliberately pronounced the word the East Coast way, the way Dreadlocks did. "You axed me a question and I'm gonna axe your head off with your buddy's knife if you don't let the girl go."

"You want me, come through her."

"Then you die," Broxton said.

Dreadlocks cut into Broxton's eyes with a long stare and saw that he meant it.

"What about my friend?" he asked.

"You don't really care, do you?"

"No," he said and he relaxed his grip on the girl, thought for a second, and let her go, backing away. One step, two, three, then he turned and ran.

"Is he dead?" one of the boys said, looking at Knifeman laid out on the sidewalk.

"No, he'll be okay." Broxton didn't know or care if he was telling the truth.

"You hit him hard. That was real neat," the other boy said.

"We should move away from here, before the police come," Broxton said.

"But you're the good guy." This from the girl that had been held captive.

"They don't think so," Broxton said and the four youngsters followed his gaze to the flashing blue light coming toward them.

"Look away so they don't see your white face," one of the boys said. Broxton did as instructed. The two girls linked arms around him, one on each side. The boys moved in front and they slowly walked away from the man laid out on the sidewalk.

The police car sped by ignoring what appeared to be a group of kids leaving the movies and a passed out drunk. Neither unusual for Port of Spain on a Saturday night.

"Are you hurt bad?" one of the girls asked. He hadn't realized it till she asked, but he was holding on to them for support.

"Don't know," he said, economizing both words and strength.

"Can you walk?"

"Think so."

"What do you want us to do?" One of the boys asked, he wasn't sure which one.

"I need to go to the Normandy Hotel. I have a friend. Waitress in the restaurant."

"Kind of far," the same boy said.

'Shut up, Leon. We're gonna help him," the girl said.

"Bleeding," Broxton said.

"Alex, take off your shirt. Julia give me that little knife you always got in your purse."

"Since when you the boss, Wendy?" Leon said.

"Since now, cause I know what to do and you don't," she said. Julia was digging in a small purse. She came out with a Swiss Army knife.

"I said I need your tee shirt, Alex," Wendy said, and Broxton winced as the boy nodded and pulled it off.

"What you doing?" Leon wanted to know.

"I'm making a compress to push against the cut. It will stop the bleeding," she said, as she cut the cotton shirt in two. Half she folded. "Here," she said, handing it to Broxton. "Hold it tight against the wound. Not so much that it hurts, just enough to stop the flow of blood."

"Alex, take this and go over there and get it wet." She handed the other half of the shirt to the boy and pointed to a water tap in front of a bakery. The bakery was closed, but the tap was dripping. She wiped Broxton's brow with the damp cloth, then she ran the cool rag around his neck, under his shirt and along his shoulders. It gave him a quick chill.

"Take a few easy breaths," she told him, "and try to calm down." She couldn't have been any older than fourteen, but he obeyed, bringing the air in slowly and letting it out the same way, while she held his hand, giving him a gentle squeeze with each breath.

"It's quite a ways, think you can manage?" Wendy asked.

"I'll make it."

"Okay, you can lean on me." Broxton wrapped his arm around her and they made their way through the dark streets toward the Savannah, the Normandy Hotel and a girl he'd met only a few hours ago.

Every step cut into the fire in his belly, like smoldering steel through ice. He bit into his lower lip to divert the pain and tightened his arm around Wendy's waist. She didn't seem to mind. He counted the driveways they passed, then he counted parked cars, then every step he took, but no amount of counting countered the pain and finally he gave into it, closed his eyes and passed out.

"Wake up." He felt the slap on his face. "We're almost there." It was Leon speaking, "Don't quit now."

He opened his eyes. He was still on his feet.

"Only a few more blocks. You can do it," Leon said. "First I didn't think you could an' I didn't care, but you stuck your neck out for us, and you made it this far. You got guts. We gonna get you to your girl, but you gotta hold on just a little more."

"I can," Broxton grunted.

"Sure you can," Wendy said, and they started up again. Step after step. Wendy's arm was wrapped all the way around his waist. She was holding the compress tightly against his stomach. He must've dropped it when he passed out. "I know it hurts," she said, "but it's not bleeding so bad now, you're going to be okay," and her soft sweet voice soaked into him, giving him strength.

He matched her small strides, eyes closed, faith open, the fire in his belly consuming him. Two blocks, five minutes, an eternity.

"There," Leon said, and he opened his eyes.

"Back table," he said.

She saw them come in as she was making her way through the tables toward the bar. She ordered a bottle of Cabernet for a party dining on the balcony, but kept her eyes on him as the two girls helped him into a seat with his back to the wall. He smiled at her and nodded his head, she nodded back, met his eyes, held them, then returned the smile.

Maybe he shouldn't have come, but he had nowhere else to go. He watched her as the bartender handed her the wine. Her smile was sincere, her eyes understanding, she saw he was hurt. She would help.

He leaned back about to close his eyes when he caught movement to his left. Two men, both white, were approaching from across the room. They moved with a purpose, like police. Both had close cropped hair, both were young, both strong. Not police. Marines. They were from the embassy and they were coming for him.

His first thought was that the running was over. He'd be safe with the Marines. He'd tell his story and they'd protect him. Whoever was after him might be able to maneuver the DEA and the local police, but nobody outside of the President of the United States was powerful enough to control the Marine Corps.

But his second thought belayed the first. Why were they here? Who sent them? Halfway across the room the marine on the right pulled a forty-five automatic from under his coat. He was bringing it up to fire. The marine on the left was following suit, a hair slower.

"No!" Jenna screamed, grabbing the wine bottle by the neck. The marines hesitated, turning toward her, both surprised. She rolled her shoulder forward, arm extended like a cricket bowler, and she whipped the bottle around as if she was bowling for the stump.

Her aim was true.

The bottle flew like a comet, bottom first, red wine splashing across the room and connected with the head of the marine on the left. He went down like lead. He never had a chance to pull the trigger.

The second marine turned away from Broxton and started to bring his gun to bear on Jenna, but Leon, Trini macho, was across the room, hitting him like an American footballer, his shoulder to the marine's chest. He tumbled over the falling man, grabbing onto the gun as they rolled.

The marine would have made short work of Leon, but Alex was right behind his friend. The marine was on his back, starting to rise, when Alex stomped on his groin. The marine doubled over and relaxed his grip on the gun and Leon jerked it out of his hand. Alex jumped away from the fallen man, grinning.

"Nobody moves!" Leon pivoted and moved the gun back and forth, covering the room in large sweeps of his extended arms.

Broxton passed out, his head thudding against the table.

"Are you all right?" The voice was soft and friendly.

"I hurt." He opened his eyes and met her smile through a soft haze.

"You'll be okay," she said, and he started to get up. "Whoa, back down." She gently pushed him back against the pillows. "The doctor said you're to stay put for the next few days."

"Doctor?" He started to get up again.

"No." Her voice was as firm as the hand pressing against his chest.

"How?"

"You told the kids to bring you to me."

"That much I remember." His throat hurt, he wanted water. And he remembered the man on the phone. It was stupid coming back to the Normandy.

"The kids and I got you out just before the police came. You've been asleep for the last eighteen hours." She moved from the bed and brought a glass of water from the bathroom.

"Here," she said, helping him to sit up. He took the offered glass and drank. When he was finished he set the glass on the nightstand beside the bed and she helped ease him back onto the pillow.

"I'm in trouble," he said.

"No kidding."

Gingerly he felt his wound.

"Wendy's father is a doctor. Twenty stitches, it's gonna be a great scar."

"Twenty," he whispered.

"Lots of blood. Your clothes are ruined."

He looked around the room taking in the expensive furnishings. Two book lined walls, teak bookcases, a large rolltop desk, teak also, facing a large window. The curtains were drawn. It was a man's room, covered in wood grain and browns. The bed seemed out of place.

"How's the patient?" The voice was deep, baritone and reassuring. A doctor's voice.

"Better than before," Broxton said.

"That's what a doctor needs to hear."

"You're Wendy's father?"

"Indeed I am. And you're the infamous young man everybody is looking for."

"I don't understand."

"I don't think he knows," Jenna said.

"Really? How interesting." The doctor was short and thin, a combination that made his baritone voice all the more noticeable. His close cut grey hair stood out like snow on a mountain top against his high, dark forehead. He wore a soft white silk shirt over a pair of faded Levi's.

"You should tell him," she said. Broxton watched her hands. She was squeezing the fingers of the left with the right and they were shaking slightly.

"Yes," the doctor said, "I suppose I should."

"Tell me what?"

"Do you know what happened to Mr. Chandee our last attorney general?"

"He was assassinated, about six months ago."

"They're saying you killed him."

"They have a man in custody."

"They released him this morning. Seems they have a couple of witnesses who say you did it. Your picture is on the front page of the *Guardian* and you were all over the news last night."

"I didn't do it," Broxton whispered, "and they know it."

"Oh, I believe you. You stood against two strangers just to see that a fourteen year old girl was safe. A real assassin would have minded his own business and turned away, leaving my daughter and her friends to whatever fate awaited them."

"I have to get out of Trinidad."

"That is being arranged," the doctor said. "Wendy is out buying you clothes as we speak. In a few hours you'll leave on a sailboat bound for St. Martin. Normally, for a wound such as yours, I would prescribe bed rest for at least a week, but in your case it would be very bad for your health. There is talk of a reward and once the figure is announced, and I'm sure it will be quite large, we can expect those boys to start talking. Nothing stays secret in Trinidad for very long."

"I don't have my passport," Broxton said.

"Don't worry. You won't be on the crew list. None of the islands board boats as policy. The captain takes the ship's papers and crew's passports to customs and immigration. The papers are inspected and the passport is stamped. It's sort of like an honor system."

"How do they control illegal immigration, drugs, cocaine, marijuana."

"Simple," the doctor said. "They don't."

"That's crazy," Broxton said, then added, "What about the US Coast Guard."

"Ah, yes, there is always them. This boat will take about two months getting to St. Martin, stopping at all the popular anchorages along the way. It will very much look like a normal cruising sailboat enjoying the ever popular Caribbean. It will do its utmost to avoid your Coast Guard.

"Why?"

"It's carrying an awful lot of marijuana."

"A drug boat?"

"What can I say, it's my brother's boat. He smuggles marijuana into the British Virgins and alcohol back into Trinidad."

"I don't get it. You can get grass in Tortola and there is certainly no shortage of rum in Trinidad."

"There are taxes and duties on alcohol in Trinidad and our marijuana is much better than that up north. My brother does all right. He won't make millions, but he likes his work and the sense of adventure that goes with it."

"I can't go on a drug boat." Broxton said.

"And you can't stay here. How long do you think it will take even our inept police to figure out where you are. Besides, my brother has made arrangements to get you a British passport."

'You're kidding?"

"Certainly not. T-Bone knows people, slips them a few extra dollars, so to speak, to guarantee the smooth flow of his goods. You will have your passport. Now if you will excuse me, I have to be at the hospital in half an hour. Jenna will see to everything."

"Saying thank you hardly seems like enough."

"No, Mr. Broxton, it is I who should thank you. You came to my daughter's aid when most would have turned their backs," he said. Then he was through the door and gone.

"And you?" Broxton said, turning to Jenna, "why do you help me?"

"I don't know. I've always had a space in my heart for the underdog, and it's partially my fault you're here. I want to make up for it."

"I don't understand." he said.

"I called my sister and told her you'd been by the restaurant and that you might be coming back. The police went by her house, and not knowing any better she told them."

"Aren't you afraid you'll get in trouble?"

"Dr. Powers will fix it. After it's obvious you're no longer in Trinidad the pressure will be off and it will all blow over."

"Pressure?"

"Of course. You don't think Trinidad's finest is behind this, do you? My lord, they couldn't find Long Circular Mall on a clear day if an informant told them where it was. It's the United States that wants you, Trinidad could care less. They know you didn't kill Chandee. Once you're gone, you'll be forgotten."

"How soon before I leave here?"

"In the morning, you set sail just before dawn." She got up from the side of the bed and started for the door. "Get as much rest as you can."

It was ten to midnight when Jenna woke him. He rubbed his eyes and ran his tongue over his teeth. He needed a toothbrush, a shower and a lot more rest.

"The police have been to Leon's. We have to go."

He sat up. He was naked under the covers.

"Put these on." She handed him a pair of worn, work jeans. He pulled off the covers and slipped into the jeans without underwear. She didn't avert her gaze and he didn't care. "Now this." She was holding a batik print shirt, about a size too large. He put it on.

"My shoes," he said, and she bent over and picked them up.

"No socks," she said.

"It's okay." He put on the loafers and stood up slowly. A dull fire burned in his stomach.

"Where's the doctor?"

"He's gone. He decided to take the family up to the Asa Wright nature center for a few days."

"Good time to see the birds," Broxton said.

"He didn't want them here."

"I guess I can understand that," he said, and he could. The man had done enough, risked enough. He steadied himself on his feet, feeling light headed. He took a deep breath and winced as he felt his stomach muscles expand against the stitches. Then he took a step forward, stumbled and caught himself, grabbing onto the desk, rattling the roll top.

"Quiet," she whispered, and he carefully followed her out of the house. They stopped on the front porch, where he inhaled the cool night, tasting the air. It smelled like a storm was coming soon, but it wasn't the electricity in the air that set his arm hairs tingling. Something wasn't right. Why did he have to be quiet?

"That's my car, there," she whispered, pointing to a white mini van, parked under a giant weeping willow. The street lights were out, the neighborhood was dark. All the better to kill someone, he thought.

"Nice," he said as they made their way down the walk toward the van.

"Two weeks old. I'm going to use it in my business."

"I thought you were a waitress."

"Not forever. I've got plans."

"And ambition."

"Right," she said, adding, "I'm going to do day tours for the yachties, you know, Caroni Swamp, the vegetable market, stuff like that."

"And up to Asa Wright Nature Center," he said.

"Yes, that, too."

She unlocked and opened the left hand, passenger door for him and he felt a chill run up his back as he wondered who was watching. He reached over and unlocked the driver's door while she walked around the front of the vehicle. He watched while she put the key in the ignition, but he reached out with a gentle squeeze and stopped her from starting the engine.

"What?" she said, startled.

"I'm not getting very far tonight am I?"

"How did you know?"

"You were whispering in the house. If nobody was home, why whisper?"

"Ah."

"Why?" he asked.

"For the money," she said, and he flexed his arm. She gasped, then he relaxed and let her have her hand back.

"Where is it going to happen?"

"I'm supposed to jump out of the van when we stop at the light just before the highway."

"Do they know about the yacht club?"

"No."

"Where do they think you're taking me?"

"To the Hilton. I didn't want to involve the doctor's brother."

"Why not?"

"Because I have some money invested in the cargo."

"Small country," he said.

"What are you going to do now?" she asked.

"Go a different way," he said. He saw the car parked up the block. It was a hot night and they gave themselves away by having the windows down. Nobody left their car unlocked anywhere in Trinidad, not unless they were police officers and they were sitting in it.

"Okay," he said. "The damage is done. I can't go back inside, because they know about the doctor and I can't go with you because they're waiting for me up the road. I guess my only option is to run for it."

"You don't have a chance," she said.

"Not much of one, you're right, but better than if I let you drive me into their waiting arms."

"It was a business deal. They offered a lot of money. Nothing personal." She was cool, not the least ruffled that he caught her out.

"They offered Judas money, too."

"You're not Christ," she said.

"I'm going to step out of the car," he said, "and start running. Maybe I can get myself lost before you get to that traffic light." He didn't know what else to do. He couldn't hurt her, he didn't have it in him. If he took off at an angle, away from the van, keeping it between him and the policemen down the street, and if she took off straight away for the traffic light, maybe the police would follow her thinking he was still in the car.

But he needed an edge. A few seconds was all he could ask for. Any more and the police would come looking. He took the key out of the ignition and tossed it into the back of the van. She was scrabbling after it even as he went out the door. He tried to run, but he didn't get far. He was woozy and wobbly from the drugs the doctor must have given him and the stitches in his stomach felt like he was being beaten with a whip. Every step another lash.

The heat of the blast slammed into him before the sound of the explosion that blew up the van woke up the night. He threw his arms out to break his fall, but landed on his stomach anyway. Fighting for air, he rolled across the cool grass till his body thudded into the doctor's front porch. He kept low and crawled around to the side of the house.

In seconds the neighborhood was up and the street was crawling with police cars, their blue lights flashing.

"You okay, Mister?" It was Wendy, tugging on his sleeve.

"I think so"

"Come back inside," she said, and he followed her up onto the porch and back into the house.

CHAPTER

EIGHT

JULIE SLID INTO THE WATER and ripples of chilling current ran from her skin to her core. This was the deep, home of the great white, the hammerhead and who knew what other species of shark. She was in their territory now. She spent a few seconds floating on the surface, relaxing her nerves and gathering her courage. It was dark down there, and cold.

She took a deep breath from the regulator and exhaled, the sound of her own breathing offered small reassurance. She was not an experienced diver, but she wasn't a novice either. She'd been diving for the last few years, but never at night and never alone and always in calm conditions.

She yanked on the tether and was rewarded by Meiko's answering tug. At least if she got in trouble, three rapid jerks and they'd pull her out. She took another breath and held it this time, listening to the silence and seeing the dark. She was stalling and she couldn't do it forever, she was going to have to go down there.

They could lose the boat if she didn't. Worse, they could lose their lives. It was up to her, all up to her. There was nobody to take care of her now. Nobody to tell her it was going to be all right. Nobody to lean on. She exhaled and bit into the regulator, took another breath, held it and dropped a few feet under the surface, into the black water.

She was alone with only the sound of her breath and her beating heart for company. She held her hand up in front of her face. She couldn't see it. She brought it closer, till she was touching the face mask and still she couldn't see it. She looked toward the surface, but it was gone. There was no up, no down. She was trapped in the vertigo.

She chewed into the regulator with clenched teeth, tasting salt water on her gums. Mucus dribbled from her nose over her lip. She wanted to blow it out, but not in the dark. She didn't want the snot inside the face mask for even a second, but moving the mask away from her face to clear her nose was out of the question.

She felt the pressure building in her ears and she reached up and pinched her nostrils closed through the mask, forcing the air out through her blocked nasal passages, clearing herself. And then it hit her, something was wrong. Why should she have to clear herself? And then she understood. She was going down. She had too much weight on and she was going down.

She cleared herself again and fought the impulse to lash out toward the surface. If she was down far enough a rapid assent would be dangerous. Then she thought she felt something move by her in the dark and all she wanted was out of the water. She sucked on the regulator, filling her lungs, straightened her arms above her head, and brought them back to her sides. She moved through the water, but was she going north, south, up or down? She couldn't tell.

All she saw was more dark and she was hyperventilating, using up the air. She wanted out. Now. She was getting too much oxygen and she wasn't thinking. Then she remembered the weight belt and with trembling hands she managed to get it off. She let it fall toward the ocean below, feeling less confined without it and a whole lot safer as she started to float upward. But she couldn't wait. She lashed out with a great kick toward the surface, pulling the regulator from her mouth and gasping for air as she broke through.

And then she was back under and gagging on sea water. A rolling wave pushed her against the boat and she pushed off, feeling the ablating bottom paint, slimy and slippery, as she shoved against it. A second wave rode under her and this time there was a loud thunk when the scuba tank banged into the fiberglass hull and she swallowed more water.

She was right under the boat. Safety so close and she was going to drown. She tried to call out, but only gagged on more water. She had to do something. What? The flapping regulator banged into her head. In her panic she thought it was something from the deep. She tried to push it away, but it wouldn't go, and she finally figured out what it was. She stuffed it back into her mouth, and took a long pull on the sweet air.

She heard someone shouting, but she didn't know from where. She tried to swim away from the boat, but she was no match for the current and the rolling waves. It was like trying to walk up a steep hill with roller skates on, no matter how fast she ran, she just slid back on the rolling wheels.

A second breath and she started to calm down. She allowed herself to float just below the surface. She was there now. No more vertigo. Her head was clearing and she was starting to think straight. She was never in danger, she had the safety line. She was never going to the bottom. She grabbed the line and jerked on it, three times.

She grabbed another breath and tried to swim alongside the boat, toward the swim ladder, but another wave sent her crashing into the hull and knocked her breath out. She swallowed water, gagged again, and felt even more air pulled out of her, as the rope around her waist tightened, and Meiko and Victor struggled to pull her from the sea.

"The swim ladder, the swim ladder!" Meiko screamed. It finally got through to her, and she let them pull her toward it. She held on to the ladder for a few seconds, then with shaking arms, tired legs and their help, she climbed up and stepped over the lifelines.

"Couldn't do it. Sorry," she said. "So dark." She arched her back and Meiko helped her slip the buoyancy control vest and the tank off. Once the weight was off her back she started to breathe easier.

"You couldn't see anything?" Victor asked. He was standing with his hands in his pockets. Julie thought he looked at home on the deck of a sailing vessel. She wondered why he never learned to dive. Then she thought of Tammy. She didn't swim, maybe her brother didn't either. It would be just the thing a macho Trini wouldn't want anyone to know.

"Not a thing," Julie said. "Too dark." She bent low and grabbed onto the lifelines and worked her way back to the safety of the cockpit. Meiko followed with the scuba gear, setting it in on the port cockpit seat. Victor walked across the rocking, rolling, slippery deck like he was walking in the park.

"Not even with the torch?" he said.

"Shit." Julie coughed. "Got scared, didn't think." She had the flashlight clipped on to the weight belt. It was on the bottom now, along with the Vaseline soaked rags. She felt like kicking herself for panicking.

"You didn't use the torch?" Victor said. He was scowling. She didn't like the look. It was like she was a little girl and she'd done something wrong.

"No, sorry." And she was apologizing. She didn't like that either.

"What are we going to do now?" Meiko asked.

"The leak has to be stopped," Victor said. "It's the only way." He was still looking at her with that dark scowl, forehead knitted, eyes squinting.

"I can't go back down there," Julie said. "I just can't."

"I understand," Victor said, "but someone has to."

"I can do it," Meiko said, "I'm an excellent swimmer and I'm in great shape."

"No," Julie said. "I'll do it." The thought of going back down there sent shivers slicing through her, but she wouldn't let Meiko do it. No mother would. "Just give me a few minutes to catch my courage." And gather a little common sense. She couldn't believe that she hadn't used the flashlight, how stupid.

"I can do it," Meiko said. "I know I can."

"Your mother should be the one," Victor said. "She's the only one of us that's qualified." In her mind, Julie knew that he was right, but in her heart she hated him for saying it. He was able to fly jets during the Gulf War, but he couldn't dive under a boat and stuff a few rags up a rudder post. It didn't seem right.

"Just let me have a cup of courage and I'll go back down," she said.

"How? The weight belt and torch are gone," Victor said.

"You make the rags," she told him. "Meiko, you get the coffee, black. And I'll get the other weight belt and flashlight."

"You have another underwater torch on board?" he asked, almost like he didn't believe it.

"Yes, Hideo's. And I think that this time, Victor, why don't you stay in the generator room and keep a light shining down those holes."

"Good idea," he said. She was surprised at how she was taking charge of the situation. She was beginning to feel like she really was the captain.

She drank the coffee quickly. Caffeine probably wasn't the best thing to use to calm shaky nerves, but Julie wanted something hot in her before she went back down. Besides, she told herself, this time she wasn't going to panic.

"Arms back," Meiko said. Julie obeyed and her daughter helped her back on with the BC and scuba tank. Then she slapped the back of the tank and Julie zipped up.

"This time I stay down till the job's done," she said. Brave words, she thought, as she stepped over the lifelines and onto the swim ladder. Then she was in the water.

She floated, face down, staring into the dark, breathing through the regulator again, getting used to the feeling. She didn't want to be in the water any longer than she had to be, but she didn't want to panic again, either. She closed her eyes, then opened them, it made no difference. She reached for the flashlight, turned it on and watched the dark eat up the light. She turned it toward the boat and smiled when she saw the red bottom paint.

Then she swam under the boat, guiding her way with the torchlight shining on the keel. The boat seemed huge, larger then it did when they were on the hard. It was like swimming under a great whale.

She made her way to the stern with short strokes and rapid breaths. She shifted the light to the rudder. She knew Victor was in the generator room above with another flashlight, waiting to see if she was able to stop the leak.

The black water seemed to swallow up the small amount of light coming from her flashlight. She had to keep it pointed at the underbelly of the boat or she couldn't see anything at all. She studied the rudder. It was swaying back and forth as the boat rocked with the waves. She grabbed onto it and looked up. She saw light shining down from above, from the holes around the rudder post. So round, so perfect, so sinister. She stared at the light for a few seconds, but the dark and the cold clouded her ability to think clearly. She wanted out of the water.

She fished in the bag tied to the weight belt, pulled out a fistful of rags and jammed them up toward the light above. After she stuffed all the rags up the tube and around the post, she let go of the rudder and kicked toward the surface, pulling on the line to let Meiko know that she was ready to come up.

She broke through and floundered against the waves with Meiko hauling her toward the swim ladder. The scuba tank pulled against her, but she didn't want to take it off in the water, so she fought its weight and struggled up the ladder, reaching the top without any breath to spare.

"Did you do it?" Meiko asked.

"Yeah," Julie answered, smiling. "I did."

"Atta girl, Mom," Meiko said. Then she helped her out of the BC for the second time that night, but this time Julie felt like she was walking on top of the world. Let's see if he's wearing that scowl now, she thought.

Victor came up from below. "You did it," he said. And his grin was about eight miles wide. Julie felt a glow of excitement and satisfaction sparked through her. She couldn't imagine any better praise out of him than that smile.

"That was the second most physically demanding thing I've ever had to do," she said.

"What was the first?" Meiko asked.

"Having you," she said. Meiko laughed, and so did Victor, his smile getting even wider, showing off his gleaming teeth.

"You really did it," he said. "I'm proud of you." God, she was being killed with his praise.

"Then we can head on to Grenada?" Julie said.

"I still don't think that's a good idea," he said. "Trinidad is the only place south of Antigua that can haul you out. Those rags aren't going to keep the water out for very long. We should head back."

"How far is Antigua?" Meiko asked.

"About four hundred miles north," Victor said. "Seven days if we sail by day and anchor at night."

"Where would we stop?" Julie asked.

"Grenada, then the Grenadines, Rodney Bay in St. Lucia, then Martinique, Dominica, Guadeloupe and finally Antigua. It's a long time to count on those rags."

"I shoved them up in there good. We'll be okay," Julie said. "I want to go for it."

"You're the captain," Victor said, then added, "If you don't mind I'll take the first watch. Meiko can spell me and you can get some sleep. You've earned it."

"How long are the watches?" Meiko asked.

"Two hours should be about right," Victor said, and Julie thought that he was making an awful lot of decisions, but it was clear to her that even though she was the captain, she was going to have to rely on him a lot, at least until she knew what she was doing.

"I'm not the least tired," Meiko said, "so I think I'll stay on deck if that's okay."

"Fine with me," Victor said.

"Make sure you clip on," Julie said.

"I'm clipped on now," Meiko said and she lifted up her tether, showing Julie that it was both clipped to her inflatable life vest and the binnacle. If she fell overboard she'd be tied to the boat.

"Okay," Julie said, and she went below and lay down in the salon. She heard Victor and Meiko talking and laughing as she drifted off to sleep. She slept poorly, waking often, and always she heard the two above. They seemed to talk the night away and finally, after what seemed an endless time, Julie fell into a deep sleep.

"Your watch in fifteen minutes, Mom," Meiko said, gently shaking her awake. "We let you sleep an extra two hours."

"Okay, I'm awake." She sat up and stretched her arms above her head. It seemed like she'd only been asleep for a few seconds, but if she'd had an extra two hours that meant that six hours had gone by.

"You're gonna love it up there," her daughter said. "Not a cloud in the sky. The water's almost flat and the wind is perfect. A gentle beam reach."

"You're learning the lingo," Julie said, on her way to the thermos in the galley.

"Victor's teaching me. There's really a lot to this stuff. You can't just get in a boat and sail away."

"Don't I know it," Julie said, sipping at her coffee.

"Bring it up with you," Meiko said, and Julie followed her up to the cockpit and gasped. Meiko was right. She gazed above, she'd never seen anything to rival it. No city lights to pollute the night. The stars wrapped around the sky and she felt like she was in a fairytale.

"If only your father could have been here with us," Julie said, and Meiko moved close to her and squeezed her hand.

"He's watching over us. I know he is," Meiko said. "We're going to get to Grenada by morning and the next day we'll be somewhere else, even farther away from Trinidad. Dad won't let anything happen to us. I really believe that."

"I do too, honey," she said, and she wondered if she'd ever learn to live with the ache in her heart.

"All right," Victor said. "Everything is all set. The wind is out of the southeast, and the current is with us. The self steering gear is set. All you have to do is sit back and enjoy yourself."

"I can do that," Julie said, "but what if the wind direction changes?"

"It won't, but don't worry, I only take catnaps at sea. I'll pop up every fifteen minutes or so and see how you're doing."

"Great," Julie said, and that's the way she felt. She took a deep breath of the ocean air and held it,

Victor was on his way below before she let it out. "You can get some rest, too," Julie said, "I'll be okay."

"I'll have a cup of coffee with you, before I go to sleep," Meiko said, and she went below, returning with the thermos and a cup for herself.

The two women drank the hot coffee under the stars, and enjoyed the quiet evening as the boat sliced through the calm sea.

"Victor's asleep on the starboard settee," Meiko said, "and he looks like he's sleeping pretty solid. I don't think he's going to be popping up every fifteen minutes."

"That's okay," Julie said. "I'll be fine. You go below and get some rest."

"Sure?"

"Yeah, honey, I'm sure."

"Okay, Mom, but you call if anything happens or if you get lonely."

"I will," Julie said, as Meiko went below. And then she was alone. To share the night with the man in her heart. Tomorrow she was going to have to bury him a little bit, but tonight she wanted to grieve.

She sat in the cockpit for over an hour, staring out to sea and crying. Small sobs at first and then she let go and buried her face in her hands. It was so unfair.

When there were no more tears, just an ache, she wiped her eyes, and a dolphin shot out of the water and did a tail dance across the waves. She laughed as the mammal danced and she hugged herself when it slipped back into the sea.

"Goodbye, Hideo," she said.

And then the wind started to pick up. She glanced at the knot meter, seven-point-five knots. They'd picked up half a knot. She checked the self steering gear and it was working fine. She glanced at the compass, on course, and the sails were full. Everything was fine.

And then it started to blow a little harder. Eight knots. She thought about waking Victor, but didn't. She didn't want him to think she was a complete washout, so she picked up a winch handle and brought in a little of the jib. She grinned as the boat slowed back to seven and a half knots.

Then she saw the clouds and the rain off on the starboard side and she realized that the increase in the wind speed was due to the squall. She looked back at the knot meter. Eight-point-four, then she turned back to the squall. It looked like they were going to miss it, so instead of waking Victor she rolled in a little more of the jib, but the boat didn't slow down, so she rolled it almost all the way in, and the speed dropped back down to six-point-five. Slower than they were going before she saw the squall. She felt secure.

But the squall shifted course. It looked like it was going cross their path after all. She felt a few drops of rain as the squall approached. The speed climbed up to eight-point-seven. She started below to wake Victor.

Then the roller furling line snapped. The wind caught the sail and the jib unfurled with blazing speed and Herculean force. *Fallen Angel* lurched to port, with the huge popping sound of flapping sails, and the knot meter climbed to nine-point-five. She was in trouble. The self steering gear was being overpowered by the wind and then the rain was upon her. She scooted behind the wheel as Victor burst into the cockpit.

"What's going on?" he yelled to be heard above the wind.

"Squall," Julie said, as Meiko came up into the cockpit.

"We have to roll in the jib," he said.

"We can't, the furling line's broken," Julie said, and he looked at the slack line.

"Too late to reef the main," he said. "We have to ride it out. Let me take the wheel."

She felt like she could handle it, but he was the one with the experience, so she moved away from the wheel when he grabbed it. And for the next twenty minutes the two women watched as Victor handled the boat. Even though they took a lot of water over the side as the boat slammed through the swells, Julie wasn't worried, because he seemed to be enjoying himself.

Then, as quickly as it was upon them they were through it and the night was clear again. The sea flattened out, the wind was back from the southeast.

"Okay, Julie, you can take the wheel again. I'm going to see what I can do about the jib," he said, then he went up front with Meiko behind him. Five minutes later he was back in the cockpit.

"How is it?" Julie asked.

"Mom, he fixed it simple, dimple. He just tied two bowlines together. Now we can roll it in." She may be a genius in school, but she was still a child, Julie thought.

"It's just a temporary fix," Victor said. "You'll have to replace the line when we get to Grenada. It wasn't an accident, somebody was at it with a knife. Sooner or later it was going to go."

"First the rudder leak and now this," Julie said. "Somebody really doesn't like me."

"When we get to Grenada we'll check the boat over and make sure there aren't any other little surprises," Victor said. "Till then I'll stay up."

"I'll stay up, too," Meiko said. "There's no way I can get back to sleep. Not a chance."

"Then I'm going below for a little sleep," Julie said, and five minutes later she was dreaming about shooting stars and dolphins.

"Mom, we're almost there," Meiko's voice rang down from above and Julie opened her eyes. Five minutes later she was on deck. Victor and Meiko looked as fresh as if they'd slept the night away. Julie felt as if she hadn't slept at all. She stretched and gave in to a yawn.

"That's Grenada, dead ahead," Victor said, giving the wheel up to her.

"You guys didn't wake me for my watch," she said.

"We thought you should get some rest," Meiko said, and she ducked as some water came splashing over the side. The spray hit Julie full in the face. "That'll wake you right up, Mom."

"I'm awake." Julie wiped the salt water from her face. "What did you guys talk about all night long?"

"Oh, the usual. We solved all the world's problems. Politics, religion, sex, you know."

"Coffee," Victor said, passing her the thermos.

Two hours later they were laying anchor in Prickly Bay. The water was clear, the sun was hot, and Julie was aching for a swim. But first she had to check into customs and then she had to go over to the boatyard and see if there was anything they could do about the rudder.

"I have an idea," Victor said, as Julie was stepping over the lifelines to get into the dinghy.

"Yes," she said.

He rubbed the back of his neck, then ran a hand through his thick hair. "We could stuff some packing up the rudder tube, then fill it with underwater epoxy. That stuff gets hard in water. It won't be a perfect fix, but it'll stop the leak for a while."

"How long?" Julie asked.

"I've heard of underwater epoxy repairs that lasted years."

"We'll try it," she said, thinking that once again, Victor had saved the day.

Victor and Meiko took a taxi to Georgetown to buy supplies and Julie had two men from the local shipyard come to the boat, and within an hour the rudder leak was fixed.

"Bad thing, that," the heavy man said, wiping sweat from his forehead with an oily rag. His skin was about the same color as the oil, so Julie hardly noticed.

"Whoever did it should be hung," the big man's assistant agreed, "but you're wrong about one thing. Those itty bitty holes wouldn't have sunk the boat."

"Really?" Julie stared into the boy's blue eyes.

"True," the big shipwright said. "I seen a lot a things on a lot of boats, but never deliberate sabotage. You're lucky, though. Either the bastard didn't know what he was doing, or he didn't want to sink you. I think he just wanted to scare you."

"What do you mean?" Julie asked.

"Not enough water coming in to sink the boat."

"But the bilge pumps were going off."

"Well they would, wouldn't they?" the boy said. "Soon as enough water came in to set off the switches, but they're set real low. You could've sailed to Miami and back and been okay with them tiny holes."

"Mind you," the big shipwright said, "it's always better to fix a leak. It's never good when the ocean comes in your boat from the bottom."

She had the men go over the boat, checking everything she could think of, the lines, blocks, sails, and thru-hulls. They couldn't find anything else wrong, but the big man warned her saying, "There's lots someone can do to mess up a sailboat that you can't see right off, so you best be careful."

After they left she thought about Victor's insistence that they either fix the leak immediately or head back to Trinidad, and she concluded that maybe the great Victor Drake might have panicked a little himself.

She didn't like his attitude and she had reservations about his offer of help, but she knew she needed somebody and she had to admit that he was a competent sailor. When they returned she asked him if he wouldn't mind staying on for a few days and show them how to handle the boat.

"I'll be glad to stay with you for as long as it takes," Victor said, "and this is a perfect place to learn. The wind is always blowing."

"Not here," Julie said. She squinted against the sun as Meiko was sweeping the marina with the binoculars.

"Why not?" Victor sounded disappointed.

"We're too close to Trinidad. The farther away we get the better I'll feel."

"Grenada is a separate country. Nobody's going to take your boat away here."

"I just don't feel safe this close to Trinidad." She picked her sunglasses up off of a cockpit cushion and put them on.

"Okay, when do you want to leave?" he asked.

"How quick can we set sail?"

"As soon as we get the rudder fixed," he said.

"Already taken care of. Two guys form the local yard came by."

"They put a diver in the water and use under water epoxy?" he asked.

"Yes they did."

"Then we can go now. We can spend the night somewhere in the Grenadines if that's what you want."

"Mom," Meiko said, "look at this." She handed the binoculars to her mother. "Check out the black schooner, *Snake Eyes.*"

Julie slipped off her sunglasses and gazed into the binoculars, following the direction of Meiko's pointed finger. "It looks like *Challenge*, except it doesn't have the white stripe."

"Let me see," Victor said, and Julie handed him the long glasses. "Same kind of boat," Victor said, "but that one's American. Nice paint job, looks new, better than Kurt's." He handed Julie back the binoculars.

And an hour later they weighed anchor.

CHAPTER NINE

THE SECURITY GUARD WAVED THEM BY and Dr. Powers drove between two long rows of covered speed boats and into the parking lot. Bright stars glowed through the scattered clouds and it was sprinkling lightly. Powers parked behind the bar, but he left the engine running with the wipers going. "The boat's name is *Obsession*. You'll find it on the west wall. Go down the jetty till it ends, turn left and keep going, it'll be the last boat, you can't miss it. It's a forty-five foot sloop, white and fast looking."

"I know the way," Broxton said, remembering his encounter with Julie Tanaka.

"Then this is goodbye." The doctor held out his hand. Broxton shook it and met his crooked grin with one of his own. He liked the man, there weren't many like him.

"Will you be okay?" Broxton didn't want Powers suffering because of what he'd done for him.

"I don't think anyone will be bothering me. At least not till they find out you weren't in the car. Then they might come around, but it's nothing I can't take care of. In Trinidad it's who you know and who knows you. I know a few people and everybody knows me."

"I thought she was such a nice lady," Wendy said from the back seat.

"She was, Wendy," Broxton said, turning to face the girl, "but they offered her a lot of money. It was just too tempting."

"I would never tell on a friend, not for a million dollars," she said. She was leaning forward, with her elbows on the back of the front seat, and she was holding up a silver crucifix on a gold chain. "This is for you. For luck. I think you might need it."

"Thank you, Wendy." He lowered his head. She slipped the crucifix over it and he felt the warm chain on his neck.

"Keep it on," she said, "It works."

"Catholic?" Powers asked.

"Father was," Broxton answered, feeling the cross.

"We'll say a mass for you come Sunday, can't hurt," Powers said.

"It'll help," Wendy said. "We'll pray that nothing bad ever happens to you."

Catholics and Jews. Broxton thought of his parents, and he smiled as Wendy held out her hand, copying her father. He shook it, feeling the warmth in her grip. "I'll write and let you know how I'm getting on."

"And I'll write back," she said, still holding on to his hand, "cause we're friends forever." Her deep brown eyes were boring into his and he knew that he would be writing letters to this little girl for the rest of his life.

"Forever," Broxton said.

"It's time," Powers said. Broxton opened the door and stepped out into the early morning. He smiled as Wendy climbed into the front seat and waved to him. He waved back and watched till the car was past the speedboats and going through the security gate. Then he turned away and walked around the outside bar toward the pier.

The yellow lights along the dock cast an otherworldly glow on the sailboats and their tall masts bobbing back and forth with the gentle morning swell. As he walked between them Broxton couldn't help thinking about the people living aboard. Older retirees, middle aged couples that had sold everything for the dream, and younger people just starting out, the hippies of the 90s. Gypsies all.

He stopped at the end of the dock and stared at the empty slip where *Fallen Angel* had been docked. Somehow she was connected to what was happening to him. It had to be. It was the only thing he was working on when it all started to go wrong.

"You looking for me?" The baritone voice startled him, but he got a bigger surprise when he turned toward it. His reaction didn't go unnoticed. "I get that a lot, when people knowing Jimbo first meet me," the man with Dr. Power's voice said.

"I wasn't expecting..."

"What, a white man? You can say it, we're in Trinidad. You don't have to be politically correct here."

Broxton blinked away his surprise. "Spitting image. I'd've thought you were twins."

"Good one." The man laughed. "Name's T-Bone. Glad to have you. I was beginning to think I was gonna have to sail up island alone. I hate that."

"I'm Broxton." He offered his hand. T-Bone took it in a firm grip and Broxton squeezed back. They were playing the male game, *who can squeeze the hardest*. It only lasts a few seconds and someone has to give and relax his hand first. Broxton never did. Apparently T-Bone didn't either, because the men stood on the dock squeezing each other's hands for an obscenely long time. Finally Broxton said, "You want to call it a tie?"

"On three," T-Bone said. "I'll count." He counted to three and both men relaxed their grips at almost the same time. T-Bone held his a fraction of a second longer, and laughed.

"Cheated," Broxton said.

"Nature of the game," T-Bone said. Then , "Broxton? That a first name or a last? I don't like last names."

"First name's Bill."

"Okay, Billy Boy, mine's T-Bone, not Tee, and not Bone, can't shorten it." He pushed his shoulder length hair out of his eyes.

"T-Bone," Broxton, said. He hated being called Billy Boy, hated it all his life, but somehow coming from a man named T-Bone, with a natural twinkle in his eye, it wasn't so bad.

"Like the steak," T-Bone said. He reminded Broxton of a fugitive from a Grateful Dead concert, beard, tie-dyed shirt, faded Levi's and bare feet.

"You're really his brother?"

"Daddy was a sailor, girl in every port." The man started toward the end of the dock and Broxton followed. He guessed that T-Bone was several years younger than Dr. Powers, but it was hard to tell. The doctor looked young for his age, and T-Bone had to be younger than he looked.

"We're ready to go," T-Bone said when they neared the boat. "You wait here. I'll start the engines, then you take it off the cleats and hop aboard."

Broxton looked down at the stern lines. "Those?"

"Yeah." T-Bone looked at Broxton the way a high school principal frowns down at a wayward student.

"I just unwind the rope?"

"You ever been sailing before?"

"Twice. I didn't have much fun either time."

"Christ," T-Bone muttered through his beard.

Half an hour later they were sailing toward the Bocas. Broxton sat back in the cockpit, while T-Bone steered, and watched the land on the right and the Five Islands off to the left. He thought about Julie Tanaka, then he turned toward the prison island out past the Five Islands, Trinidad's version of Alcatraz, and wondered if he was going to wind up behind bars for crimes he didn't commit, or if he was just going to wind up dead.

"Gorgeous, isn't it?" T-Bone said.

Broxton nodded.

"I love the early morning. The sun coming up, shimmering seas, makes one glad to be alive."

Broxton nodded again, but he didn't feel that way thirty minutes later when they were going through the Bocas. The passage from the gulf into the ocean was narrow and choppy, and he grabbed onto the lifelines as the worst nausea he'd ever experienced caused him to vomit over the side.

"Nothing to be ashamed of," T-Bone said. "Happens to the best of us. Still get seasick myself sometimes."

His stomach was in knots and his head was clamped in a vice. He wiped sweat off his brow with the back of his hand and felt the wig and whipped it off, thankful for the rush of cool air across his head.

"Whoa, it's Kojak." T-Bone laughed.

Broxton wanted to laugh with him, but instead he cut loose with some more bile over the side.

"Use this." T-Bone handed him a hose.

"Thanks," Broxton said, and he depressed the handle on the nozzle and sprayed his face.

"A lot of cruisers think it's a waste but I like a fresh water hose on deck," T-Bone said.

"I don't understand," Broxton said.

"Living on a boat's not like living on land. On a boat you have to make everything last. But I like fresh water on deck. In the end I think I use less, cause I'll jump in the ocean and wash off with Joy, then rinse with the fresh from the hose, rather than take a hot shower below."

"You wash with dishwashing soap?"

"You will too, and you'll be surprised. Wash yourself with that stuff in salt water and it does something to your hair. Makes it comb out shiny, better than any fancy shampoo."

Broxton ran a hand over his head and felt the stubble starting to grow.

"Well not on your head," T-Bone said. "But if you had hair you'd notice."

Broxton laughed and kept laughing till they were out in the open ocean.

"Most folks make this passage at night," T-Bone said, "but I like to see where I'm going and the boat's fast enough that I can make all the Caribbean passages during the day."

Broxton looked out at the sea and shuddered at the thought of sailing through the rolling waves after dark. "I don't think I'd like night sailing," he said.

"Tell me about it."

Broxton saw something off the bow and pointed.

"Good eye," T-Bone said, but the right thing to do would have been to say, "Sailboat at eleven o'clock. Then you don't have to use your hands. It's always better to keep them free for the boat."

Broxton nodded.

"Say, you wanna learn to sail, or are you just along for the ride?" Broxton saw the way his face lit up and knew there was only one answer he could give.

"I think I'd like to learn."

"That's great. I used to teach it, but what I'm doing now is easier, and besides I like living on the edge."

"I know what you mean. Anybody can live in a house with a picket fence and work at a factory."

"Right." T-Bone nodded his head, smiling at Broxton with crystal blue eyes you could almost see through. "We could go straight up north, but it'll look much more natural if we take our time. I think we'll spend a week or two in Grenada. Good winds there and lots of bays to sail into. In a week I'll have you sailing like you were born on a boat.

A week later, Broxton felt like killing T-Bone Powers, but he knew how to sail, his wound was well, and he felt better than he had in over ten years. They spent the week in Grenada's Prickly Bay, up before dawn every day, oatmeal only for breakfast, before a grueling five hours sailing in the rough waters around the southern part of the island, then a lunch of cold rice and beans, before another four hours tacking and jibing, ending every night with a vegetarian dinner.

He had never argued with, admired, hated, loved, respected or wanted to shoot anyone more than T-Bone, and he'd never been closer to another human being. Not the two partners he served with, not his team mates when he played college ball, not even his ex-wife.

And five pounds fell from his stocky frame like water from a rock. Hard as it was to admit, he had been going soft. Too much television and too many hamburgers. He was already leaner, getting stronger, and his white skin was turning darker as the days flew by. The wig, tossed over the side one night by T-Bone, was no longer needed, his hair was coming in, light brown and bleached by the sun.

Nights ended with a couple of glasses of rum and grapefruit juice and conversation. They talked about all the usual things. Politics, religion, sports, boats, sailing, the day's adventures and misadventures, but the past, other than ex-wives and old girl friends, was never brought up.

The marijuana stuffed in the bilges and packed away in the forward locker was another subject not discussed, and after the first few days Broxton was able to bury it in a back corner of his mind.

Then one day it roared out of the dark corner and presented itself front and center.

They were sailing under a reefed main in twenty-five knots of wind, the jib was rolled in halfway and they were headed for the narrow opening into Hog Island, Broxton's favorite bay on Grenada's south coast. The waves were cresting at ten feet and it didn't look like they were going to reach the protection of the bay before the storm was upon them, but it wasn't the storm that had them worried. It was the white and orange Coast Guard cutter off their stern.

"Won't be long before they're on us," Broxton said.

"Grab the main sheet. We'll jibe and see what's what."

Broxton started hauling on the main sheet until the boom was centered, then he cleated it off. "Ready when you are," he said.

"Okay, jibe ho," T-bone yelled and Broxton released the starboard jib sheet and started hauling hand over hand on the port sheet as T-Bone swung the boat around. "All right," he yelled when the jib came over and Broxton released the mainsheet. "You don't need me anymore," T-Bone said as the boom slipped over the top and they were on the opposite tack.

T-Bone grabbed a glance over his shoulder. "They changed course," he said, then added, "Let's jibe back," and they repeated the maneuver and were back on course for Hog Island.

"What's the plan, Captain?" Broxton knew if they were boarded T-Bone would lose the boat and wind up in jail, probably in Grenada. But he wondered what would happen to him. Were the long knives still out and looking, or was he yesterday's news?

"We can't let them board, that's for sure." T-Bone said. "That would be very bad."

"They might not find it." Broxton said.

"Oh, they'll find it. They'll take one look at this old hippy and they'll tear the boat apart. Now, if I looked like you I could probably bluff it out, but I don't so let's pretend we don't see them and let out the jib."

"In this weather?" Broxton said.

"Speed, we want speed," T-Bone said.

"You're crazy. We'll never out run them, they have four times our speed."

"We'd never let out the jib if we knew they were back there, would we?" T-bone said.

"No."

"So let's pretend we haven't seen them and act like all of a sudden we're in a hurry to get back."

"What have we got to lose?" Broxton said, and he took the jib sheet off the winch and watched as the big foresail unfurled. The boat leaned over and picked up speed.

And the Coast Guard cutter added power and started closing fast.

"Will the white sloop ahead heave-to, and prepare to be boarded." The voice crackling over the radio sounded young and inexperienced.

"Shit," T-Bone said and it started to rain. "Good omen," he said, then he slipped the winch handle into a winch and started to crank on the jib sheet, tightening it, moving their speed from seven to eight knots. No match for the cutter, but it would get them into the bay five minutes earlier.

"Are you going to answer?" Broxton asked.

"Not just yet."

"When?"

"When we get a little closer to land," he said, then he started to move away from the wheel. "She's yours, I'm going below."

"What?" Broxton instinctively took the wheel.

"If they see me, we're gonna be boarded. We don't want that," T-Bone said. Then he slipped down the companionway, out of sight. "I'll talk to them, all you have to do is wave."

"I repeat, will the sloop heave-to and prepare to be boarded." The young voice on the radio was more insistent.

T-Bone waited a few seconds with the mike in hand, then he clicked the talk button, "Negative." He released the talk button. "Let's see how they like that."

"This is not a request. Heave-to and prepare to be boarded."

"Guess they didn't like it," T-Bone said, "and they're not going to like this even more." He clicked the talk button. "This is the sailing vessel *Obsession*, bound for Hog Island. I repeat, I will not heave-to. Can you put on someone a little older. Someone that understands radio etiquette, and begin your next transmission by identifying yourselves. *Obsession*, standing by."

"Shit," Broxton said. T-Bone was laughing. The wind picked up to thirty knots, their speed picked up half a knot and it continued to rain. Broxton wasn't wearing foul weather gear, but the electric situation kept his mind off the wet and the cold.

"This is Captain Andrews on the United States Coast Guard cutter Puerto Rico, operating in concert with the Grenadian Government, and we are ordering you to heave-to, and stand by to be boarded." This voice was older and from the timbre of its delivery Broxton knew it was a voice used to being obeyed.

"This is the sailing vessel *Obsession*, out of Hog Island. Captain Powers speaking. I am a sailing instructor and I have a sixteen-year-old student on board. Presently said student is below heaving his guts out all over the salon. I would love to accommodate you, but as captain of this vessel I have to put the safety of the crew and the vessel first.

However I will gladly accept your boarding party in about thirty minutes, after we are safely at anchor in the bay."

"Negative. We will send a launch along side and board you under way if need be."

"If you send a boarding party over in these conditions you will be putting your young men at risk. If I was on this boat alone I'd follow your orders and heave-to, but I will not put the life of my student at risk. Surely the safety of your men is as important to you?"

"I will evaluate the risk."

"Now I have to give him a face saving way not to board us," T-Bone said up to Broxton, then he clicked the talk button. "I'll tell you what. I'll alter course to Prickly Bay. The water is deeper there, you should be able to motor in right behind me. By the time I get the anchor down you can have your launch in the water, and by the time I snub the hook your men can be safely along side."

"You say you're out of Grenada?"

"Registered in the BVI, but operating out of Grenada. I teach sailing. A lot of the charter customers that come down here need a refresher course before they're qualified to take a boat out by themselves. If there was more people like me down here then there would be a heck of a lot less work for you guys."

"I hear that, Mister," Captain Andrews said, seeming to warm to T-Bone. "Too many people come down here, charter a boat, get in trouble and yell for help. The charter companies should be more responsible."

"If they were then I'd be out of a job." T-Bone laughed into the mike.

"All right, Captain Powers, continue on your course for Hog Island. We won't molest you any further today," Captain Andrews said, as the cutter motored along side the sailboat.

"Put your hand to your mouth, like you have a mike in it," T-Bone said to Broxton, and Broxton put his right hand up to his face as T-Bone clicked the talk button. "Thanks very much, Captain Andrews. Fair winds to you and if we meet somewhere down the line I'll buy you a beer."

"And fair winds to you, Captain Powers. Maybe I'll drink that beer someday."

"Wave," T-Bone said to Broxton, who turned toward the cutter and waved. Several crew members on board waved back. It was impossible for Broxton to single out the Captain through the rain. Then the cutter turned off and Broxton knew that his friendship with T-Bone was soon to be put to the test.

For the past month he'd put the drugs on board and his past out of his mind. He'd been living and learning sailing. He hadn't been off the boat and he hadn't minded, but now it was time to move on, time to start putting things right. His enemies, whoever they were, were still out there. And they would still be looking. By now they must have figured out that he was no longer in Trinidad.

"Okay, Billy Boy, let's get her in before that storm catches us." T-Bone came back up on deck.

"I don't know where you've been, my friend," Broxton said, "but it's caught us."

"Yeah, it is a little too windy out here, let's roll in some of that jib." T-Bone laughed and snapped Broxton away from his own problems.

Broxton grabbed a winch handle and started cranking in on the jib, but after a couple of turns it started getting harder to crank and then he couldn't move it at all. He let a little out and then tried grinding it in again, but he met the same resistance at the same spot in the line. "I think it's jammed," he said.

"It happens sometimes, the line bunches up on the roller. I need to change the lead, something I've been meaning to do. I'll go up and fix it." Broxton watched as T-Bone grabbed onto the running backstay and pulled himself out of the cockpit. He bent low to grab onto the lifelines but a wave crashed into the side of the boat before he got a handhold and he went flying over the side and into the water head first.

"Shit!" Broxton threw over the life ring, then he grabbed onto the cockpit cushions and tossed them over, then the second life ring and the man overboard pole. He did a quick check to see if there was anything else that would float and threw over T-Bone's life jacket. He wanted to give T-Bone as much to grab onto as possible, and he wanted the spot good and marked in case he lost sight of him. Then with nothing else to throw over, he went back behind the wheel and spun it to the right, away from T-Bone and into the wind, keeping his head turned toward his friend as the wind brought the boat to a stop. T-Bone was too far away for him to get a line out to, he was going to have to tack back.

He turned the wheel to the left and let the wind fill the head sail. The boat started to come around and Broxton let out a little of the mainsheet to allow the main to fill and the boat started to move. Broxton kept his eyes on T-Bone the whole while and shuddered each time a wave rolled under him, and he sighed with relief when T-Bone grabbed on to a floating cockpit cushion.

As he fell off the wind, the boat picked up speed and once he was on course for T-Bone's position in the water, Broxton realized that he was going too fast. He had to reduce sail or he'd go right over his friend, and the headsail was jammed. With no way to bring in the jib, he'd have to drop the main.

He stepped out of the cockpit, holding onto the boom for support, and moved as quickly as he could across the slippery deck up to the mast. Like T-Bone he wasn't wearing a life jacket. At the mast, he uncleated the main halyard and let the main drop. Even as it was falling he was making his way back to the cockpit. There was no time to tie the main onto the boom, it was just going to have to flog around on deck till he got T-Bone out of the water.

Back at the wheel, he pointed *Obsession* toward T-Bone, who now had a cockpit cushion under each arm. The wind was gusting up to thirty knots and he was still going too fast. For a second he thought about calling the cutter, but that was the last thing T-Bone would want.

He kept on course until he was two boat lengths from the man in the water, then he cranked the boat into the wind and lost sight of T-Bone as the headsail started flapping and blocked his vision. He could only hope as the boat slowed to almost a stop, but with the wind and current it wouldn't stay stopped long.

He looked over the port side and saw T-Bone, close enough to throw a line to, and still hugging the cushions. He had both cushions wrapped under his left arm and he was waving his right hand in the air. Broxton tossed him a line and he almost screamed as his friend tied it around the cushions.

Then he started laughing. He put the line on a winch, and started grinding his friend toward the boat. Once T-Bone was alongside he pulled himself aboard and hauled the cushions up after himself. Then he grabbed Broxton and planted a wet kiss on his forehead, "Billy boy, you are the bloody best sailor in these waters, and I'll knock the block off anyone who says different."

"The fucking cushions?" Broxton said.

"Hey, I got a hard butt," T-Bone said. He wasn't even breathing hard.

"And a harder head," Broxton said.

"Guess I better fix the jib," T-Bone said, and he moved up forward and fixed the jam and raised the main. Then he stood there, holding on to the mast, with his long hair and beard blowing in the wind, and yelled back to Broxton. "You don't really want to go back to Grenada, do you?"

Broxton shook his head.

"Where do you want to go?" he yelled to be heard over the rising storm.

Broxton pointed up island.

"You don't want to wait for better weather?" T-Bone was laughing.

Broxton shook his head, no, and he was laughing, too, as he spun the wheel away from Hog Island and the protection of the bay, and out into the storm.

CHAPTER TEN

THEY MOTORED ALONG GRENADA'S COASTLINE, then sailed on a single tack until the mountains on the leeward side of Carricou killed their wind and they had to turn the motor back on. Julie watched everything Victor did, trying to learn as much as possible. Meiko just watched Victor.

Since they had only enough daylight left to make the southern Grenadines they decided to motor on to Union Island, where Victor raced the sun through the reefs. He won and they set anchor with the sun fading from the horizon.

And the engine died.

All three turned toward the stern.

"Could be nothing," Victor said, but after several failed attempts to start it back up he said there was water in the fuel, "And that is a bad thing. Maybe a blown head gasket."

"How can that be? We just had the engine rebuilt. In your yard."

"Even my guys aren't perfect."

"What are we going to do now?" Meiko asked.

"I'll have my mechanic fly up tomorrow and check it. It might be something simple, but if it is a head gasket, or worse a cracked block, you're going to be here a while."

"Can't your mechanic fix it?"

"Sure, but you might have to wait for the parts."

A week later and Julie was sitting in an outside restaurant overlooking the anchorage, waiting for bacon and eggs. Victor and Meiko had taken the day charter over to Palm Island and wouldn't be back till sunset. Victor had a charter flight back to Trinidad at six-thirty. His mechanic's son had been in an auto accident and he didn't want to leave Trinidad until the boy was well. Victor had some business to take care of that he said would take a couple of days. He promised to return in less than a week with the mechanic in tow.

Julie was beginning to think she was stuck forever.

The waitress brought her breakfast and set it on the table, but Julie didn't notice, because she was watching the black schooner *Snake Eyes* wind its way through the reefs.

"Doris," she called out to the retreating waitress.

"You called?" the tall woman turned toward Julie.

"If you wanted a diesel engine fixed, who would you call?"

"I thought you was never gonna to ask. Sittin' here waitin' for a lazy mechanic to come up from

Trinidad, dumbest think I ever heard. Call Henry. He be da best. He there, down da way." She pointed a bony finger toward the street. "Green building, yellow door, can' miss it. He been waitin' all week for you to come by him."

"Thank you, Doris," Julie said, and she put the money for her breakfast, along with a generous tip, on the table.

"Not gonna eat da eggs?" Doris said, with a toothy grin, scooping up the money.

"Not this morning." Julie pushed her chair away from the table. She stood and pulled her clammy tee shirt away from her body. It was early and already her clothes were sticking.

"They not too good today, anyway," Doris said, but Julie didn't hear her because she was already out of the restaurant and hurrying down the street.

She knocked on the yellow door.

"He not home," said a little girl about seven. She was standing by the side of the building and she was selling fresh vegetables.

"When will he be back?" Julie asked.

"Just now," the girl said.

"Does that mean the same here as it does in Trinidad?"

"What it mean in Trinidad?"

"Oh I don't know, five minutes, a half hour, maybe next week."

"Yeah, it the same." The girl was laughing. She pulled at a braid and asked, "You wanna buy some vegetables while you waitin'?" Her smile was like a quarter moon on a dark night, perfect white teeth and two twinkling stars for eyes.

"How much are the tomatoes?" she asked.

"One dollar EC a pound?"

"A dollar a pound?"

"Yes ma'am and you get to pick your own." Julie looked at the man sitting under a shade tree not too far away and recognized his smile, it matched the little girl's.

"How many you want?" Her smile grew and Julie was hooked.

"How many should I buy?"

"Many as you need."

Julie picked up two tomatoes and put them on the scale. The little girl dropped a pound weight on the other end.

"Not enough, you need more, has to make a pound."

Julie put two more on the scale.

"Oh, no, over a pound," she picked up the pound weight and replaced it with a two pounder. "Oh, lady, you need more, has to make two pounds."

"How about if I take one off?"

"Oh, no, you can't do that. Once you put them on you have to buy them."

"Then how about you put a half pound weight on and I pay you a dollar fifty?"

"I only have these two weights."

Julie looked over at the girl's father who was flashing a lot of bright teeth from the inside of the largest smile she'd ever seen.

"I guess I should pick some more tomatoes," she said.

"I guess." He laughed.

She dropped two more on the scale.

"Whoops, over two pounds." She dropped the one pounder back on. "Now it has to make three pounds."

"I don't think I want three pounds."

"Has to make three pounds," she insisted.

"This time I'm only gonna put one tomato on."
She did and it was just under three pounds. "That's
all." Julie handed her a five dollar bill.

"Oh, no, lady, I don't have no change."

Julie looked over at her father. He shrugged.

"Okay, keep the change," she said.

"Oh, no, I couldn't do that. Do you want a
cucumber?"

"How much?" Julie was on to her game now.

"Only two dollars." She knew Julie had wised up.
No more money out of her. She took her bag of
tomatoes and her one cucumber, walked over to the
girl's father and held out her hand. He shook it.

"She's quite a salesman."

"She put me out of business, now I just watch."

"I can see why."

"You come back in a few years, I'm gonna be a
rich man. But till she makes me rich I have to repair
diesel engines. My name's Henry and I bet you be
lookin' for me."

"Yes, I am. I have a diesel engine that doesn't
want to run."

"I can come later today."

Julie thought about Victor and Meiko enjoying
themselves at Palm Island. Victor would be back by
sundown. She didn't know why, but she felt
intimidated by him. He called her the captain, but he
made all the decisions, and he'd decided on bringing
his mechanic up from Trinidad. He didn't like it
when he didn't get his way. He wouldn't want Henry
on the boat. There would be an argument and she'd
give in for harmony's sake.

"Can't you come earlier?"

"Can't, gotta wait till Darla sells her vegetables.
It's my morning job."

Julie looked over the vegetables on the small table, tomatoes, cucumbers, white radishes, she loved those, and a few heads of lettuce. "How much for the lot," Julie asked.

Darla's eyes lit up, but she caught a sharp look from her father and frowned.

"You don't have to buy it all," he said. "That wouldn't be fair to you and it wouldn't be fair to Darla."

"I can't wait till this afternoon," Julie said.

"You want me to look at it before the ferry comes back from Palm Island?"

"Yes." How had he figured that out? "Is it that obvious?"

"I tell you what," he said, "you stay and watch Darla. She be too young to be selling by her lonesome, an' I'll go look at your motor."

"Let me get this straight. You go and look at my engine and I take your place under that tree?"

"Yes ma'am." His smile was a block wide.

"My dinghy is parked at the dinghy dock."

"I have my own boat. It's got all my tools on it. Here, you might want this. Our sun is powerful hot." He was holding out his wide brimmed straw hat.

"You get thirsty, we got lemonade, jus' ask Darla." She accepted his hat and then he was off, ambling toward the dock with a stiff-legged limp.

For the next two hours she sat under the wide willow tree, her back against its bark and the passing day shielded from her eyes by the broad brim of Henry's hat. Every time she heard a customer she opened her eyes and made sure that Darla was all right, then she dozed back off. Twice Darla woke her when her mother brought out fresh lemonade. Julie was in heaven.

"How much for tomatoes?" Julie opened her eyes at the sound of the high pitched German accent, and peeked out from under the hat. There were three of them. The one speaking was blond, with his back to her. The other two had black hair and rippling muscles.

"A dollar a pound," Darla said. The blond man spoke in German with his two muscleman companions, and the men looked at Darla, and laughed. They looked like body builders, thick chested and thick necked.

"My friends are saying a dollar is too much," the blond man said. He waved his hands when he talked and he stood ramrod straight, like he was pushing his shoulders skyward, trying to be taller. Kurt did that.

Darla's smile faded to false. There was something about the blond man she didn't like. Julie pushed the hat back, not wanting to miss anything, and one of the musclemen caught her stare and started babbling in German. The blond man glanced over and saw Julie and frowned. Julie bit into her lip to keep from screaming. Then the German stalked away with the two heavyweights in his wake.

The blond man had Kurt's face, without the scar. It must be a twin. And that black schooner that looked so much like *Challenge*, now she knew why. Twin boats for twin boys.

"Do you speak anything beside English?" Darla asked.

"I speak Japanese," Julie said.

"Is that because your daughter is Japanese?" Darla asked. There really are no secrets on a small island, Julie thought.

"In a way. My husband was Japanese."

"Where is he?"

"He died."

"Oh," Darla said. She thought for a few seconds, then said, "I can speak German."

"Really?"

"We used to live in Germany, till Daddy hurt his leg. He used to fix all the engines on the big boats, but after the accident he couldn't work any more and we had to come home."

"What happened to your island accent?" Julie asked.

"If I don't sound like everybody else the other kids think I'm stuck up."

"How good is your German?" Julie asked.

"I was born there. I'm nine years old, we only came back last year."

"So that's why you lost your smile, because of what those men were saying."

"He said I was pretty, for a black baby. Only he didn't say it so nice."

"I see," Julie said.

"But when that big man saw you, he said, 'Look, it's her,' and the man with the funny voice looked at you and said that they should leave, 'right now.' Then they left. They didn't sound like they like you very much."

"It didn't look like I was his most favorite person," Julie said.

"They came on that black boat that came in this morning."

"How can that be? I don't even think they've come ashore yet."

"They've been anchored at Chatham Bay, on the other side of the island, for the last three days. There's five men on that boat. It's only two miles from here. They could have walked easy, or took a taxi. They don't have to go back, cause now their boat is here."

"Really?" Julie said.

"I don't think they're nice men," Darla said. "I think you should go away. In the middle of the night, when they're not looking." And Julie thought that Darla was one smart little girl.

"How can I? My engine isn't working."

"It will be," Darla said, "My dad can fix anything that runs." Her pride in her father was evident and Julie was struck by the difference between her and Victor. Victor cultivated and affected a British accent because he thought it elevated him above his peers and Darla talked with an island accent so that she sounded like her peers, not better. In some ways Darla was the more adult of the two.

"There's your father now," Julie said, "I hope he has good news for me."

" 'Course he does, I told you if it's an engine, my Dad can fix it." Darla waved and her father waved back. "It hurts when he walks," Darla said. "He pretends it doesn't, but I know better."

Julie pushed herself up and dusted herself off. Darla was right. She could see the grimace in Henry's eyes as he walked, but he grinned at her and his eyes lit up when Darla ran to him and took him by the hand.

"Got it running," he said.

"What was wrong?" she asked.

"Water in the right fuel tank."

"From a cracked block?" Julie asked, remembering what Victor had said.

"Nope, nothing wrong with the engine, just water in the tank."

"I don't get it, we have a Raycor."

"The best filter in the world won't handle the water I found. Water to fuel ratio was about fifty-fifty."

"That's not possible."

"It is if someone put it in," he said.

"Nobody would do such a thing."

"If somebody wanted you to think there was something wrong with your motor, all he would have to do was sabotage one tank. When he wanted the engine to quit he'd go below and switch from one tank to the other and the engine would stop. The danger is that he could cause permanent damage, but he didn't. Your engine seems to be okay."

"Would you do me a favor and not tell anyone the engine's working?"

"You don't want the White Trinidadian to know?" Henry asked.

"Not so much him as the Germans on that black schooner. But you're right, I don't want him to know either."

"But he's your daughter's boyfriend," Darla said.

"He is not," Julie said, but she was starting to think otherwise. She'd been wanting to talk to Meiko about it, but the only thing they ever argued about when she was growing up was boys. It seemed like whenever she didn't like one, Meiko went out of her way to like him more. So she'd learned to keep her mouth shut.

"Yes he is. You should see them holding hands when you're not around."

"It's true," Henry said.

"In that case I really don't want him to know. Shit, he's my age. We'll leave tonight, if we can get out of here without the Germans seeing us."

"They've been spending every night at Sophie's bar. I'll ask her to let them drink for half price tonight, and I'll ask her to serve them doubles."

"Now all I have to do is get past the reefs after dark," Julie said.

"Very dangerous," Henry said.

There was a steel band playing in the background as they brought up the anchor. Julie hung over the bow pulpit with her foot on the windlass button and watched the anchor rode come up. The sound of the band on shore helped cover the sound of the rattling chain as it clanged over the bow roller.

She wanted to leave the bay with as little attention as possible. The black schooner was dark, the crew was ashore. Henry had reported that they were drinking heavily at Sophie's.

She stepped away from the bow roller as the anchor came up and thudded into place with a clang that reverberated through the bay. She was a second slow off the button and now everybody knew someone had an anchor up. Julie hoped the Germans were sitting close to the pan players and not looking out over the anchorage.

Meiko added a little forward throttle and they started to weave their way among the boats, paralleling the reef. Julie knew that only the experienced or the foolish left Clifton at night, but she was more afraid of *Snake Eyes* and her crew than she was of the reef.

There was a breeze battling the current and the water was choppy. Boats were bobbing at anchor, their anchor lights, atop the tall masts, weaving patterns in the night. Julie bent over and held on to the lifelines as she made her made her way back to the stern. She grabbed onto the mainsheet, hanging off the boom for support and swung into the cockpit.

"The marker," Julie said. "Left, left, left," and Meiko started spinning the wheel. They heard and felt a crunching sound as the keel scraped the bottom. The boat shuddered and for a second Julie thought it was all over, but the shuddering and scraping stopped and the boat moved back into deeper water.

"That was close," Meiko sighed.

"See the lights on the south end of Palm Island?" Julie said.

"Sure, that's the hotel," Meiko said, and Julie wondered how she knew that.

"Try to stay halfway between them and the red buoy on the left. That should keep us off the reef until we get out of this channel."

"Then what?" Meiko asked.

"Then we're through the most dangerous part."

Meiko steered and Julie kept watch. The wind increased and Julie wished she had gotten a weather report. It was turning into a chilly night. Then the rain came, but not hard, just enough to keep them cold and uncomfortable.

"Mom, we're in twenty feet of water." Meiko was bobbing on her toes and heels.

"It's okay, as long as we stay between the lights," she said, trying to sound more confident than she felt.

"Mom, it's fifteen feet." Meiko stopped bouncing, but her knuckles were white on the wheel. She was waiting for them to hit bottom again.

"We'll be all right," Julie said. "Stay between the lights."

"Twenty-five feet, forty, forty-five. It's getting deeper," Meiko said, reading the depth sounder. Then they were through the reefs.

"Turn a little to the left," Julie said, "and aim for Mayreau. We still have another set of reefs to negotiate. There should be a lighted beacon. Keep your eye out for it." She had to go to the bathroom. "I'm going to the toilet, will you be okay up here for a minute or two?"

"Sure, no problem."

The boat was rocking gently in the five foot swells and Julie held onto the bulkheads as she made her way forward to the head. She pumped some water into the bowl, pulled down her shorts and sat on the toilet. She finished and was pumping fresh seawater into the bowl when a screeching sound assaulted her and the boat shook. She felt like she was in an earthquake and she braced herself between the walls for support.

"Mom, help!" Meiko called out.

The small bathroom rocked back and forth, knocking Julie into one wall, then another. She felt like she was the clangor inside a giant bell. She pulled the door open, and with hands against the walls for support, she scrambled to the cockpit.

"Turn right and full power," Julie yelled as she came up the ladder, and Meiko obeyed, sliding the throttle forward and spinning the wheel away from the reef. The scraping continued as the boat grated on the coral bottom, and they were barely moving.

"Are we going to be all right?" Meiko asked, eyes wide. Then the boat broke free, and for the second time that night they moved into deeper water and off of a reef.

"What happened?" Julie asked. Meiko backed off on the throttle.

"There wasn't any light. By the time I saw the beacon it was too late. I'm sorry."

"It's okay, we're all right now."

"Thank God," Meiko said.

"Keep your current course. I'm going to run below for a second and look at the chart." She saw the look in her daughter's eyes. "It'll be okay, we're a mile away from any more reefs."

"That's comforting," Meiko said, and Julie went below. The boat was rocking more, because they were away from the shelter of the reefs. Julie held onto hand rails for support and made her way to the chart table. It took her less than a minute to decide what to do.

She scooted out from behind the table and went topside. "Turn left," she said.

"But it's the wrong way."

"We're going out to sea."

"But I thought we were going to hug the islands. You said it was safer."

"We've come a hair's breath from running aground twice. We might not be so lucky the next time. If we head up toward Martinique we'll have better winds and we won't have to worry about any reefs."

"Martinique, that's at least two days away."

"I know," Julie said, "and it's the last thing *Snake Eyes* will suspect. They'll be looking for us in the Southern Grenadines, Bequia or St. Vincent. Meanwhile we'll be in the French Islands, where they have real law and real police. If they try anything there they'll go to jail for a long time."

"We'll have to sail during the night." Meiko pushed the hair from her eyes. The wind blew it right back. It was a constant battle she couldn't win, but she kept trying.

"We're sailing during the night now, well, we're motoring anyway," Julie said and mother and daughter laughed. The sky was clear behind, but there were clouds ahead, covering the stars and blocking the moon. Julie hoped they wouldn't bring more rain.

"You know what I mean. Two days without rest, just the two of us. Do you really think we can do it?" Meiko asked. She had one hand on the wheel and the other holding her hair back.

"Of course we can. People do it all the time," Julie said, and she pulled a band out of her hair, "Here, you need this more than I do."

"But we're so inexperienced," Meiko said. She held the wheel with her foot while she put her hair back with the band.

"Can you think of a better way to learn?"

"Sure, Victor could be here teaching us."

"Helping us is more like it," Julie said.

"What do you mean?" Meiko asked.

"He did all the work, he never really showed us how to do anything." And that bothered Julie. Every time she asked him a question he put her off. As if he didn't really want to teach her. As if teaching a woman was beneath him.

"Come on, Mom, we learned a lot."

"By watching."

"That's just his way of teaching. He wanted us to learn by experience, not by being told."

"Well I didn't like it. Every time I asked him why he did something he just said, 'Because, that's the way you do it.' It felt like he was putting me off, and it was beginning to feel like he was in charge."

Thunder rumbled ahead and Julie shivered as they started to move under the clouds. In a few minutes they'd be far enough from the reefs and they could turn toward a course for Martinique.

"We wouldn't be here now if it wasn't for him. We owe him a lot," Meiko said.

"I know that," Julie said. "He's been a great help. I keep forgetting he's a Trini. They all have that macho Trini attitude, black or white. I've never been able to get used to it."

Thunder rumbled again, louder, closer.

"Think we'll get more rain?" Meiko asked, and Julie sensed that she wanted to change the subject away from Victor. She ached to tell her daughter that she was too young for him, but she thought it best to hold her tongue.

"Maybe not," she said. "Turn to zero three zero."

"Turning to thirty degrees," Meiko said, and she slowly spun the wheel to the right until the compass needle told her she was on course. Now the dark skies were off to the right and the wind was from the east, on the beam.

"I guess it's time we got our feet wet and raised a sail."

"You want me to turn into the wind."

"No, I don't think we'll use the main just yet. Lets see how she does with just the jib." Julie freed the port jib sheet, then she freed the furling line from the self tailing jaws, but she kept four wraps on the winch as she cranked on the starboard jib sheet. She stopped cranking when the sail was halfway out, and she cleated off both the furling line and the jib sheet.

Wind filled the sail and the boat picked up speed. Meiko shut off the engine. "Wow," she said, "it's like magic." Rain was falling on the left, but the squall wasn't affecting them. It was clear on the right and clear ahead, the waves were coming from behind and Meiko was wearing a smile that would light a Christmas tree.

"We're doing seven knots with sixteen knots of wind and the jib is only halfway out," Julie said. "This boat can sail."

The winds aloft shifted and the cloud cover moved over them, blanketing their world in darkness, but they were steadily moving away from the squall. "It's kind of spooky," Meiko said. "Like one of those Jack Priest horror stories. I can see it now, mother and daughter abducted by women starved aliens."

Then she turned and scanned the horizon. "Hey, Mom, I saw a light."

"Where?"

"Behind us."

Julie turned. "There's nothing there now."

"There was," Meiko said. "It was on for a few seconds, then off. It looked far away."

"It could have been fishermen. They go out horribly far in those little boats."

"At night?" She was behind the wheel, and Julie heard the tension in her voice.

"Easy, we're both a little jumpy. There's no way they could have followed us. We're safe from them. We only have the ocean to worry about."

"And the wind and the rain," Meiko said, loosening up.

Six hours later Meiko was back on watch, and she saw the light behind them. "Mom, I saw it again," she said, softly.

"What, honey?" Julie said. She was waking from a dreamy sleep on the starboard cockpit seat. She sat up, stretched and yawned.

"The light behind us. It's still on."

Julie turned and this time she saw it, too. Then it winked out. "Could be fishermen," she said.

"It's not," Meiko said. "Not this far out. Not this late."

"You want to let out a little more sail?" Julie asked.

"Yeah," she said, and Julie rolled out a little more head sail. Their speed increased from seven to seven-point-eight. "Roll it all out, let's see how fast we can go with just the jib," and Julie rolled it all out.

"How's that?" she said.

"Look at the knot meter," Meiko said, "and see for yourself."

"Eight-point-five. We're smoking," Julie said, and they sailed like that, a perfect beam reach at eight and a half knots, till morning, when the wind shifted to just off their nose.

Meiko saw it first. The white sails against the dawn. About a mile behind. "Sails at six o'clock," she said, and Julie turned to look.

"Check with the binoculars," Julie said, but her words weren't necessary, Meiko already had the long glasses to her eyes.

"It's them."

CHAPTER ELEVEN

FOR THE LAST TWO HOURS a speedboat had been shadowing them at the edge of a normal man's sight, but Broxton had better than excellent vision and he knew they were there. Had been for over an hour. It was a bad sign.

He pushed himself up from his seat in the cockpit, faced to the sea and into the afternoon, onshore breeze. He shivered against the early chill and ran his hands through his growing hair, enjoying the feel of it. He thought about the new couple on board. Something about them wasn't right.

He stretched, ignored the familiar ache across his stomach and took in a deep breath, holding it in his lower abdomen, and with eyes closed he took himself away from the island coastline. He thought about

Julie Tanaka, her glistening green eyes, her golden brown hair, her strong, tanned body.

And he opened his eyes. The speedboat was still there. Fast. Powerful. Holding back. Waiting.

For what?

He closed his eyes again and exhaled, letting the breath pass his lips in a trickle as he relaxed his shoulders. It was an art. With the air out of his lungs he took in a normal breath and blinked away the tears caused by the stinging wind. He moved toward the binnacle and slid around the wheel. There was no need to look at the compass or GPS, he knew where they were and what direction they were headed. He wanted to steer, to feel the wind in the sails with his hands, so he flicked off the autopilot, gripped the wheel and took in another long, slow breath.

He picked up the binoculars as he exhaled and grabbed a quick look. One of the men was holding what looked like a Mach Ten machine pistol.

"Hey, Mr. Broxton, how's she going?" Jimmy said, as he climbed out of the companion way. Jimmy was Australian and sounded like it. T-Bone found the couple, forlorn and lost in Fort de France four days ago. He was young and strong, his wife was pregnant and they looked down and out. They said they'd work for a ride up to St. Martin. T-Bone felt sorry for them and took them on.

"Fine, and Susan?"

"The little nipper is kicking up a storm like you wouldn't believe. It's gonna be a boy, sure as God made thunder." He shook his hand in mock pain and Broxton pictured him holding Susan's swollen belly, jerking the hand away when the baby kicked.

A gust of wind came up and Broxton corrected for it as the sails flapped. It took him a few seconds to fill them again. He glanced at the speed indicator, they were doing eight knots. He moved his gaze to the GPS, they were doing six over the surface of the globe, they had a two knot current against them.

"I've done loads of deliveries with loads of blokes and you're the only one that steers every chance he gets," Jimmy said.

"Can you put the dinghy in the water?" Broxton asked.

"Now? At this speed? No way, too dangerous."

"If your life depended on it?"

"Not a chance."

"Susan's life, and your strong, kicking son?"

"Maybe," he said.

"Go below, wake up T-Bone and have him bring up the pump," Broxton said.

Jimmy looked into Broxton's weathered eyes. "Am I in a hurry?" he said.

"I believe so," Broxton answered. "And tell T-Bone to bring the thirty-eight he has hidden in the port head."

Broxton turned to look at the speedboat. Red. Fast. Still hanging back.

T-Bone poked his head out of off the companion way, his long hair hidden under a wide-brimmed, floppy hat. He dropped the pump in the cockpit, disappeared, then reappeared with the gun in his left hand.

"Stick it in your pants," Broxton said.

"I'd feel better if I was holding on to it."

"They may have binoculars," Broxton said, and T-Bone jammed the gun between his belt and his belly.

"Who?"

"Speedboat. Been following us a long time."

T-Bone roamed his eyes around the sea. It was Antigua. It was Friday afternoon. There were a lot of boats on the water, though they were the farthest out. "I see it," he said.

"I have a strong feeling they don't want us to get to St. Martin."

"And you want us to jump into the dinghy, out here, going eight knots, on a hunch?" Jimmy said, coming back up on deck.

"That and the machine pistol I saw one of the men holding."

"I'll blow up the dinghy," T-Bone said.

"What's wrong?" Susan asked, coming through the companionway.

"Mr. Broxton says we have to get off," Jimmy said.

"My god, why?"

"The speedboat back there has been shadowing us. He thinks they're going to pirate the boat," Jimmy said.

"We're getting off, because of that?" she said. Broxton noticed her slight shiver.

"If I'm wrong. We'll be embarrassed, but alive."

"This is insane," she said.

"They've got guns," Jimmy said.

"It's gonna be harder than hell getting the bloody thing blown up, I've no idea how we'll get the engine on her," T-Bone said.

"We have to try," Broxton said. T-Bone nodded and went forward. The dinghy was deflated and lashed upside down to cleats between the staysail and the main mast.

It started to rain.

"That's all we need," T-Bone said.

"It'll give us some cover," but as he said it the speedboat moved a little closer, and Broxton turned the autopilot back on.

The boat was sailing close hauled, healed over at a twenty-five degree angle. Broxton, even after a month on the boat, still hadn't gotten used to moving around in a world where nothing was as it should be, but T-Bone and Susan moved forward like the boat was motoring in flat calm.

"We'll have to turn it over," T-Bone said, and Broxton and Jimmy removed the line from the cleats at the port and starboard end of the dinghy, while T-Bone held it steady. "It's heavy," T-Bone said, "I'll take the front and you two take the back."

And they started to lift it when a wave crashed over the side, drenching the three of them. The dinghy started to slide toward the water, but Broxton dove between the dinghy and the lifelines, blocking it from sliding under and into the sea with his body.

It took the three of them to manhandle the dinghy back to the center of the boat, then T-Bone and Broxton flipped it rightside up.

"Let's lash it fore and aft so we don't lose it again," Jimmy said. Sitting upright the deflated dinghy rocked back and forth on the hard fiberglass vee of its bottom with each swell that jolted the boat and Broxton had a hard time with the line.

"I'll do it," Jimmy yelled to make himself heard over another crashing wave. He had the line cleated off before the water cleared the deck. Broxton cursed his inexperience.

"Go below and get your gear while we blow it up," Broxton told Jimmy, he at least could do that.

Lightning splashed through the sky as another wave washed over the deck. The boat was jerking and the autopilot was correcting with each wave. Broxton listened for the thunder that didn't come. Then the rain stopped, presenting them with an Antiguan rainbow.

"Take it off the wind a bit," T-Bone said, "or the dinghy will fill with water once we inflate it." Broxton nodded and worked his way back to the cockpit and set a new course for the autopilot, pointing them an additional fifteen degrees away from the shore. The boat flattened out and the waves stopped drenching the deck.

"How's that?" he yelled forward, and T-Bone gave him the thumbs up sign.

"Think they'll come in closer once they see we've changed course?" T-Bone asked him.

"I think it'll take them a few minutes to figure it out," Broxton said.

T-Bone trimmed the sails and the boat picked up speed, gliding through the water like a dolphin. This was the kind of sailing that Broxton had come to love, a beam reach, the wind at the side, the sails full, slicing through the waves instead of them breaking over the bow.

Broxton pumped on the hand pump until the port side was inflated. He was breathing heavily when T-Bone took over and filled both the front and starboard chambers.

"We'll have to drop the dinghy in the water, then lower the engine down. It weighs seventy pounds, do you want to hand off or receive?" T-Bone asked.

"I'll hand off," Broxton answered.

Jimmy and Susan came back on deck with a carry-on bag each. Susan went forward and dropped them in the dinghy, then she tied them in with a bowline, looping the line through the bag's handles and the port handle of the dinghy.

"We have to move fast now. We don't have much time," Broxton said.

"We'll get the dinghy ready while you get your gear," Susan said.

"I'm not going," Broxton said.

"What?" she said.

"I'm staying, too," T-Bone said.

"Maybe we should also stay," Jimmy said. "You can't know for sure that we're in any trouble?"

"Believe me there's a lot of reasons you want to get your wife off this boat," Broxton said.

"Lots of reasons," T-Bone echoed.

"You could be wrong." Jimmy said.

"If it wasn't for your wife, you'd be dead right now," Broxton said.

Jimmy turned ashen.

"It had to be you. How else could they have known where we were. What did you do, call them from the restaurant last night?"

"You son of a bitch," T-Bone said, advancing on Jimmy.

"No, stop. It wasn't him. It was me. I'm sorry," Susan said. "Jimmy didn't know."

"Why?" T-Bone asked.

"He said they just wanted to know where you were going. Nothing bad was going to happen," she said.

"He lied," Broxton said.

"How'd you do it?" T-Bone asked.

"A man approached me when we went ashore in Dominica. He said he just wanted to know where *Obsession* was going to be. He said he was an insurance man and he was investigating a lawsuit. He gave me two hundred dollars and a cell phone so I could let him know where we were."

"So you sold us out for two hundred bucks."

"Don't worry about it, T-Bone, "Broxton said, "I've been sold out before. There's nothing we can do about it now."

He looked at the speedboat still hanging back, almost at the edge of sight. Then he turned back to the couple. "We should get you off, before we get too far out to sea."

Broxton and T-Bone lifted the dinghy up and dropped it over the side, while Susan held on the to the painter to keep it from floating away. Once it was in the water she wrapped the painter around a cleat.

"The speedboat hasn't moved," Jimmy said.

"I'll get the gas tank." Broxton went to the storage area under the cockpit seats, as T-Bone lifted the outboard off its wooden perch on the aft port side.

Susan took the gas tank from Broxton and lowered it into the dinghy. Then she went over the side and jumped in herself.

"They may come looking for you, so stay out of sight as long as possible," Broxton said.

"Righto," Jimmy said.

"Good luck." Broxton held out his hand. "Don't be too hard on her."

Jimmy took it and answered, "You, too."

Then he was over the side and in the dinghy. Broxton helped T-Bone lower the motor. Jimmy struggled to fasten it to the dinghy's transom, but the sea was too rough for him to slide it into place.

"The speedboat's coming in closer," Susan said.

"If the bloody boat would just stay still a second," Jimmy hollered. A rolling wave slid under them and he almost lost the engine to the sea, but he held on and between waves he slipped it into place and clamped it down.

"Quickly," Broxton said, as Jimmy snapped the hose from the gas tank into place.

The speedboat eased a little closer and Broxton suspected that they were using binoculars and wanted a closer look.

Jimmy pulled on the starter cord.

Nothing.

The speedboat moved closer.

He pulled again.

Still nothing.

"Use the choke," Susan said as the speedboat roared to life. Jimmy pulled the choke and pulled the cord and the engine coughed.

"Pump the gas," Susan said and Jimmy squeezed the ball pump in the center of the gas hose.

They could see the spray shooting up from behind the speedboat. It was coming full throttle now. Jimmy pulled on the starter cord and the engine caught. He gave it a little gas and it purred, then he revved it and it roared.

Broxton uncleated the painter and tossed it to Susan. Despite the fact that she'd sold them out he couldn't bring himself to want anything but the best for her. He liked Jimmy and she was his wife. He flashed her the piece sign with his left hand. She flashed it back. Jimmy gave his familiar thumbs up sign. Broxton pointed to a group of three sailboats halfway between them and the shore. Jimmy nodded as he put the dinghy in gear and then he was off, planing the dinghy over the rolling waves. The speedboat would have no trouble cutting them off before they reached shore, but they had a better than even chance of reaching the safety of the sailboats.

With them away, Broxton went back to the cockpit and released the autopilot. The speed boat was coming fast and Broxton pointed the boat out to sea and let out the main sheet. With the wind at her side, *Obsession* was again on a beam reach, her best and fastest point of sail.

The men in the speedboat had a problem, go after the dinghy and risk losing sight of *Obsession* as she made for the open sea, or go after *Obsession* and lose the dinghy for certain. Broxton gambled they'd go after the prize, and he smiled with satisfaction when the speedboat changed course to follow.

He set the autopilot and went forward to join T-Bone. He knew now they were watching them with long glasses or they wouldn't have charged forward when the dinghy went in the water.

"Drugs gotta go overboard," he said.

"I know," T-Bone answered, and he opened the hatch to the forepeak and jumped below.

Broxton stood above as T-Bone handed out the bales, one at a time, and one at a time, Broxton tossed them into the sea.

The weather was changing, for the worse. The wind was picking up and so was *Obsession's* speed. They would have a devil of a time boarding.

Broxton picked up the binoculars from the bracket on the binnacle and smiled when the speedboat slowed to pick up a bale. There were four of them. Two large and Teutonic looking. The other two looked Hispanic. Dark hair, dark eyes, both holding machine pistols. One of them was driving the boat, the other was watching Broxton through a set of binoculars of his own. Broxton flashed him the piece sign. The man gave him the finger in return.

The speedboat circled the drugs. A mistake, because that made it even harder to grapple the bales on board as they bobbed in the boat's wake. The two big men were forced to set their weapons down and fish for them with their hands.

"Stupid," T-Bone said. "they should let them go."

"Greed," Broxton said. "Go below. Fill a glass with catsup and add about twenty-five percent soy sauce and mix it up good."

"You got a plan?"

"When you're finished it should look like blood."

"Yeah, Billy Boy, you got a plan. I can tell." T-Bone went below.

Broxton stood in the cockpit and watched the speedboat as they fished the bales out of the sea. Till the day he died, he'd never understand that kind of person. For whatever reason they were after him, it had to be more important to whoever was paying them than a few thousand dollars of marijuana, but there they were, just the same. Not much brighter than children.

The last bale was giving them trouble, and Broxton laughed as the men in the boat struggled to get it. Every time they came around to it, it floated away, almost like it was eluding them on purpose. After the third attempt and the third failure, Broxton thought they were going to give up, but when they made another circle and came up on the bale again, he realized that it had become a challenge. They wouldn't quit until they had the bale on board.

And it galled him that they were so sure of their quarry that they would take the time out to fish the grass from the sea. They must think they were dealing with sitting ducks. So stupid, because these ducks were intelligent. They weren't going to wait and go like lambs to the slaughter.

"Okay, got it," T-Bone said from below.

"Come up, but stay low," Broxton said, and T-Bone slithered out of the hatch like a snake out of a hole. He kept sliding till he was fully in the cockpit and staring up at Broxton.

"Now what, Billy?" Broxton couldn't believe it. The man was smiling, laughing, like he was having a good time. He'd just lost thousands of dollars and the men in the speed boat would shortly be upon them. T-Bone had to know they weren't coming for tea and crumpets. Most men would be shaking with sweat, but his friend was tingling with excitement.

"Slide across to the back of the boat and pour the fake blood on the deck. Then lay down with your head in it."

"Shit, that doesn't sound like much fun."

"Think you can keep your eyes open for a few minutes without blinking?" Broxton asked.

"What happens if I can't?"

"We'll probably be killed."

"Shit, I can keep 'em open all afternoon. Who needs to blink?"

"Can you shoot a man?"

"What happens if I can't?"

"We'll probably be killed."

"Sure, I can take out an army if I have to," he laughed.

"Can you hit what you're shooting at?"

"Shit, let's just do it," T-Bone said, and he slid to the stern and poured the catsup-soy sauce mixture out of the jar. "Gooey," he said, before dropping his head into the mixture. "How's this?" He stared up at Broxton, eyes wide, tongue hanging out.

"Don't make me laugh, they're coming," Broxton said, and T-Bone pulled his tongue back in his mouth and lay there, looking dead. "Keep the gun tucked out of sight," Broxton said, and he bent over his friend, picked up the jar and tossed it over the side.

"Pollution," T-Bone mumbled. "Can get in big trouble for that."

Broxton smiled and reached under T-Bone and pulled his cigarettes out of his pocket along with his wooden matches.

"You don't smoke," T-Bone said.

"I do today," and he cupped his hand, struck a match and lit a cigarette. "Okay," he said. "It's showtime."

The speedboat was moving closer and Broxton squinted over the side. That last bale was drifting toward shore. So there weren't able to get it after all. He wondered if it was a good sign. He didn't think so. He was counting on their greed.

The speedboat pulled along side. Broxton smiled and waved, like he was greeting friends. Then he unhooked the swim ladder from the front of the mast. One of the blond men was struggling to get a line around one of the stanchions, but the speedboat, not made for rolling seas, was jerking back and forth, making it a battle he was bound to lose.

"Wait a minute," Broxton yelled down at them. The second blond man pointed a pistol at Broxton, expecting resistance, but Broxton, with his cigarette clamped between his lips, ignored him as he set the swim ladder in place.

Once he slipped the pins in, securing the ladder, he stood up, flipped the cigarette into the ocean and yelled to be heard over the sea, "Throw me your line." The blond man did and Broxton secured it to a stanchion with a double half hitch. By the time he was finished the man with the gun was climbing on board. Broxton offered his hand. The man ignored it.

"Move away," he said, with the gun pointed at Broxton's stomach. Broxton stepped back as the other man and one of the Hispanics climbed on board.

"I'm Broxton," he said.

"What happened to him?" the second man up the ladder asked. Both men sounded German, and they were looking at T-Bone's body and the pool of red around his head.

"He died," Broxton said.

"How?"

"I killed him."

"Why would you do that?" the Hispanic said. Broxton thought he had a Cuban accent.

"I thought maybe we could make a deal."

"What kind of deal?" one of the Germans asked.

"I know where he buys the drugs and I know where he sells them. With a little financial backing we can make a fortune."

"You really don't know anything, do you?"

"I know we can make a couple hundred grand each in a few months. I know that. That should interest you."

The man laughed, turned and said something to his friend in German, then he turned back to Broxton, still laughing, "Time for you to go," he said, bringing a pistol out from inside his shirt.

"One question, please," Broxton said.

"Sure." The German pointed the gun at Broxton's chest. "What could it hurt?"

"Why?"

"Such a small word and such a big question." The German was enjoying himself. "*Stardust* was a drug boat."

"Impossible. I searched that boat myself," Broxton said.

"The cocaine was glassed into the hull, packed in between the bulk heads and buried into the bilges, false bottom. Millions of dollars."

"Too bad," Broxton said.

"They don't know what caused the explosion, but Dieter thinks it was your big mouth." And Broxton had to fight a smile, he had a name now, and he knew who Dieter was.

"I don't get it." Broxton said, playing for time and more information.

"They think the competition blew the boat. That way they keep their prices up and our stuff out of California."

"No honor among thieves," Broxton said.

"None," the German said, bringing up the gun.

"Wait, one last quick question."

"No."

"Like you said, what could it hurt?"

"Ask."

"A German accent, male with a little girl's voice?"

The man with the gun laughed. "Our man inside the DEA, Kurt's twin, Karl," he said. Then T-Bone shot the laughing German in the belly. He flew backwards, dropping the gun, clutching his stomach and screaming, until he collided with the mast and fell forward, bleating like a calf.

Broxton dropped to the deck with fear-crazed speed, grabbing the German's gun. The Cuban fired his machine pistol, but he was caught by surprise and his shots went wild. T-Bone shot him in the chest. He was dead before his body hit the deck.

The Hispanic in the speedboat was busy sliding a fender between the speedboat and *Obsession*, his machine pistol out of reach on the stern seat when Broxton shot him between the eyes.

Both Broxton and T-Bone trained their weapons on the German still standing and he threw his hands in the air. The other one was still wailing on the deck, hands clutching his bloody stomach.

"Oh, put him out of his misery," T-Bone said, and Broxton turned the man over with his foot and shot him through the heart.

"I want to know more about the man with the little girl's voice," Broxton said.

The German glared at Broxton and Broxton blew off his right knee cap. He sank to the deck without a whimper, hate filling his eyes.

"Tell me about the man with the little girl's voice."

The German glared up at Broxton, who aimed the pistol at the man's groin. "No more," he pleaded. "His name is Karl Schneidler. He works for the DEA." He bit into his lip to help fight the pain. Both his hands were clutching his bloody knee.

"How, if he's German?"

"He's an American citizen. It's not so hard."

"Tell me more," Broxton said. Now he knew who the traitor was. He knew who'd set him up.

"He sails a forty-five foot sloop."

"Boat name? Color? Where can I find him?"

"*Snake Eyes*. Black. Don't know," he said.

Broxton raised the gun.

"I don't know," he wailed. "Dieter has them out chasing two women in a big race boat. He's mad like hell that they haven't caught her."

"*Fallen Angel*?" Broxton asked.

"Yes," the German said.

"Why?"

"She's like *Stardust*. Only more valuable"

Broxton looked at T-Bone and nodded. T-Bone shot the German in the back of the head.

"Billy Boy, we gotta talk."

"Soon as we clean up the mess," Broxton said. T-Bone nodded. Then the two men went to work. T-Bone tightened sail and pointed *Obsession* away from the island and out toward the sea. Then they dumped the three bodies in the speedboat still rafted to the side.

"When we get far enough away, so that we can't be seen, we'll cut it loose."

"You don't want to dump the bodies? Get rid of the evidence?"

"No."

"You want to send a message?"

"Yes."

"Better than a postcard," T-Bone said, and he picked up the salt water hose and started hosing down the deck.

"Okay, Billy Boy," T-Bone said when the deck was clean. "Tell me about the German with the little girl's voice."

"I really hate that name," Broxton said.

"Really? You never said."

"Just call me Broxton."

"Keep calling me, T-Bone, like the steak," he laughed and Broxton joined him.

"I work for the DEA." Broxton said.

"Sheeit."

"Yeah, it was my job to bust guys like you."

"I heard what you were talking about back there. There's lots bigger fish."

"I'm not out to bust anyone anymore. I'm just giving you background."

"Okay."

"I was working out of the American Embassy in Trinidad when an informant tipped me that the boat *Stardust* was dirty. But I had no proof, so one night I went aboard and had a look for myself. Nothing. Clean. Now you know why.

"Then I get a call from an old partner of mine. He was working in the Director's office and he tells me that I'm on the agency's most wanted list. Someone put a lot of money in my account and everyone thinks I'm dirty. My name's on everyone's list, and a lot of folks start trying to make me dead.

"So I get paranoid and start trying to get out of Trinidad, and just before meeting you I call Dawson, that's my partner, and this girlie sounding German answers the phone and tells me he's killed my friend.

"I told the bastard that I'd be coming for him, and it's a promise I'm going to keep. Especially now that I know he works for the DEA. He set me up and killed my friend. I'll get him. If I never do anything else on this earth, I'll get him."

"And the other boat?" T-Bone said. *"Fallen Angel."*

"There's a couple of pretty ladies on board I wouldn't want hurt for anything."

"Damsels in distress?" T-Bone's eyes sparkled.

"They're somewhere in the Caribbean and they're in trouble. I want to help."

"Damsels in distress, being chased by evil Germans. Very bad," he said. "Where will they go?"

"I don't know."

"Then we'll head south, to St. Lucia. Everybody goes through Rodney Bay. There's a nice beach bar. Typhoon Willie's. We'll wait there. We'll ask questions. I know everybody in the Caribbean that can be trusted to keep his mouth shut. We'll have a lot of eyes looking, a lot of ears listening. We'll find those damsels and we'll slay those dragons."

Broxton shook his head. If T-Bone was your friend, he was your friend.

"Okay, Billy Boy, cut that fucker loose and lets go south."

"I really hate that name," Broxton said.

T-Bone just laughed.

Chapter Twelve

SOUTH OF THE CAPE VERDE ISLANDS, *off the west coast of Africa, the winds at sea level were pacing the winds aloft, blowing away from the giant continent. The sea breeze converged with a rapid wind headed toward the Island group. The water below was unseasonably warm and the colliding winds curved upwards, taking evaporating moisture from the ocean below toward the heavens and a westward moving high pressure area.*

Lightning flashed, thunder roared. A storm was born.

"HOW COULD THEY HAVE KNOWN? How could they have followed us?" Julie said, lowering her hand from her forehead. She looked west and saw the steep green of St. Lucia through the early morning light.

They were far enough away that the mountains didn't cut off their wind, but the wind had shifted and was now out of the northwest. Almost on the nose. They were sailing close hauled, and they were down to five knots.

"Radar," Meiko said, looking through the binoculars. "They've got all their sails up, and I think they must have the engine on, too, because their jib is sort of luffing."

"And we've only got the jib up," Julie said. She glanced at the wind speed indicator, eighteen knots of wind, then she turned to study the boat in back.

"I think they're gaining," Meiko said. "What are we going to do?" She turned toward her mother. Her ponytail was whipping around and she was biting her lower lip.

"Put up more sail," Julie said. She didn't have any illusions about what those men would do if they caught her. At the very least they would take the boat back to Trinidad, dropping them off along the way. She didn't want to think about the worst.

Meiko started the engine and after a few seconds she added some power. The rumbling of the diesel was music to Julie's ears. Henry knew his business. She stole another quick look at the knot meter and frowned. They'd picked up less than a knot.

"Okay, darling, turn into the wind and I'll go up and start hoisting the main." Julie had never pulled the sail up by herself before, but she'd seen Victor and the men from the shipyards do it a number of times. She thought she could handle it.

"They'll gain on us when we slow down," Meiko said.

"We're just going to have to be quick about it," she said. "Once we have the main up, turn back on course and give it the gas. We're going to use all we have."

Meiko eased the boat into the wind and the headsail started to luff as the wind fell out of it. By the time she had *Fallen Angel* all the way around the big jib was making cracking sounds, like thunder, as it flapped across the deck. Julie knew it would be suicide to go up there with the sail snapping like a dragon's tongue. One hit and she'd be over the side.

"Mom, we forgot to roll up the jib." Meiko was bobbing on her toes, straining to see around the whipping sail.

"We'll have to take some of it in," Julie said, and she grabbed a winch handle and started cranking on the furling line.

"Hurry, Mom!"

"I'm going as fast as I can," Julie huffed. She was hunched over the top of the winch, both hands on the handle, turning for all she was worth. When she had the jib halfway in she pulled the handle out of the winch. "That should keep it out of my way," she said, then she crawled on her hands and knees up to the main.

"You didn't clip on!" Meiko yelled after her.

"No time," Julie called back, but she was facing away from her daughter and Meiko couldn't hear.

The wind gusted, giving *Snake Eyes* a burst of speed and Julie trouble as the boat started rocking with the waves. She uncleated the main halyard and started to haul up the sail. She struggled it about a third of the way up the mast, but she wasn't strong enough to get it any further.

She pulled on the halyard, using it to help pull herself into a standing position. Then she wrapped her hands around the line and used her weight to pull on it, but she was only able to raise the sail a few feet more.

"I need help," Julie shouted back, and Meiko came forward, holding onto the boom for support.

"If we both pull we should be able to get it up," Julie said and both women grabbed onto the main halyard and pulled.

"Mom, Victor took the reefs out, we have to pull it all the way up."

"We have to get it on a winch," Julie said. She dropped back down onto her buttocks and wrapped the mainsheet around a winch, put in a winch handle and started grinding.

"I need help here," she said, and Meiko dropped to the deck and they both grabbed onto the winch handle and cranked.

"We gotta hurry, they're getting closer."

"Just a little more," Julie said, and she pulled on the handle with an effort she didn't know she possessed. "Got it," she said, and the sail was up.

"Okay, let's get back there and get her on course."

They crawled back to the cockpit, fighting the slippery deck and the rocking boat.

Julie took the wheel.

"They're so close," Meiko said. The boat was coming toward them at an alarming rate. Julie turned back on course. Another fifteen or twenty minutes and they would have been on them, but the wind filled *Fallen Angel's* sails and she healed over onto a starboard tack, gliding though the waves, just off the wind.

But it wasn't enough.

"Look at the knot meter," Meiko said, and Julie smiled when she saw that there were doing six and a half knots. "And we're almost into the wind," Meiko added, "they'll never catch us now."

"They're still back there," Julie said, "We don't seem to be losing them."

"But *Fallen Angel's* faster."

"Kurt has a huge Caterpillar diesel in *Challenge*, he can power through anything, I'll bet his brother has one too." Meiko was right, she thought, *Fallen Angel* was faster. A lot faster. She'd been sailing on Kurt's boat and she knew that it was built for cruising, not racing. His brother's boat couldn't be any faster. Without that big engine they'd be sitting still back there.

"But our engine's on," Meiko said.

"Our engine is tiny compared to his. We're just wasting fuel," she said and she shut off the engine.

"Mom, we're not giving up?" Meiko was holding on to the binnacle, looking over her mother's shoulder. Her fingers were as white as when she was holding the wheel.

"Hardly." Julie smiled. "We can still roll out the jib."

"Yeah," Meiko whirled around and took the furling line off the winch and eased it out. The wind caught the big sail with a loud whoosh, and it billowed and flapped in front of the boat.

"Tighten it up," Julie said.

Meiko stuffed a handle in the sheet winch and ground the jib tight.

"Look," Julie said, "nine-point-seven knots." She was as tight as the jib, muscles rippling, sweat dripping from her brow.

"We're losing them," Meiko squealed.

Julie grabbed onto her hair to keep it out of her eyes as she turned around. They were steadily pulling away from *Snake Eyes* and her German crew.

"I'd say we have about a knot, maybe a little more, on them. At this rate it'll be ten or fifteen hours before we're out of radar range." But she didn't think it made any difference, because by then they would be in Martinique. And the first thing she would do would be to notify the Gendarmes about *Snake Eyes*. She sat back behind the wheel and spent a few seconds enjoying the morning. The sun was glowing yellow-orange on the left. Whitecaps on top of three to four foot swells were quartering them from the right. The wind was fresh on her face and they were leaving *Snake Eyes* in their wake.

It wasn't a pleasant sail, and only a few days ago she would have found the constant spray uncomfortable, but now that they were sailing hard on the wind, doing almost ten knots, and outdistancing a boat with a powerful motor, she was beginning to appreciate the fact that *Fallen Angel* was built more for speed than comfort.

"I'm gonna go down and get some coffee, you want some?" Meiko said.

"Sure, black and strong." Julie tossed her daughter a smile.

"Is there any other way?"

"Coffee's on," Meiko said, coming back into the cockpit and handing her mother a warm mug. She was smiling and Julie liked the way the early morning sun bounced off her clear brown eyes. She was a woman, but she was a girl, too.

Julie took a welcome sip of the strong coffee. The warm mug in her hand was a pleasant contrast to the cold, spray filled, morning. She looked over her shoulder and the wind whipped her hair around her face. *Snake Eyes* was getting smaller in the distance.

"I'll bet they figured they'd just sail alongside and snatch the boat," Meiko said.

Julie took another sip of her coffee and nodded.

"But they won't give up, will they?"

"Not if he's like Kurt. He'll be like a pit bull and he'll keep coming and coming, waiting for us to relax, or make a mistake. Then he'll be there and he'll pounce."

"What are we going to do?"

"How would you like to learn French?"

"You know I've always wanted to do that."

"Well now you're going to get a chance. We'll go into a marina in Martinique and stay put. Kurt's brother and his friends can nose around all they want, but they won't be able to do a thing. You can't bribe the French to look the other way like you can a lot of these other island governments. One wrong move and our German pals will be learning the language, too. From the inside of a French jail."

"I'm in love with Victor," Meiko said changing the subject.

"I'd guessed as much," Julie said.

"You didn't say anything."

"I didn't want to lose you," Julie said.

"You would never lose me."

"When your father and I got married we both lost everyone we loved. His family was as racist as mine. I didn't want that to happen to us."

"So you don't approve?"

"But I'll never stand in your way. It's your life and I'll always support you."

"But you don't approve?" Meiko looked away from her mother and studied the boat behind them. They were still pulling away from it. Before long they wouldn't be able to see it at all.

"It's not for me to approve or disapprove, that's your job."

"But I want you to like him."

"Honey, that's between me and him. I'll try, for your sake."

"Thanks, Mom, I couldn't ask for more." She stepped behind the wheel and hugged her mother.

"We have some problems to work out," Meiko said.

"Like Charlene?"

"That's the main one."

"And her father's money?"

"No, Victor doesn't need her family's money."

"Her father owns the yard," Julie said.

"No, it's Victor's."

"The government leased Victor the land. Charlie Heart put up all the money. It's his travel lift, his equipment, his company, his yard."

"It's got nothing to do with Charlene. It's just business," Meiko said. Julie sensed that she wanted it to be true, but maybe she didn't quite believe it.

"Honey, Charlie Heart is the richest man in Trinidad. He owns oil wells, supermarkets and God knows what else. Why do you think he wanted a shipyard?"

"To make money." She was clutching the binnacle again, but this time she was looking deep into her mother's eyes and not at the boat behind them.

"No."

"Then why?"

"To finance his daughter's fiancé, the Gulf War hero."

"Mom." Meiko was almost shouting, and Julie knew how she hated to raise her voice.

"I'm sorry, honey. I don't want to fight with you."

"If that's the way it is, then how come they're not married?"

"Her father wanted her to go to college first, and what Charlie wants, Charlie gets."

"That's not the way Victor tells it. He said that she wasn't sure, and wanted to wait awhile. He says they've grown apart and they don't love each other anymore."

"Does she feel that way too?" Julie asked.

"He needs some time to work it out. A few months, he said. Maybe three or four."

"And what about school?"

"Mom, this is love."

"You were going to be a doctor."

"I know, but things change." Her daughter's words hurt. Meiko was a near genius. Twenty-one and in her second year of medical school. She had so much potential.

"So what do you want now?"

"I want to marry Victor and raise his kids," Meiko said, and Julie struggled to keep calm. She knew how destructive an argument would be, so she turned and looked over her shoulder.

"It looks like they've picked up some speed. Maybe we ought to tighten sail." She couldn't hide the tremor in her voice, she could only hope that Meiko mistook it for concern about *Snake Eyes* and not about Victor.

Meiko followed her mother's gaze and she tightened sail by bringing in some of the main sheet.

"Good," Julie said.

"Jib, too?" Meiko asked.

"Couldn't hurt," Julie said. But it did. Meiko cranked in the jib and the boat picked up speed. Then a blast like a gunshot ricocheted across the deck and the jib sheets shot away from the snapping jib.

"Roll it in," Julie said.

"Got it," Meiko yelled to be heard above the popping sound and she started winding on the furling line. She started to tire when it was halfway in, but she kept grinding and Julie recognized the dogged determination in her daughter. She wouldn't quit turning the winch and she wouldn't ask for help. It was a personal challenge. When she set her mind to something, she did it. Julie was going to have to tread softly around the subject of Victor Drake. She'd said her piece, now she was going to have to let her daughter work it out for herself.

Once the sail was furled in everything quieted down. They were sailing almost straight up. They weren't pointing as close to the wind. They'd lost half their speed. And Julie knew they would never make Martinique without the engine. They weren't going to make it before dark and she was afraid they might not make it at all.

"What happened?" Meiko asked.

"The clew blew out."

"What's that?"

"It's the round hole at the bottom of the sail that the line is attached to, and I'll bet that if we examine it we'll find that it's been cut or the stitching was undone, something."

"Can't we fix it?"

"No, the line ripped clean through the sail. It'll take a sailmaker to repair it."

Meiko looked at the knot meter, "Four knots and we're not even on course." She turned and looked behind. "It looks like they're closer already. Can we get to Martinique before them?"

"No."

"I wish Victor was here. He'd deal with those guys." Meiko said, and Julie clenched her fist and held her tongue, because she was beginning to think that Victor might be part of the problem.

"Take the wheel, honey. I'm going to go below and get the staysail."

"What's that?" Meiko asked.

"A sail that goes between the jib and main."

"We'll get our speed back?"

"I hope so," Julie said, and she went below. Like raising the main, she had never put up the staysail, and although they hadn't used it on this trip, Dieter and Kurt always sailed with everything out. She'd seen them use it enough to know how to hank it on and haul it up.

She pulled the blue sail bag out from the forward sail locker and dragged it through the boat and back to the cockpit. "Meiko," she called out. "I'll push it up and you pull it out."

"Okay, Mom." Meiko left the wheel and pulled the sailbag up from below.

"All right," Julie said, coming up the ladder after the sail. "I'll drag it up and hank it on. When I give you the thumbs up sign, turn into the wind. She glanced back, *Snake Eyes* did look closer. Then she grabbed onto the sailbag and heaved it across the deck, thankful that the sea had calmed down and that she didn't have to slide on her butt.

When she reached the inner forestay she pulled the sail out of the bag and clipped it on. Then she clipped on the staysail halyard, steadied herself, and tied the loose jib sheets to the staysail's clue with two bowlines. Then she clipped the foot to the deck, turned toward Meiko and pointed into the wind. She started hauling as Meiko started turning, thankful that the sail was less than half the size of the main. She had it up by the time Meiko had the boat in the wind. It was full and they were back on course by the time she was back in the cockpit.

"Okay, let's see what she'll do," Julie said, and they glued their eyes to the knot meter.

"Seven knots. It's not fast enough, is it?" Meiko said, and they both turned to look at *Snake Eyes* in the distance. Her sails we're still luffing, but she was holding her distance, maybe even gaining some.

"I was afraid of that," Julie said. "It's almost like they knew that clew was going to go. Without the jib we can't out distance them. At least not on this tack."

"What are you saying? Are they going to catch us?"

"They wouldn't have a chance if the wind was right."

"But is isn't," Meiko said.

"Then we'll just have to make it right," Julie said.

"How?"

Julie looked at the compass, then she turned her face into the wind. She grabbed a breath of the crisp breeze, then turned till her right shoulder was in the wind and she was facing ninety degrees away from it. She extended her arm and pointed. "Go that way."

"But that's away from everything."

"No, Puerto Rico is that way."

"How far?"

"I don't know. Maybe six hundred miles."

"Can we do that? Go all that way without stopping?"

"It's the last thing they would expect, and it's something I'm sure they didn't plan on. It'll be a perfect beam reach. No more hard on the wind. No more spray in the face. And once we're sure we're out of their radar range we can turn back toward the islands. And maybe if we're lucky the wind will change and start blowing like it's supposed to.

"Okay." Meiko spun the wheel, and in a few seconds they were pointed away from the island of St. Lucia and out toward the Caribbean Sea.

Snake Eyes turned too, but *Fallen Angel* had the wind and in less than a minute she was up to ten knots. Julie tightened sail and they picked up another knot. An hour later *Snake Eyes* was a speck in the distance, an hour and a half and she gave up the chase and turned back toward land. Two hours and she was out of sight. Now it was just Julie, Meiko, *Fallen Angel* and the open sea.

"Mom, I've been thinking," Meiko said. "Even if they knew that clew was going to blow out, they couldn't have known about the wind coming out of the northeast. Maybe it was just an accident."

"No, I don't think so. If the wind would have been its usual self and been behind us we would have needed the jib even more. It's our main downwind sail. No, it wasn't an accident. Somehow they weakened that clew, like they frayed the furling line and drilled those holes under the rudder and added water to the fuel. I only hope we don't have any more surprises."

"What do you mean, water in the fuel tank?" Meiko asked, eyebrows arching, "You're not implying Victor had anything to do with any of this, because he's the one that figured out that the furling line had been tampered with. Remember?"

"Honey, I didn't think for a second Victor had anything to do with it," Julie said. She hated lying to her daughter, but she had no choice. To tell her what she was really thinking would drive a wedge between them, and that was the last thing she wanted to do.

"Then why didn't you tell me about the water in the fuel?" Meiko said.

"I don't know, there was so much going on, I didn't think about it."

"How'd you get it out, the water?" Meiko asked.

"I had a mechanic look at it while you guys were over at Palm Island."

"But Victor was going to come back with his mechanic," Meiko said.

"And he was going to have him fly out the first day we were in Union Island, but he didn't." Julie had to fight to keep the testiness out of her voice. For an instant she felt like taking her daughter over her knee, but she bit it back.

"You didn't tell Victor that the engine was fixed?"

"Come on, honey, no matter what you think of him, he's still a macho white Trini. He can never be wrong, and a woman can never be right. I just wanted to avoid a scene, that's all."

"Victor's not like that," Meiko said.

"Honey, I told you, it'll take me a while to get used to the idea of you two. Maybe if you had told me earlier about your feelings for each other I wouldn't have felt that I had to hire a mechanic on my own, and I might have said something about the engine being fixed. But you didn't and I didn't, and it's over. Let's not make anything out of it. Okay?"

"Okay," Meiko said. Julie had a feeling that she'd be hearing more about it later, but at least the subject was closed for now.

They sailed the day away, both lost in their own thoughts. It was the closest they'd been to a fight in years, and neither of them wanted to take a chance of it turning into one. They took two hour shifts at the wheel. When one was on the other napped, and they sailed further and further from land.

But Julie knew it couldn't go on that way. She was going to have to say something, and she spent the better part of the day formulating her plan of attack. Finally, when the sun hung low in the sky, she began.

"I've been thinking," she said. "You said that it was going to take Victor three or four months to work everything out between him and Charlene."

"Something like that," Meiko said. Julie couldn't believe that a daughter of hers could be so naive. The more she thought about it the more she was convinced that Victor was leading her on. He would never abandon Charlene Heart and all of her father's money. But she couldn't figure out why he was doing it. There didn't seem to be anything in it for him, unless of course he really was in love with Meiko. But if that was the case, he'd tell Charlene and her father right now and damn the torpedoes. Of that she was certain, because if there was one thing in all the world that Julie Tanaka understood, it was love.

"Summer vacation is over in September. Right?"

"Right," Meiko said.

"Well, I'll make you a deal. You help me get the boat up to St. Martin and safely tucked into the yacht club. Then you go back to school and I'll fly back to Trinidad and make sure that old Charlie Heart won't throw a monkey wrench into your future.

"You can do that?" Meiko said. The smile on her face tore into Julie's heart. Victor didn't deserve it.

"Charlie is a good friend. If anybody can make him see reason, I suppose I can."

"Then you could talk to him right away." Meiko said.

"No, I can't. The last thing I want to do is to go to a friend and explain why he should look the other way while my daughter marries his daughter's fiancé. It is marriage we're talking about, isn't it?"

"Yes."

"Then it's Victor's job, and if he says it's going to take three or four months, you go back to school in September. That'll give you a month in the Caribbean. When you go off to the States, I'll fly back to Trinidad. If Victor can't work it out I'll use my wiles on Charlie."

"But Mom, I don't want to go back."

"That's the deal. You tell Victor you want to do one more semester while he works things out, and you go back to school. I don't want you hanging around like a lovesick child. If Charlie found out it would spoil everything. I think the last thing you want is for him to yank the rug out from under Victor."

"I don't like it so much, but we have a deal," Meiko said, holding her hand out.

"Deal." Julie took her hand and shook it.

"So that gives us a month, what are we gonna do?" Meiko asked.

"As soon as it gets dark we're going to turn this boat around and go back the way we came."

"We're going back to Trinidad?"

"Hardly. We're going to Venezuela. Let Kurt's brother and all of Dieter's other Germans knock their socks off looking for us up island, we'll be down south sitting in Los Testigos, sipping rum and swimming in the cool, cool ocean."

"Can I call Victor when we get there?" Meiko asked.

"Sure you can, honey." Julie didn't tell her that there were less than two hundred people in the Los Testigos island group and that there were no phones. More importantly, she didn't tell her that she didn't know Charlie Heart. They'd never even met.

CHAPTER THIRTEEN

THE STORM COVERED THE SKIES *above the oil tanker Caribbean Girl. On deck, seaman Paulie Hearst felt the hair on his arms rise and chills shivered at the base of his neck when he saw his finger tips sparking. He turned to his mate, Johnny Dunne, and pointed a glowing finger. Dunne's mustache was shining white and he was looking up at the bridge. Paulie followed his gaze.*

The radar antenna atop the bridge looked like it was sending fire skyward. Then the lightning hit, shattering the radar tower and shutting down the boat's electrical system. Seamen Hearst and Dunne locked arms as they were blasted to the deck, but they survived their brush with St. Elmo's fire.

And the storm grew stronger as it moved west, showering lightning and rain as it gathered up smaller storms that crossed its path. Wind started to swirl at twenty knots around a common center as the thunderstorms formed into a swirl.

Faraway in Coral Gables, Florida, the National Hurricane Center noted the storm, and weathermen were calling it a tropical depression that deserved watching.

THE SUN WAS SETTING off to their right when Julie spun the boat around and headed south. If Dieter wanted to get her boat bad enough to send Kurt's brother and a full crew after her, she knew he wasn't going to give up just because *Fallen Angel* was able to out run *Snake Eyes*. By morning he'd have a plane in the air.

They would be looking for her up north, so she would go down south. They'd never think of looking in Venezuela. She'd be safe from them and Meiko would be away from Victor. She hated lying to her, but she could see no other way. Because despite what she'd told her she was going to do her best to keep them apart. The thought of Meiko with creepy Victor just made her skin crawl.

Meiko was up front, hanging on to the mast, watching the sunset.

"Mom, I saw it. Did you see it?"

"No." Julie had been trying unsuccessfully for over a year to see the green flash. Almost everybody she knew in the yachting community in Trinidad had seen one, and now Meiko had, too. Someday. Then she faced right, into the wind. It was on their beam, the rolling waves were under three feet, the moon was going to be almost full, and they were moving along at eight knots. It looked like it was going to be a perfect sail, and Julie prayed nothing else would go wrong.

And her prayers were answered. After a day and a half of a pleasant beam reach they sailed into the rising sun with the Los Testigos island group just off their bow.

"We did it, Mom. Just you and me. No help. Are we a pair of sailor ladies or what?" Meiko's smile was huge and Julie hoped it wasn't because she was expecting to call Victor any time soon.

Twenty minutes later the boat was safely at anchor and they were sitting in the Guardacoasta office facing a young officer in a starched uniform. He was talking in rapid Spanish and punctuating his words with quick and jerky hand gestures. Every other second or two he'd pick their passports off the desk in front of him then throw them back down.

"*Quiero hablar con su jefe.*" Julie said. The man was momentarily stunned into silence, meeting Julie's innocent green-eyed expression with an ice-cool, brown-eyed stare.

"What did you say?" Meiko said.

"According to the Spanish book on the boat I said I wanted to talk to his boss," Julie said, smiling at the official. She reached forward and took a tissue out of the box on the officer's desk and wiped the sweat from around her neck. Then she balled it up and tossed it into a waist basket halfway across the room.

"Two points," Meiko said. The guardsman smiled. That he understood.

"Okay," Julie said, "let's leave while we're ahead."

"You mean we're just going to walk out of here?"

"*¿Donde esta sus visados?*" the man said.

"Whoops," Julie said. "I think he just asked us where our visas were."

"Ouch," Meiko said. "Does that mean we're in trouble?"

"I don't think so," Julie said. "We're two pretty women in an Hispanic country. They may have piles of rules, but chivalry isn't dead here. Come on, let's go. We'll let his boss sort it out later."

"But our passports?"

"They're not going anywhere," Julie said. She stood. Then Meiko stood. Then the young guardsman stood, jabbering his fast Spanish again, waving their passports in the air, like he was shooing flies, but Julie just turned and walked out the door.

Meiko attempted a brief smile at the guardsman, gave him a quick wave, then she turned and ran after her mother. Neither woman looked back, but it wouldn't have made any difference, because the guardsman didn't go to the door. Instead he sat back down at his desk and shook his head.

It took Meiko about ten more minutes to figure out there were no phones on the island, or any of the Testigos, and her enthusiastic mood faded to disappointment.

"How am I going to call him and tell him we're okay?" she whined. Julie wanted to throttle her, but instead she bit her tongue.

"I don't know, honey, I hadn't counted on this." She lied again, but she reasoned it was for her daughter's own good, and for a brief second she wondered if her parents felt that way when she ran off with Hideo, but then she put the thought aside. The past was past, she was living for the future.

"I'll bet he's worried sick," Meiko said.

"When the kid's *jefe* gets here and we get everything straightened out, we'll tell him to call Victor and tell him that we're okay. We're only a day's sail from Trinidad, he can come visit if he wants."

"Really?" The little girl in Meiko was back.

They spent the next three days getting up with the sun, swimming, and dinghying to shore in the mornings, where Meiko and Julie allowed three old men to teach them how to fish and clean their catch. At first Julie found cleaning the fish repulsive, but soon both women could have a fish ready for the pan in a flash. They swam in the afternoons and ate the morning's catch for dinner. It could have been such a great life, Julie often thought.

On the fourth night Julie was sleeping fitfully. Jarring, dismal dreams kept shaking her awake throughout the night, keeping her in a hot sweat. Twice she got up to change her wet tee shirt, once to take an aspirin and three times to go to the bathroom. When she heard the deep rumbling outside she thought it was another nightmare growling in her subconscious, trying to jerk and jar her awake.

She was beginning to think it wasn't a nightmare when *Fallen Angel* was suddenly awash in light. She blinked at the bright reflection coming in her open hatch and put her hands to her eyes, both to rub the sleep out of them and to shield them from the light.

"Mom, what is it?" Meiko said, coming into her cabin.

"Someone's out there." Julie grabbed a pair of shorts from the foot of her bed and jumped into them.

"Who do you think it is?"

"Let's find out." Julie stuck her head up through the hatch, her hand in front of her eyes, still trying to block the light.

"You the vessel," a deep voice boomed through a bullhorn. "Step out onto the deck."

"I think the *jefe* has arrived," Julie said to Meiko, then she pushed herself up through the hatch. Meiko came up behind her.

"Can you turn the light away," Julie yelled.

"Are you the master of this vessel?" The voice was still booming, electronically amplified to an ear piercing wail.

Julie flattened her hand, like she was going to salute, ran it in front of her eyes, then extended her arm and pointed away. The man behind the light got the message and turned it off. It took a few seconds for her eyes to get used to the darkness. Then she said, "You don't need the bullhorn."

"Are you the master of this vessel?" The voice was nicer, and amplified only by a healthy pair of lungs.

"I am," Julie said.

"Name, please." It wasn't a question.

"Can't you come back in the morning? We're not going anywhere." Julie said.

"Mom," Meiko whispered behind her, "You're gonna make him mad."

"Name, please?" This time it was a question, and Julie thought she detected a hint of laughter.

"Julie Tanaka, and it's the middle of the night. I'm not feeling well and you must have better things to do than to roust two innocent women out of bed."

"How many on the boat?" This time she definitely heard laughter in his voice.

"Two," Julie shouted back. "Now, can I have your name, Captain?"

"I ask the questions around here."

"Come on, Captain, have a heart and give a girl a break. I just want to know who I'm talking to." She could see him clearly now. He was a big man, with a wide, bushy mustache, and from the looks of his pot belly she didn't imagine he let too many beers pass him by.

"Sanchez," he rumbled, his voice the same timbre as the cutter's engines. He was grinning like someone told him his favorite bar would be serving drinks on the house for the rest of his life.

"Can I come in and talk to you in the morning, Captain Sanchez?"

"We are here but to serve," Captain Sanchez answered. "But I will expect you both promptly at nine."

"We'll be there," Julie said.

"Of course you will," he boomed back, then he saluted and the cutter rumbled off.

"I think we'll check in with the Guardacoasta tomorrow about nine," Julie said.

"Good idea," Meiko said. They went down below and Julie slept the sleep of angels for the rest of the night.

"Let me see if I have this correctly," Sanchez said the next morning. "You come to Venezuela with no visas. You want to stay here without going to the mainland to check in. And you want me to look the other way and pretend that I don't see you. Is that about it?"

"That's it." Julie smiled. She told him everything that had happened to her since they found the dead body floating by the Five Islands in Trinidad. When she got to the part about the water in the fuel tank in Union Island, he interrupted her.

"This mechanic, Henry, did he have a limp?" he asked. His mustache started an upward curve and Julie thought she was seeing a smile in his eyes.

"Yes, he did," Julie said.

"Henry Waller. Best diesel mechanic in the Caribbean, possibly on the planet. A good friend," Sanchez said.

"Yes, a good friend," Julie said, and at that point she thought it was going to be all right. If he was a friend of Henry's, then he'd help.

And she went on with her story.

"So it's sanctuary you're seeking?" Sanchez said when she finished, boring into Julie with his deep brown eyes.

"Kind of," Julie said, hands clasped in her lap, fingers white.

"Why should I do this?" he asked.

"Because you're a man and we're two women in trouble. Because you're a kind of policeman and these men, these Germans, they're bad. They probably killed that man we saw floating in the ocean, probably also killed Trinidad's attorney general, and maybe they're trying to kill us. Because you know I'm telling the truth and you won't let them take my home. It's all I have left and I'm counting on you to help guard it."

"You can stay, but do not move your boat without telling me," he said, handing over the passports.

"Thank you," Julie said.

"Is there anything else I can do?" Sanchez asked, his bushy mustache bobbing over his smile.

"My daughter would like to get a message to someone in Trinidad, if that's possible." Julie said.

"It is," Sanchez said, and Meiko told him about Victor and how she wanted him to know they were well and safe. Sanchez promised to send a man to the mainland the following day to make the call.

The women got up to go and Julie turned toward the big man and said, "I have two cases of Carib on board. I wouldn't think of offering them to you, because you might think it was a bribe of some kind, but if you drop by evenings after work, you could help me drink it. Those cans don't last too long in this heat and I can only keep a couple of six packs cold at a time in my refrigerator."

"A beer or two after work. I would be delighted," Sanchez said, and the women left.

"Mom, he's gross. Fat and old. How could you invite him on the boat?" Meiko said as soon as they were out of the Captain's earshot.

But Julie guessed right. Captain Sanchez turned out to be a great friend. He came by that first night and they drank beer, talked, and watched the sun go down. And they discovered they had a mutual fascination for chess. The next night he brought the beer.

He was a dedicated player and sometimes their games lasted well into the night. They quickly became settled in a routine. The captain addressed her as Mrs. Tanaka and she called him Captain Sanchez. The friendship was fast and Julie knew he was a man she could trust, but she also knew the government in Venezuela was as corrupt as the government in Trinidad. Everything was for sale. He could only do so much.

"Hey, Mom, look who's here," Meiko, said, interrupting them as Captain Sanchez was setting up the board one evening, nine days after their arrival. Julie followed Meiko's pointed finger and smiled. *Left Home*, Alice and Chad's thirty-two foot sloop was sailing toward them, anchor hanging from the bow, Chad up front ready to drop it.

"I'm gonna dinghy over and say hello," Meiko said, and Julie and Captain Sanchez watched Meiko climb down into the dinghy and motor over to *Left Home*. Julie was looking forward to catching up on all the yacht club gossip.

"Don't you want to see your friends?" Sanchez asked.

"I do," Julie said, but I want to get even for the way you trounced me last night first. Tomorrow's soon enough.

Sanchez smiled through his mustache and set up the board.

The next afternoon, while Julie and Meiko were fishing with the old men, Sanchez interrupted their sport.

"Both *Snake Eyes* and *Challenge* left Chaguaramas Bay early this morning. Headed this way.

"How'd they know?" Julie said. Then she looked up at *Left Home* anchored peacefully off shore. They had an SSB. She turned to Meiko. She wanted to scream, but it was too late.

"I just wanted to talk to him for a minute," Meiko said. "I wanted to know why he hadn't come. Captain Sanchez's man never called him." Meiko was glaring at Julie.

"I gave the order," Sanchez lied. "It's true I wasn't there personally to see that it was carried out, but I gave the order. It's not my fault," he added, and Julie was thankful that he could lie so gracefully. And he was lying, because that first night she'd asked him not to notify Victor, and after she told him why, he readily agreed.

"How do you know this?" Julie asked him.

"I've had them watched ever since you first came here. I have been in the Guardacoasta a long time. I have some yachtie friends, like you, that I can trust. I get an SSB update on those two boats every morning, in code of course, right after the Caribbean net."

"Meiko," Julie said, "anybody can listen in on SSB traffic. When you told Victor where we were you told the world."

"I didn't know."

"It doesn't matter," Julie said. "We have to go."

"Can't you arrest them when they get here?" Meiko asked.

"For what?"

"You can keep them away from us, though, can't you?" Meiko said, and Julie truly felt sorry for her. She looked devastated.

"What if they have legal papers impounding the boat?" Sanchez said.

"But this is Venezuela, not Trinidad," Meiko pleaded.

"We're a country of laws. I would hate to have to hand your boat over to those men. It pains me to say this, but you should go, now. When Dieter Krauss's Germans get here, I'll tell them that you left for Margarita."

"You know Dieter?" Julie said.

"I know of him," Sanchez said.

"There's another thing," Julie said. "We've been laying around enjoying ourselves while Rome burns."

"What do you mean?"

"We blew out the clew on the jib, remember? I told you about that."

"I remember."

"We need that sail. It gives us our speed. We need it fixed."

Sanchez spoke in Spanish to the three old men.

"They'll fix it for you," he said, turning back to Julie.

"It's thick cloth, the clew has to be tough. Do you think they can do it?"

"They've spent their whole lives weaving and stitching the long fishing nets, I'm sure they can handle your sail."

Then Sanchez handed Julie more bad news. "By my calculations they are three hours away, maybe a little more, maybe a little less. You maybe could get away without them seeing you, but if they have their radar on, and if they're watching?"

"What should we do, Enrique?" It was the first time she'd addressed him by his given name.

"I could send your friends on to Margarita right now. If they are looking on their radar they will see a boat going exactly where I will tell them you went."

"And what about us?"

"You hug the southwest side of Testigo Grande, right under Testigo Pequeño, and when they come around the south side of the big island you motor around the small island on the north. The anchorage is not so pleasant, but you will be out of their sight. Then when they leave, you wait until they are out of radar range and shoot, like a bullet, up north."

"That could work," Julie said.

"The water is deep over there. And there's no protection against the swells."

"How deep?" Julie asked.

"Sixty, seventy feet."

"I've got four hundred feet of chain and we've been in rolly anchorages before. We'll do it," she said, and she stepped forward and gave Sanchez a hug that started his mustache twitching.

"Okay, get that anchor up," Sanchez said, and Julie and Meiko hustled to the dinghy and motored out to *Fallen Angel*.

"You don't really think it was Victor, do you?" Meiko asked.

"No, honey, I'm sure it was just a coincidence," Julie said, but she wasn't so sure.

"Because Victor would never do that."

"I believe you honey."

"Really, I know him."

"Can we talk about it later? We've got a lot to do right now," Julie said. The words came out more harsh than she intended and Meiko clenched her fists, but she dropped it.

On board Meiko started the engine, while Julie leaned over the side with her foot on the windlass button, watching the chain come up. She heard the sound of an outboard and saw Sanchez motoring out with the three old fishermen in their pirogue. The anchor clanged into place and Julie stood, holding onto the rolled up jib.

"Your sail," Sanchez said, and Julie remembered the blown clew.

"Do I have time?"

"These are three of the best net men in Venezuela. It will only take a few minutes, you don't even have to put the anchor back down."

Sanchez was right about the quality of the work, wrong about the time involved. It took an hour, but the sail was stitched and the clew reinforced, as well, if not better, than any sailmaker would have done the job.

"All right," Sanchez said when they were finished. "We go now,"

Julie hugged him again, then she hugged each one of the fishermen. Then Meiko hugged Sanchez and she too, hugged the fishermen, kissing each one on the cheek. All three men were blushing and smiling as they climbed down into their pirogue.

Sanchez was the last and before he started down he said, "listen up on eighty-eight, just in case." It was a little used channel and the chance that *Challenge* or *Snake Eyes* would be on it was rare.

"Okay, let's get the jib sheets reattached," Julie said, as the men were motoring away. Meiko grabbed the port sheet and Julie the starboard, and they fed their lines through the clew, tying them off with bowlines. That done, Meiko took her place behind the wheel. Julie stayed up front, to guide her into the shallow water between Testigo Pequeño and Testigo Grande.

Meiko motored *Fallen Angel* into position, going dead slow, as she followed Julie's hand signals. When they were as close to the island as she dared, Julie dropped her arm and Meiko put the boat into reverse for a second to stop it, then she put it into neutral.

Julie dropped the anchor, turned, gave Meiko the thumbs down sign and Meiko killed the engine. With an arm wrapped around the jib, she wiped the sweat from her forehead. The sun was straight overhead. If there was a devil, Julie thought, this was the kind of day he'd be out and about in. And then she thought about the German devils headed her way and shivered despite the heat.

Her tank top and shorts were covered in sweat and the sun was scorching her shoulders red. There was no wind and the water was flat calm. Her world was silent, like the middle of the desert, only she was seeing water, not sand.

She ran her a hand through her hair, like her clothes, it was wringing wet with sweat. A fly landed on her arm and she shooed it away. Another followed and she swatted at it, but it was too fast. Hot, muggy and flies, not her favorite combination.

She wasn't looking forward to a long conversation about Victor and she hoped Meiko wouldn't bring him up. She was tired of lying. And although she had only been running and hiding for a little over a month, it seemed like she'd been doing it forever.

"Now, I guess we wait," she said, stepping into the cockpit.

They didn't have to wait long before the radio crackled to life. "I can see them," Sanchez said. "You have an hour or so."

"Thanks, Enrique," Julie said and then they were back to radio silence, waiting and swatting flies.

After a few minutes Julie wanted to scream the quiet was so loud. Her daughter never brooded, but she was brooding now. Sitting, head in her hands, looking down at the cockpit sole, acting like a misunderstood, lovesick child. But still, Julie preferred the roaring silence to conversation about Victor.

"Problems." Sanchez said, his voice over the radio breaking the lull.

Julie clicked the talk button, "What is it?" she asked.

"They split up, one's coming around the north end the other the south."

"What are we going to do?"

"Do you think you can squeeze between the two islands?"

"How deep?" Julie asked. The small island was fifty feet from the larger one.

"Seven feet in the most shallow," Sanchez said.

"Then that's a negative," Julie said. "We draw nine."

"Standby I'll get back to you," he said, and again they were waiting.

A minute later Sanchez was back. "Julie," he said.

"I'm here."

"We're going to create a diversion, just as the boat on the north comes around Pequeño." Then he said, "You should tuck in as close to Pequeño as you can."

"I'm pretty close now."

"You have to get closer."

"I'm in fifteen feet."

"It's soft mud. You can power into seven. I've seen boats dig into two feet of it lots of times. Get closer."

"Right," she said. Meiko started the engine, while Julie brought up the anchor, and once again Meiko was following her mother's hand signals as she called out the depth from the cockpit.

"Fourteen-eight," she said and Julie was pointing to a tiny inlet. Fourteen-three, and Julie was still pointing. Thirteen-two, twelve-six, twelve, Julie still had her arm extended, but now it was shaking. "Eleven feet," Meiko said. She was driving the boat, slow, slow, alternating between forward, neutral and reverse to keep it at a crawl.

Then Julie pointed off to the right and Meiko cranked the wheel all the way over and the boat started to turn. Meiko worked the gears, alternating between the shift lever and the throttle lever, to bring *Fallen Angel* around in a tight circle, so that they were facing away from the island, and Julie came back into the cockpit.

"We're in ten feet of water," Meiko said.

"We have to be in closer or they'll see us when they come around, so let's back it up," Julie said. Meiko put it in reverse and added a touch of power.

"The depth gauge doesn't work in reverse," Meiko said.

"Keep backing up, till we can't see the point."

"I feel the drag. I think were in the mud." Meiko kept her hands tight on the wheel and the wheel straight.

"A little more," Julie said, and Meiko increased the power.

"Okay, neutral."

"Just in time," Sanchez scratched over the radio. "They'll be coming around in about fifteen minutes. You'll hear machine gun fire as they round the bend. Don't be alarmed. It's intended to keep their eyes forward."

"Mom, look," Meiko said, and Julie turned to see their fishermen friends' pirogue motor toward the southern part of Testigo Grande. All three of the old men were in the boat, and they were all waving. Then they stood and one of them dropped the small anchor. They waved again, then all three jumped into the water and swam toward shore.

"What are they doing?" Meiko asked.

"The diversion," Julie said.

"But all three of them, and they're so old."

"They wanted to say goodbye again."

The women watched as Sanchez motored the Guardacoasta cutter into place. It would be the first thing the crews of *Challenge* and *Snake Eyes* saw when they came around the islands. There were two young sailors at the guns. Sanchez was on the bridge, mike in hand. "Shut off your engines," he said, and Meiko obeyed. "Ten minutes, maybe less," he said.

They heard the stereo rumble of diesel engines, the cutter's in front and another coming from behind. The one from behind was getting closer. Julie moved back behind the wheel with her daughter. Meiko took her hand, clutching tightly.

"Mom," Meiko whispered, "they're here. Look," And they saw the bow of the black schooner, less then fifty feet away. The sound of its diesel rumbled through Julie and she fought an impulse to duck.

Then a new sound tore up the morning as the cutter's machine guns opened up on the pirogue. The black schooner was around the bend. Kurt, or his brother, Julie couldn't tell which, was behind the wheel. Three crew. They were all looking forward, straining to see what was behind the gunfire. Then the pirogue blew with a sound louder than any thunder Julie had ever heard and the fishermen's little pirogue vanished, turning into flying bits of wood and splinters.

Dynamite, Julie thought. Sanchez had filled the little boat with dynamite, and like the crew on the black schooner, she had her eyes clued forward as the smoke was clearing and pieces of wood, large and small, rained down on the water.

"Now," Sanchez said over the radio, and Meiko started the engines and motored out behind the schooner. Julie read the name *Snake Eyes* on the stern. If any of the men turned around, they would be caught. *Fallen Angel's* engines sounded so loud to Julie, she was surprised the men on *Snake Eyes* couldn't hear, but the guns on the cutter were still blazing away at the place where the pirogue had been as Meiko turned the wheel toward the right. A couple of minutes later they were around the bend and behind Testigo Grande.

Julie went forward and dropped the anchor in seventy feet of water. They had a long uncomfortable wait till dark.

"Think we'll be okay?" Meiko asked.

"I do." Julie said, "We should try and get some sleep. It's going to be a long night."

Five hours later as the sun was going down Sanchez motored the cutter around. Julie and Meiko were both on deck. "They stood and waved. They just left my radar," he called over and the cutter stood by as Julie brought up the anchor.

"Sail safely." Sanchez waved and Julie blew him a kiss.

The next morning, two hours after sunrise, they set anchor off Hog Island in Grenada. Both women had been up all night and were exhausted. Twenty minutes after the anchor was down they were fast asleep. Julie woke at sundown and finally saw her green flash. Then she went back to sleep, never knowing that *Challenge* and *Snake Eyes* passed ahead during the night. This time they had anticipated her move and they would be waiting for her up island.

CHAPTER FOURTEEN

THE TROPICAL DEPRESSION *hung east of the Bermuda High, in the mid Atlantic, for a full week, gorging itself on smaller storms, forcing them below and above it, turning itself into a multilayered, slow moving monster that turned the sky dark above the cruise ship Norwegian Venture.*

Her captain, a veteran of many storms, radioed his position to the Coast Guard as lightning lasered into the surging sea around his ship. But he was spared a strike as he plowed through the waves, thankful that he encountered the storm before it was fully formed.

BROXTON AND T-BONE were sitting in Typhoon Willie's, sipping Red Stripe Jamaican beer, about an hour before sunset, when T-Bone smiled and said. "I've got a present for you."

Broxton turned away from the bay. He'd been watching the boats come and go for the last three days. "Another beer?" he asked.

"This." T-Bone slapped a blue passport on the table between them. "Now you're Daniel Arthur Steele. Danny Steele. Hey I like that, Danny Boy. Got a nice ring to it."

Broxton picked up the passport and opened it, and looked at the picture of himself staring back. He smiled and looked up at T-Bone.

"It's even got a five-year multiple entry visa for the States," T-Bone said. "You couldn't ask for better, except US maybe, but a Trinidad passport with a US visa is pretty fucking golden." He was grinning like he knew Broxton was buying the next round.

"How?"

"Well, Danny Boy, you didn't look in the dead men's pockets. I did. The two Colombians had Trini passports. Lucky for you they're not as tamper proof as ours. I borrowed your funky looking photos, and, voila, now you're Danny Steele."

"You think they were Colombian? I thought they were Cuban," Broxton said, thumbing through the pages.

"Colombian."

"You can't even tell. T-Bone you're an artist." Broxton slipped the passport into his shirt pocket.

"You can thank me, Danny boy, by picking up the next round."

"I have the feeling I'll be paying all night."

"Fair exchange, Danny Boy, fair exchange."

"I didn't like Billy Boy, I hate Danny Boy."

"Sorry, you're stuck with it. Be good to me or I might start singing."

Broxton raised his hand to get the waitress's attention.

"No singing?" T-Bone said.

"Please, no," Broxton said.

"They're here," T-Bone said.

Broxton turned to look and saw the two black schooners weaving their way through the bay, looking for a place to drop anchor.

"Is there going to be more killing?" T-Bone asked.

"One, for sure," Broxton said.

"That I understand, but the others?"

"I don't know."

"You ever killed anyone before, Danny Boy?" T-Bone asked. With the lone exception of the dead man's passport, neither man had brought up the killing of the men on the speed boat and why it appeared to come so easy to both of them.

"Once. In self defense," Broxton said. "Not long ago. You?"

"I spent four years in Vietnam."

"You don't look that old."

"Fifty-five." He raised his wrist and looked at it. In about six and a half hours."

"Tomorrow's your birthday?"

"Yeah, tomorrow."

"I'll have to get you something," Broxton said.

"You already paid for half of the new dinghy. Don't think I don't appreciate it. I know it took most of your money."

"You spent four years in Vietnam? Why so long?

"They taught me good. Point and shoot, send the kid, he never misses. I was a grunt for the first thirteen months and the brass saw something in me they liked. They spoon fed me America the Beautiful, and better dead then red, and I bought the whole lot. For the next three years I was their good little shooter. After the war they had a job for me at Langley."

"CIA?"

"Central Fuckin' Intelligence, yeah, and for ten years they sent me places and had me doing things that nobody should ever have to do. Somewhere around year five I started to wonder about what I was doing. I started drinking a little at year six and by year ten I was a bloody drunk and no good to them or myself anymore.

"They cut me loose with a hundred grand golden handshake, and it took me about two years to drink it up. Then Dad died. He was seventy-nine. He had a good estate, but he left all the money split equally among my seven brothers."

"Seven?"

"Eight sons, five wives, four countries. I told you, Daddy was a sailor man. He didn't leave me a dime, cause he knew I'd drink it away and maybe kill myself. But he left me something better than money. He left me his boat, and here I am, God bless him. He stepped out from the grave and he saved me. Now I only drink when I want to. I never get drunk. And I only kill people I don't like."

"So I was never really in charge the other day?" Broxton said.

"Sure you were, Danny Boy, cause your plan made sense. Shit, I probably would have shot them all before they boarded the boat, but then you wouldn't have learned anything about your German with the girlie voice."

Their conversation was interrupted by the waitress and Broxton ordered two more Red Stripes as they watched the crew from the two black schooners climb into their dinghies.

"How do you want to play it?" T-Bone asked, after the waitress had left.

"I've seen Kurt, the twin with the man's voice, a couple of times around the boatyards in Trinidad. I'd recognize him if I saw him again, but I don't think he'd know me with the hair." Broxton grinned and ran his hand through it. "I think I'd just like to hang out awhile, drink beer and see what we can pick up."

"And the one that sounds like a girl?"

"He'll die before your birthday."

"Need help?"

"Maybe later, with the others, but not with this. It's kind of an honor thing."

"I understand," T-Bone said as the waitress brought the drinks.

The two men sat and sipped beer and watched the Germans pull their dinghies ashore. They were still sipping as they came in, boisterous and laughing. Kurt asked for a seaside table, louder than he had to, and was more upset than he had to be when told they were all taken. They waitress said she could put two tables together for the eight men, but it would be toward the back. Kurt didn't stop complaining until the tables were joined and she was taking the drink orders.

"Another round?" Broxton said.

"You still buying?" T-Bone said.

"You know I am."

"Then I'm still drinking."

Broxton got up and went to the bar. He wanted to get a look at the man he'd promised to kill. He studied him through the mirror behind the bar, both twins caught him looking and met his eyes through the mirror. Broxton looked away, ordered the two beers and took them back to the table.

They were still nursing the beers fifteen minutes later when a bass voice sang out, "Hey, T-Bone Powers." A large black man slapped T-Bone on the back, then he eased himself into a chair opposite Broxton. Broxton thought he saw a grimace as the man sat down.

"Henry Waller." T-Bone smiled, standing as the big man sat. T-Bone sat back down and the two man shook hands.

My daughter, Darla," Henry said and a young girl pulled out the chair next to Broxton and sat down.

The party of four at the next table got up and left. Kurt and Karl Schneidler and two of the other Germans took the seats before the evening breeze had a chance to cool them off.

Darla pulled on Broxton's sleeve, "I got a secret," she said, crooking her finger. He bent his head low, so that she could whisper in his ear. "Show me your dinghy," Darla whispered. "Right now, show me now."

Broxton looked up at her father. Henry nodded.

"He's gonna take me for a ride in the rubber boat," Darla said. "So we can see the sunset from the water, and maybe see the green flash." She sounded excited and took Broxton's hand as he rose from the table.

"I haven't ever ridden in one of those before," she said, loud enough for the Germans at the next table to hear. She kicked up sand and was bouncing around as Broxton pulled the dinghy into the water. She jumped in at the last second and Broxton got his feet wet as he pushed it out.

He reached for the cord, but she said, "We can row, we don't have to go very far." She had the right oar in the lock before he'd finished with the left. She'd definitely ridden in a dinghy before. He sat in the center, facing her, she sat on the front tube and seemed to be enjoying herself as he rowed out toward the boats at anchor.

"Okay," he said after a few minutes, "they can't hear us. That's why we're out here, isn't it?"

"They saw the name on your boat when they came in," she said. She had his full attention. "The two twins, the one with the normal voice and the scar on his face, he recognized you. It took him a few minutes, cause he said you have hair now. Did you used to be bald?"

He ran his hand through his hair. "I used to shave it," he said, thinking about what she'd said, working it over, trying to see how it changed things.

"They're bad men," she said. "I've met some of them before, but they didn't recognize me. I sure recognize them though. You didn't ask me how come I know what they said?"

"You speak German," he said, still thinking.

"You're smarter than you look. Definitely smarter than them. They don't think anyone like me can understand a word they say. What are you going to do about them?"

"Do you always end everything you say with a question?" he said.

"No." She thought for a second. "Not always."

"How would you like to take a quick trip out to *Obsession* and see what a sailboat's all about?"

"I know what a sailboat's about," she said. "My dad is the best diesel mechanic there is. That's why we're here. He's fixing the engine on that Swan 57 over there." She pointed to a beige yacht that was anchored close to the shore. "The owner wanted him and no one else. He wanted him so bad that he paid the airfare for both of us, and our hotel room. I've been on tons of sailboats. Why do you want to go out to your boat?"

"I need to get a few things."

"Like a gun?"

"Why would you think that?"

"They said you killed the men they sent after you. All four of them."

"You learned an awful lot in such a short time."

"They're stupid. They talked loud. I was at the next table. I would have had to put ear plugs in my ear not to hear. But it's good that they're so dull. They talked in front of me once before, and I was able to warn Julie, so she could get away."

"Julie Tanaka on *Fallen Angel*?" Broxton said.

"You know her?" Darla asked.

"Yes," Broxton said. "Those men are after her."

"Don't I know it," Darla said.

"And now you warned me," he said, and he yanked on the starter cord and motored out to *Obsession*. "Coming aboard?" he asked, after he eased off the gas and they were gliding toward T-Bone's boat.

"No, I'll stand guard in the dinghy," she said. Broxton smiled, thinking that was probably a good idea. Then he climbed aboard and went straight to the salon and picked up the floor boards. There was something in the tool box he wanted to bring to shore with him.

"Did you get a gun?" she asked when he climbed back down into the rubber boat.

"No, I didn't get a gun," he said.

"Did you get a knife?"

"No."

"Well what did you get?"

"This." He showed her a small roll of wire.

"Seizing wire? What good is that going to be?"

"Think about it," Broxton said.

She was quiet for a few minutes. Then she shivered, and then for an instant Broxton thought her whole face kind of twinkled. "Which one?" she said.

"The one that squeaks when he talks."

"He's a bad man," she said.

"As bad as they come," Broxton said, and he twisted the throttle all the way, bringing the dinghy up on a plane, with Darla up front whooping and yelling as they rocketed across the bay. She was acting the excited child as he made a quick pass by *Challenge* and *Snake Eyes*. There wasn't anybody on board either ship. He turned the boat and raced toward shore. Darla stopped pretending and settled back in the dinghy, smiling, her brown eyes golden as they reflected the setting sun. He slowed when they neared the beach, leaned forward, flashed his hand in front of her face, snapped his fingers and showed the coin in his hand. "A US silver dollar," he said.

"How'd you do that?" she squealed.

"Magic." He said, handed her the coin.

"I'm gonna keep this," she said. "And I'm gonna learn that trick." She was still laughing when he hopped out of the boat and pulled it ashore.

She grabbed his hand as they walked along the beach back to the restaurant. Hazy clouds slid across the sky, taking the moonlight away, then offering it back again. Broxton looked across the bay. *Challenge* was easily visible from the beachfront restaurant, the clouds willing, but *Snake Eyes* was anchored past her twin and not visible. He grinned and squeezed her hand as a plan started to form.

"Hey, Dad, it was so much fun, but I didn't get to see the green flash," Darla said when they returned to the table. The sun was over the horizon and the dark was coming fast. Darla scooted into her place, next to Broxton and across from her father.

"Next beer, I paid," T-Bone said, indicating the cold Red Stripe. Broxton picked it up and took a long pull, then he leaned forward and T-Bone, Henry and Darla leaned into him so that the Germans at the next table couldn't hear.

"Henry, you and Darla go back to your table and order dinner. Stay in the restaurant. They saw you come sit down and say hello to an old friend, and they'll see you go back to your table. They won't think anything of it."

"You gonna be all right?" Henry whispered.

"I'm gonna be fine, thanks to you and Darla. And I'm going to make sure that Julie Tanaka comes out okay too, you can count on it," Broxton said. Then he added. "It's important, Henry, that you order dinner, act like nothing has happened out of the ordinary. Wave when T-Bone leaves, but don't get up."

Broxton leaned back and took another pull on his beer, and after a few seconds Henry and Darla excused themselves, Henry saying they had a dinner to eat. And Broxton leaned forward again.

"In a few minutes I'm going to get up and go to the bathroom. I'm betting that one of the ugly twins next door will follow. You should make some excuse to go out to the boat, but let them know next door that you're coming right back."

T-Bone nodded.

"Ready?" Broxton said.

"Any time," T-Bone said.

Broxton slid his chair out from under the table, took a swig from his beer, finishing it, and said, "Be right back."

"Okay," T-Bone said. "I'm going to shoot out to the boat and get some more money."

Broxton walked through the restaurant, winked at Darla and smiled when she winked back. Then he turned down the corridor to the toilets. He slipped into the women's toilet and waited. He heard someone pass on the other side of the thin swinging door and his instinct told him it was Karl Schneidler. He moved into the corridor, took three quick steps to catch up to the German, and slipped a loop of the seizing wire over his head and tightened it with a gentle but quick jerk.

"You can die here. Now." Broxton said, drawing back slightly on the wire, "or you can walk out that door and we can have a little talk."

The German started to speak, and Broxton pulled a little harder on the wire.

"No sound, nod your head, yes or no," Broxton whispered. "Yes, for we talk. No, for I kill you now."

The German nodded yes, and with one hand holding the wire loop around his neck, and the other in the small of his back, pushing him forward, Broxton guided him out the back door and into the dark.

Once out back, Schneidler started to turn, but Broxton brought a foot behind one of the German's knees, forcing him to kneel on the damp earth. "A slight move, that's all I want, just give me a reason to end it now," Broxton said, kneeing him in the back, forcing him forward even more, till he was face down on the ground.

Schneidler tried to talk, but could only gag with the wire around his neck. Then he squawked as Broxton's hand went up his shorts and he put a smaller loop of the seizing wire around his testicles.

"Now," Broxton said, "one wrong move and you spend the rest of your life as a girl." He stepped off the German and stood aside. "You understand what I've done?"

Schneidler shook his head, no.

"The wire around your balls and neck. Seizing wire. Very strong, easy to bend." Schneidler started to move. "Don't, Karl," Broxton said, and he leaned forward, reached his hand under the German's loose fitting shirt and removed the gun.

"Forty-Five auto, very bad. Illegal in St. Lucia. But you knew that." Broxton thumbed the release and the clip fell out. He threw it toward the ocean and grinned when he heard the splash. "Played ball in college," he said. Then he pulled the slide back. A round flew up, landing about five feet away. "And one in the chamber. Very dangerous."

He loosened the wire noose around the German's neck, then he slipped it off. "Okay, you can get up. Just remember that I've got you on a leash, one wrong move and you can kiss 'em goodbye." Schneidler pushed himself from the ground and gave a high pitch little yelp when Broxton gave a slight tug to the wire looped around his testicles.

"You'll pay," Karl Schneidler said, his voice even higher than Broxton remembered from the phone.

"We all have to pay," Broxton said, "but right now I'm holding the hand with all the aces, so to speak. And here's how I want to play my cards. You're going to walk to your dinghy with your hand on this," he shook the hand with the gun in it, like a mother shaking a baby's rattle. "You'll get in the dinghy and you'll do your best to convince your friends at the bar that I'm your prisoner. I'll get in after you and I'll drive. Your friends will assume that you're taking me out to sea to do away with me."

"You're insane," Karl Schneidler said.

"Maybe, but I don't have wire wrapped around my balls. I'll play out about ten feet. One wrong move, if I even suspect you're trying to signal your brother, and I'll jerk off your nuts."

"And they'll kill you."

"I'd rather be dead than the way that'll leave you, but hey, that's just me," Broxton said, and for emphasis he gave a slight pull on the wire. Schneidler winced, but didn't yelp.

"Here," Broxton said. "Stuff it in your pants, make sure your friends see it when we get in the dinghy." He handed the gun to Schneidler, who did as instructed. Broxton led him to the rubber boat like he was taking a dog for a walk. He risked a glance at the bar as they were pushing the boat into the lazy ocean and fought a grin when he saw the smug look of satisfaction of the face of Schneidler's twin.

"Okay, hand it over," Broxton said, after they were out of the sight of the men in the restaurant. The German handed over the gun, and Broxton tossed it into the sea.

"Stupid, it was a good gun," Schneidler grunted.

Schneidler motored up to *Snake Eyes* and kissed the side of the black boat with the dinghy. He moved carefully up the boarding ladder, with Broxton behind, holding the wire.

"I need some line to tie you with, then I can take the seizing wire off," Broxton lied.

"You're not going to kill me?"

"Not if I don't have to."

"You killed the others, and you made sure we noticed," he said. Broxton winced when he heard the squeaky high voice. He wanted to lash out at him, to jerk on the wire till the man was screaming in agony, but instinct told him that Karl Schneidler was a strong man who wouldn't break under torture.

But he would talk if he thought his manhood was at stake. He was that kind of man. With a voice like his he probably had to prove himself time and again. He wouldn't be able to live without his balls.

"They didn't give me any choice," Broxton said. "They were idiots."

"And if I give you a choice?"

"You can walk away from this. Now where's the line?"

"There." Schneidler pointed to the cockpit seats.

"Get it," Broxton ordered, and Schneidler lifted up the cushions to get at the storage space underneath. He pulled out some spare line and, Broxton, still using the wire leash to coax cooperation, led Schneidler up to the mast.

"Hands behind your back," he said, and he tied the German to the mast.

"Now you will take this thing off?"

"First we talk."

"You promised."

"What do I look like? We talk, if I'm satisfied, we both go back to shore buddy buddy. If I'm not you'll be squeaking a note or two higher." Broxton grinned as the blood rushed to Schneidler's head. The German glared at Broxton. And Broxton knew that if he ever got free he'd tear him apart, like a pit bull would a rabbit.

Broxton stayed quiet and let the blood drain from Schneidler's face. Then calmly, Schneidler asked, "What do you want to know?"

"First let me tell you what I already know. *Fallen Angel* has several million dollars worth of drugs on board. I want to know who's involved and just what I have to do to get in on the action."

Schneidler sighed and smiled. Broxton grinned back. For the first time since his capture Schneidler had to be thinking that there was a way out for him after all. "So, you want a cut of the pie?"

"Yes," Broxton lied, "but not so big a cut that anyone will be too resentful. The way I figure it there's enough to go around. Think about it. You guys could use me. I'd like to be on the side of the big money for a change."

"You have been resourceful," Schneidler said.

"Talk to me," Broxton said. "Let's be friends."

"Take off the wire."

"Sorry, talk first, trust later."

Schneidler was silent for a while and Broxton was tempted to jerk on the wire, but instead he said, "I know about *Stardust*. Too bad, but if I inadvertently caused the problem you have to remember that I was just doing my job. That's not my job anymore."

Schneidler was quiet for a few seconds more, then he started talking. "Dieter lost a fortune when *Stardust* went down, over half a million US. He's counting on making it back with *Fallen Angel*."

"How?"

"The original plan was for the Tanakas to take the yacht back to the US, then we'd find a way to get it back from them."

"How?"

"Not what you're thinking," Karl Schneidler said. "We'd buy it. Usually if you give someone substantially more than something's worth, they sell."

"But *Stardust* went down." Broxton said.

"Yes, and that amplified the problem. Dieter used his own money to finance the *Stardust* operation. Paid the Salizar Cartel cash. They were so sure his plan would work that they sold him the next batch on terms, a quarter up front, a quarter when the boat sails and the balance when he realized his profits from *Stardust*."

"But *Stardust* went down." Broxton said again.

"And the magic man ran off with the second payment and then some."

"Explain?"

"Dieter was using the shipyard to launder money for the Salizars."

"How much did he lose? Broxton asked.

"The second payment was three hundred thousand, US."

"And the Colombian's money?"

"Over eight million dollars," Schneidler said.

"Ouch," Broxton said.

"The magic man is dead and the money is missing."

"Who is this magic man?"

"Michael Martel, the Magic Man, he did an international trade in magic tricks. Allowed him free access to come and go to the States. He carried the money back."

"The prosecution witness in the Chandee murder?"

"The same."

"Magic," Broxton said, "is supposed to be a good thing. A thing for kids and adults who wish they were kids."

"This magic man wasn't a kiddy magician, he moved major money from country to country."

"So the money's gone?" Broxton said.

"Yes and no. Martel had a luggage locker in St. Martin. Dieter thinks the money is there."

"So why doesn't he just go get it?"

"He doesn't have the key."

"He could create a diversion, break into the locker," Broxton said.

"He doesn't know which locker."

"How do you know this?" Broxton asked.

"I asked Martel's wife." Schneidler said, and Broxton knew what methods he probably used to extract the information.

"So like I said, the money's lost?"

"Maybe not. His wife said that he wore the key around his neck. Find the key, find the money."

"Where's the key?" Broxton asked.

"Dieter thinks Julie Tanaka might have it, because she found his body floating in the gulf. He's a little paranoid about her because she's got his cocaine. She's on her way to St. Martin right now. Her daughter has a flight out on the fifteenth."

"So that's where you were going. To St. Martin."

"Yes."

"No." Broxton said and he jerked the wire, severing Karl Schneidler's testicles from his body with a howling scream that rippled across the bay.

Schneidler wasn't going anywhere, so Broxton left him and went below. In the engine room, He found a tool box and took out a strong screwdriver. It was hot in the small room, and Broxton wiped some sweat from his brow before he opened the door to the engine compartment. He lay down on his belly, reached under the main engine and closed the thru-hull seacock.

Then he undid the hose clamp with the screwdriver and pulled the hose off of the seacock. His lips curled up into a smile as he reopened the seacock and he was almost laughing as he scooted back, watching the ocean rush into the boat.

The engine compartment bilge pumps came on and started tossing water out of the boat. They were doing their job well. They were designed to take out more than a damaged hose would allow in. He jerked the wires from the float switches and the pumps shut down.

Satisfied, he went topside and looked out across the bay.

The cockpit cushions were still off, the hatch cover still open. He found two full five gallon, plastic jerry cans of gasoline. He took one of them below, where he stripped a sheet off the bed in the aft cabin. Then he grabbed a box of wooden matches from the galley and went to work.

The cool air coming in from the open hatch caused him to shiver as it met the sweat on his skin, but he paid it no attention as he tore the sheet in half and rolled one of the halves so that it resembled a white snake. He thought about the gasoline for a second, but he wanted something that would burn slower. Then he saw the hurricane lamp hanging in the galley. He took it down, poured the kerosene over the rolled sheet half, opened the jerry can and stuffed one end of the soaked sheet half in the spout.

Karl Schneidler was still screaming on deck, and every loud agonizing blast from the German sent ripples of pleasure though Broxton as he set the giant Molotov cocktail in the center of the salon. He looked around, saw a pack of cigarettes by a paperback book. Night Witch, by Jack Priest. A horror story. How fitting. Then he took a cigarette, lit it, laid out the rolled sheet half, doused the book in kerosene and set it on the end of the rolled sheet, broke the filter off the cigarette and set it between the pages of the paperback, thus making about a twenty minute fuse.

By the time Broxton was back on deck Schneidler was weeping. Broxton had the other half of the rolled sheet around his neck as he lowered the second jerry can into the dinghy and motored over to *Challenge*.

He left the outboard running as he climbed aboard the twin ship, opened the thru hull, poured kerosene throughout the ship and set up the gas can cocktail in the center of the salon. He lit another cigarette, found a magazine instead of a paperback, doused it with kerosene, broke about three quarters of the cigarette off, giving himself about five minutes to get away, dashed up the hatch and leapt into the dinghy.

He cranked the throttle full on and zoomed away from the boats. When he judged himself a safe distance away he cut the gas, and waited. *Snake Eyes* went first, in a blinding, blazing explosion. *Challenge* blasted apart a few seconds later.

CHAPTER FIFTEEN

THE DEPRESSION HAD A RADIUS *of over three hundred miles as it moved into the clockwise winds of the Bermuda High at seventeen knots. Still headed westward, turning day to dark, sparking lightning between the layers of storms. Winds in the depression whipped up to forty knots and the National Hurricane Center gave it a name. Darlene.*

The British frigate, HMS Leeward, cruising below the thundering sky, noted seas at twenty feet. They were on course home when they received a mayday from the fishing trawler Northern Lights, out of Holland. The trawler had capsized by the time the Leeward arrived on the scene. Darlene had claimed her first victims.

THEY MOTORED INTO RODNEY BAY on the northern end of St. Lucia at dawn. "That looks like a good spot," Meiko said, pointing into the sun. Julie nodded and stepped out of the cockpit to get ready to drop the anchor. The deck was slippery with salt water spray and she moved forward with one hand on the boom till she reached the mast, then she took two quick, cautious steps and grabbed onto the inner forestay. The morning air chilled her as she held her hand up against the bright sun, squinting into it, and she shivered when she saw the two masts sticking out of the calm water. She pointed right and Meiko turned the wheel away. Julie made sure they were well away from the two sunken ships before she dropped the anchor. Once she was satisfied the holding was good, she gave Meiko the sign to cut the engine.

"What do you think happened to them?" Meiko asked as Julie stepped back into the cockpit.

"Don't know," Julie said. She picked up the binoculars and studied the two masts sticking out of the water at odd angles. She felt sorry for the owners of the sunken boats and she wondered how long they'd been under water and if the owners had insurance.

Twenty minutes later they were having coffee while waiting for bacon and eggs in Typhoon Willie's. Julie looked out at *Fallen Angel* and for the thousandth time wished she wasn't quite so big. She couldn't handle it by herself, but she was determined not to give up the boat.

"So how are you going to get by?" Meiko said, reading her thoughts.

"I'll try to find a couple of women I can get along with in St. Martin, or maybe a young couple just starting out. I'll manage."

"I could stay."

"We've been through that. One more semester, remember?"

"I remember."

Four men pulled up chairs at the table next to theirs. They were all young, strong, European and good looking. Julie thought they'd make a good advertisement for surf wear.

"Morning," Meiko said.

"Good morning," one of them answered back. Julie detected no hint of an accent. Maybe she was wrong. Maybe they were American.

The breakfast came and Julie picked up a crisp piece of bacon. She bit into it and her lip when she heard the men start speaking among themselves. In German. She tasted the salty bacon mingled with the saltier taste of her own blood. She swallowed and ran her tongue along the inside of her lower lip, along the cut, while she glanced at the young men at the next table.

She shivered, but told herself that the possibility that these men were connected with the Schneidler twins and their twin boats was so remote as to be unthinkable. There were a lot of wonderful German sailors cruising the Caribbean. She looked away from the young men and caught Meiko's eye and she could feel the chill running up her daughter's back.

"It's okay," Julie said softly, barely above a whisper. "It's just a coincidence."

"I know, Mom, but it still gives me the chilly willies."

After they finished breakfast they went to Customs and Immigration to check in. It was a quarter to nine, but the officer was already in and willing to do the paperwork. Julie and Meiko were welcomed into his office and he bade them sit at two chairs across from his desk. He was friendly, smiled large, and when they finished the forms and had their passports stamped, Julie asked about the two sunken boats in the harbor.

"Happened last night. Deliberate."

"For the insurance?" Julie asked, feeling her own chilly willies.

"Someone didn't like them. Set them afire. Then took off."

"Who would do such a thing?" Julie asked.

"We're looking into that," he said, then he leaned forward and lowered his voice in the way Islanders do when they gossip. "They was two brothers, same kind of boat. One got killed, the other is mad, mad."

"Do you have any clues?" She leaned across his desk and lowered her voice to match his.

"We had a boat in here for a few days, anchored farthest out. Didn't check in."

"Didn't check in?"

"No, funny thing, those two sunken boats, they didn't check in either. Happens sometimes, folks don' think they have to obey the law."

"They give us all a bad name." Julie smiled at the man, wanting more information. "Are the crew still on the island?"

"Course," the customs officer said. "Only happen last night, you don' think we let them leave so quick. Besides, we wanna know why they didn' check in."

"Mom," Meiko said as soon as they were outside the door. "We have to leave right now. Once we're away from here we're safe."

"I think you're right," Julie said.

"You wanna go back in and check out?"

"No, let's just go to the boat and get the *H* out of here."

"That's got my vote, big time," Meiko said. They went straight to the dinghy dock, climbed in their inflatable and zoomed out toward *Fallen Angel*.

"There's something I wanted to tell you," Meiko said when Julie throttled back as they approached *Fallen Angel*.

Now what? Julie knew that tone, halfway between a whisper and a murmur. Meiko used to sound like that when she was a little girl and got caught doing something wrong. Julie put the outboard in neutral and waited.

"I want to go back on the fifteenth instead of the thirtieth."

"That's less then a week to get to St. Martin."

"We can be there in two days," Meiko said, if we sail straight through. We'll have plenty of time to get the boat into the yacht club."

"We'd have to change the tickets. I don't know if we can do it on such short notice."

"Actually, that's already been taken care of," she said with an even quieter voice.

"How?" Julie fought to keep the tension out of her voice as her grip tightened on the outboard's throttle.

"When I radioed Victor from Alice and Chad's boat. He's going to be at the boat show in Miami and I figured since I had to go home for that last semester, I'd see him one more time, before I started cracking the books."

"When were you going to tell me?" Julie tightened her hand on the throttle and the engine revved a bit. She relaxed her grip and the engine quieted back down.

"I'm telling you now," Meiko said.

"You know what I mean. Captain Sanchez went to a lot of trouble to get you that ticket and I was counting on your help." She was reaching and she knew it. She'd wanted Meiko to go back to the States, she just didn't plan on Victor being there.

"Come on, Mom, I'm sorry I didn't tell you earlier. I was working up the courage."

"Since when do you need courage to talk to me?"

"Since you don't like the idea of me and Victor," Meiko said.

"If you're going on the fifteenth," Julie said, "then we'd better get going." She put the outboard back into forward and eased up to *Fallen Angel*, once again biting back her true feelings. All she could do now was hope that when Meiko got to spend a little time with him she'd figure out that he wasn't the man for her. She turned the dinghy and brought it alongside, just behind the swim ladder.

Meiko cleated off the painter and went up the ladder. Julie cut the engine and followed up. She stepped over the lifelines, and stopped in her tracks. Kurt Schneidler had a hand around Meiko's mouth and a knife at her throat.

"Finally," he said.

"What do you want, Kurt?" she said, trying to sound indignant.

"Give me a break," he said.

"Are you going to try and take the boat? That's piracy, you know. You'll go to jail."

"Where's the key?" he demanded.

"What are you talking about," she said, and she gasped as three of the four young men they had breakfasted next to came up through the hatch.

"No luck, Kurt," one of them said.

"We've been conducting a little search below," he said. "Not as neat as the last time I was aboard."

"So there was someone aboard that morning."

"I suspected you heard me. I would have liked to question you then the way I will later, but I couldn't have your screams echoing through the yacht club." He dropped the knife from Meiko's throat and released her. She moved over next to her mother.

"Kurt, if I knew what you were looking for, and if I had it, I'd give it to you just so we could be on our way."

"You're never going to be on your way," he said.

"You'll never get away with this."

"You stupid bitch, look around you. I've already gotten away with it."

He was right. He had them good. She looked to shore. There would be no help from that quarter. Even if she could scream, nobody would hear. *Fallen Angel* was the last boat out. No one would notice if she just hauled up her anchor and motored out of the bay.

Two more men came up from below. "How many men to capture two women?" she asked, no pretext at surprise now, just indignation.

"We are seven. We were eight last night, but we had some problems."

"Someone sank your boat and killed your brother," Meiko said. Kurt slapped her across the face and she almost fell.

"Hold your tongue, bitch, or I'll let my men have you, then throw you overboard."

Meiko started to say something.

"Shut up, Meiko," Julie said, and her daughter bit back her words.

"Smart, Julie, smart, but then Dieter said you were smart. One more time, where's the key?"

"If I was so smart would I hold anything back from you? We're completely at your mercy. Our only hope is cooperation. I don't have any key. I don't even know what it is."

"Maybe," he said. "Tell me about Broxton."

"Why?"

"Tell me."

"He's a DEA agent. He thought my husband was a drug smuggler. He was wrong. That's all I know. He showed up the day I found out about Hideo and tried to ask me questions. Tammy Drake shooed him off."

"I'm going to kill him," Kurt said.

"I don't understand," Julie said, but she was beginning to. "It was him," she said, "wasn't it?"

"The son of a bitch killed my brother and sank our boats. He will die horrible and slow."

"Why tell me?" she said, "I don't know him and could care less what happens to him."

"You and him, we've been after the both of you. I thought there might be a connection."

"I'm just trying to save my boat," Julie said. "That's all. Surely you can understand that."

He looked long and hard at her. He started to say something, stopped, and cocked his head, kind of like a cocker spaniel, and for a moment he looked child-like, almost angelic. He looked lost and hurt. Then his eyes glazed over and he looked away. "Harris, start the engine and lets get out of here."

A few seconds later Harris shouted from the cockpit, "She won't start."

"Shit," Kurt said, and he hurried to the cockpit and started depressing the starter button.

"Go below and see what's wrong," he said.

After a few minutes that seemed like eons to Julie, Harris came back on deck. "I don't know. Starter clicks, but nothing happens."

"Any of you idiots know anything about diesels?" he screamed. Julie thought of the childish expression a moment ago and contrasted it with his clenched facial muscles and burning grey eyes and realized that he was crazy as a mad dog. The only way to deal with him would be to put him down.

None of his men spoke up.

"You're all fucking worthless!" His face was red, his right hand clenched into a tight knuckled, pumping fist. "All right, we'll sail off the fucking anchor. Can you at least do that?"

The men scrambled to do his bidding.

"You two, follow me," Kurt said and the women followed. Kurt went to the bow and opened the forepeak hatch. "Get in," he said.

"You're kidding," Julie said. "It's over a hundred degrees in there."

"It'll be uncomfortable, but you won't die." He pointed with the knife.

Julie knew there was no point in arguing, so she climbed down the hatch and Meiko came down after her. Kurt closed the hatch on top of them and Julie and Meiko looked for a way to get comfortable among the diesel jugs, bundled lengths of line, buckets and tools.

It was hot, but not dark. Plenty of light came in through the Plexiglas hatch. The hatch also had latches on the inside. If it got too hot she could open it a little and let in some air, but not if they were sailing, because water coming over the deck would flood down in the hatch and drench them.

"There are no winch handles," Julie heard Harris say.

"God dammit, yes there are, find them." Kurt was raging and Julie thought that maybe they were better off where they were than up on deck. The crew was silent except for Harris, who seemed to be bearing the brunt of Kurt's verbal abuse. Kurt became more and more unhinged as the seconds ticked by.

After a few seconds, Julie and Meiko heard Harris say that there were no winch handles anywhere on the boat, and Julie thought that was strange. *Fallen Angel* was a big race boat, sixteen winches and six handles. The winch handles all had plastic holsters, one on each side of the mast, four in the cockpit. Where could they be?

"All right," Kurt screeched. "We'll sail without the handles."

"How can we do that?" Harris tried to reason with him.

"We have enough men to pull up the main. We'll set it and cleat it off. We might not be able to tighten it, but it should get us the fuck out of here."

"Why don't I just go ashore to the chandlery and buy a couple of winch handles?"

"Why don't you fucking shut up," Kurt said. Like when she was trapped on the island, she wondered why they weren't speaking German. Then it hit her. Harris didn't speak German. He hadn't been at the table during breakfast when the young men were eating and bantering in German. She'd seen him around the yard, but she'd never had occasion to talk to him. He mostly worked in the office, with Dieter.

And then another thought assailed her. If Harris wasn't German, was Dieter? He sure sounded American that day out at Five Islands.

Julie heard the sound of the men hoisting the main and felt movement as the boat shifted slightly with the wind and tugged at its anchor.

"Cleated off," Harris said, and Julie heard footsteps overhead and then she saw Kurt step over the Plexiglas hatch and step on the windlass button to bring up the anchor. The chain started to fall into the chain locker behind her.

Think, she told herself. The rattling chain echoed throughout the small compartment. Meiko had her hands on her ears. If only she could stop the banging and clanging of the falling chain. Then she grinned, reached overhead and jerked on the DC wires to the windlass, ripping them from their terminals.

Immediately the stuffy compartment went quiet.

"Mother fuck!" Kurt screamed from above. He was stamping his foot on the windlass button and the sound of his bare foot slamming against the deck above reverberated throughout the compartment, but Julie preferred it to the chain clanging in the locker.

Kurt bent low and Julie saw the river of hatred flowing from his eyes through the glass. He opened the hatch.

"God dammit, the windlass doesn't work! What's going on with this boat?"

"I don't know," she said.

"Why doesn't the shit work, where's the fucking winch handles?"

"I don't know. The handles are supposed to be at the mast and in the cockpit."

"I fucking know that, they're not there."

"Someone must have stolen them."

He slammed the hatch shut in a rage, still screaming, "Harris, take the fucking men ashore, get winch handles, an electrician and a diesel mechanic."

"We all don't have to go," Julie heard Harris say.

"Yes, yes, yes, all of you, go. I want to be alone with these women."

Julie didn't like the idea of being on the boat alone with Kurt. She looked around her prison for a weapon, then she took some half inch line off a hook and started to uncoil it. She tied a small bowline loop in the end of it and fed the line back through it.

"What are you doing, Mom?" Meiko asked.

"When he sticks his head down here again I'm going to loop this around his neck and we're going to pull for all we're worth."

"Mom, that'll kill him. It's murder."

"He wasn't kidding when he said his men would use you. When they get tired of us they'll toss us overboard, probably with our hands tied behind our backs. You heard the man, he's insane."

"But to kill someone?"

"Him or us," Julie said, and she heard the sound of the dinghy motoring toward shore. Now they were alone with Kurt.

"I'm sorry, I just don't think I can do it."

"Okay, honey, just stay back and I'll do it myself."

Then without warning the hatch opened, but Kurt was standing and Julie had no chance to get the noose around his neck.

"Hot down there?" He laughed, then he started squirting them with the salt water hose.

"Stop it," Meiko yelled, holding her hands in front of her eyes, but Kurt laughed and kept the hose trained on her.

"Fucking mongrel child!" He blasted her in the face with the water. Then he moved the hard spray to her breasts, soaking the halter top till he could see through it. "One thing about mongrels," he said. "They fuck good."

Meiko backed away from the center of the compartment till she had her back to the chain locker and Kurt couldn't reach her with the spray, but he was a man possessed. He dropped to his knees, stuck the hose in the hatch and aimed it toward the back of the compartment.

"Missed me, missed me, you fucking pervert," Meiko yelled out.

"You fucking whore!" Kurt stuck his head down the hatch after the hose. "You won't fucking get away from me so easy." He saw them cringing against the chain locker and laughed. Like a hyena, Julie thought.

Then she looped the noose around his neck and jerked. Meiko jumped forward, grabbed onto the rope and helped her mother pull. There was a screech out of Kurt, then a crack as his neck broke, followed by a stench as his bowels cut loose as his body flopped into the compartment.. He died quick. He died fast.

"Shit," he stinks," Meiko said.

"He's dead," Julie said.

"Good," Meiko said. "I was wrong, I can do it. I just needed the proper motivation."

"We have to get out of here," Julie said.

Meiko scrambled up and out of the hatch. Julie looked at the body slumped at her feet. So Broxton killed his twin, and I killed him. She was bound up with the skin headed DEA agent, but why? It had to be more than just getting her boat so that Dieter could sell it and recover a past dept. People didn't kill for that kind of money.

"Better get up here, Mom. Dinghy's coming," Meiko said, and Julie climbed through the hatch, taking her time, thinking. She looked out over the bay. The dinghy was headed for them with only Harris and a large black man in it. The German crew was gone.

"Be right back, honey," Julie said and she dashed back to the cockpit. She pulled up the starboard cushion and then the locker cover and grabbed a flare gun. Then she hustled back to where her daughter was standing, and together they waited for the rubber boat.

Harris brought the dinghy along side. "Where's Kurt?" he asked, wary.

"Dead," Julie answered.

His hand went to his shirt, but the big black man slapped the gun out of his hand as Julie shot him in the chest with the flare gun. The big man grabbed Harris by his long hair and shoved his head over the side and under the water. He held him there until he stopped kicking, then he let go.

"Morning, Julie Tanaka," the man said.

"Morning, Henry Waller," Julie answered.

"You gonna wanna be sailing out of here real quick I think," Henry said.

"I think that's best," Julie said.

"You say the other one's dead?"

"Dead, dead."

"I'm gonna motor round to the other side, so's no one looking from shore can see. We're gonna have to haul this one up. We can dump them when we get out to sea." Henry motored the dinghy around to the other side of the boat.

Julie unclipped a spinnaker halyard and dropped it down to Henry. The two women watched as he wrapped the halyard around the dead man's waist and cinched it tight. "Okay," he said, "haul him up."

Julie wrapped the halyard on a winch.

"You'll need this." Henry held up a winch handle.

"So you took them," she said. Then she bent down and started grinding and the dead man rose from below. Meiko guided it over the lifelines and Julie lowered it onto the deck. Henry cleated off the dinghy and pulled himself on board.

"My legs may be shot, but there's nothing wrong with my arms," he said. Then he unclipped the halyard and picked the body up, one handed, by the back of the pants. "Where do you want it?"

"Kurt's in the forepeak," Julie said, and she went up front and opened the hatch. Henry dropped Harris in and they both winced as his body crashed on top of his dead boss.

"A bad business," Henry said.

"Yes."

"His crew walked out. They didn't mind the chase, but they couldn't stomach kidnapping. They were good kids who fell under the influence of a bad man."

Julie thought that was probably true.

"You fixed the engine so it wouldn't start and you took the winch handles. How'd you know?"

"Darla. She overheard them again. So when you were in customs I came out and doctored the engine and removed the handles. Just to be safe. We didn't want you to go without saying goodbye." He smiled.

"You said we," Julie said. "Are you coming with us?"

"Word is you're headed to St. Martin," Henry said.

"We are."

"Darla's always wanted to see St. Martin."

CHAPTER SIXTEEN

AFTER A DAY RIDING *in the Bermuda High, Tropical Storm Darlene began a curve to the northwest, toward the Caribbean Islands. The clockwise winds in the high fed the storm, and the winds around Darlene's center whipped up to eighty miles an hour and she became a hurricane.*

Hurricane Darlene picked up speed, pushing smaller storms on ahead of her as she drew nearer the islands. Darlene was four hundred miles across and reached upwards over fifty thousand feet through the troposphere and into the stratosphere, moving more than a million cubic feet of atmosphere every second, whipping up sixty foot waves in the ocean below.

Broxton sailed the boat through the sparkling star-filled night toward early morning. T-Bone slept below. Broxton was alone with the boat and the ocean. He saw the stars off to the right, over the land, start to wink out, but rain clouds over the land didn't bother him.

Broxton turned back to the sea ahead, a long line of flat that extended forever. A world with no borders, boundaries, bosses or businesses. A world shared with nature and all her glory. A world devoid of petty people and petty minds. A world that was never boring. Work was hard, rewards were few, friends were fast, luxury was rare, moments were enjoyed. Like now.

The sun was sliding up over the horizon. Billowing, high flowing cumulus clouds moved north. The higher cirrus clouds were glowing orange and red across the sky and Broxton thought of that old sailor's adage, *Red sky at night, sailor's delight. Red sky at morning, sailor take warning.*

He looked over his shoulder, back toward the island nation of Dominica. Those clouds weren't red. They weren't white either. But for now the dark grey rain clouds were over land. He didn't think they posed a problem.

He saw the rain in the distance, a sheeting haze coming down from the grey clouds over the island. The moisture in them picked up and reflected the sun's rays, wakening something spiritual in him. If ever there was an argument for God, that view was it.

The air had a familiar feel. It reminded him of that smell he got when he was kid, after he'd just mowed the lawn and watered the grass. That special smell that made him glad to be alive, glad to be in that place. Glad to be home.

And then he knew it. He was home. Not the boat, not *Obsession*, but the vastness around him, the sometimes friendly, sometimes angry sea. That was home. Still looking at the far off rain, he smiled. This was something people who live in houses never see, and he never wanted to go back.

He ran his fingers through his hair and scratched his head. The hair felt good under his fingers, alive. He was alive. He had a passport good for five years. He wasn't going back. Somehow he'd figure out a way to get a boat of his own and he'd sail the islands, fish for supper, share his life with the islanders and the cruisers, enjoy himself till he died. He wasn't going back.

The jib luffed, then flapped. He put a handle in the winch, tightened it up and the sail's belly filled, forming that vertical wing that gave the boat its lift and forward momentum. They picked up some speed. He turned off the wind a bit, and gained more speed. He was learning to steer by the feel of the boat and the wind on his face.

The waves picked up and he judged them to be about five feet. Large rolling waves that slipped under *Obsession*, like a cat sliding under a gate. He tingled with anticipation when the waves were higher than eye level, and he thrilled when *Obsession* floated over them.

A breaking wave splashed the side and foaming water rippled and ran across the deck. A second breaker was coming and he turned into it and sliced through it. Then he turned back on course, another breaker, another turn, then back on course. He kept it up until he was able to fine tune the turns and get in the groove, a slight turn to starboard, just enough so the wave didn't break on the side, then back to port.

Then a larger breaking wave popped up out of sequence, smacked the side and flooded the deck. The stinging water slapped him in the face, like an angry woman he'd taken for granted. He wiped the salty water out of his eyes and turned toward the far off storm, surprised to find it wasn't so far off anymore.

"Better get up here," Broxton yelled down the companion way. Then he turned back to the storm. The familiar gray squall line he'd grown used to was turning to black, and it covered half his vision. Dominica was gone, buried under black thunder clouds. The sea turned confused. No more steady rolling waves. They were all breaking now.

The storm had moved from behind to along side and the weather became a stark study in contrast. To the right, dark, murky skies, to the left, bright, white, red tinged sky. Heaven and Hell, life and death,.

"Shit," T-Bone said. When he saw the approaching weather. "We're in for a blow." Lightning flashed in the distance, lighting up the dark and dangerous sky. "Beautiful. Where else do you get to see this? Nature is out there and she's kicking ass."

"How do we keep her from kicking ours?" Broxton asked. Thunder roared and rain sprayed his face. They were at the edge of the rain. And it wasn't Sunday afternoon picnic rain. The black thunderclouds were pouring water down with the fury of a giant waterfall.

"We could heave-to and ride it out," T-Bone said, "but that wouldn't be any fun." He was holding on to the bimini bar as a breaker splashed over the side and he skillfully slid back, avoiding the water that came splashing back into the cockpit.

"No," Broxton said, "not any fun." His hands were knuckle-white on the wheel and his stomach churned at what he was afraid his friend was going to say next.

"Boat against nature," T-Bone said, "Sort of takes us out of the equation."

"But it's the safest thing to do, right?"

"Probably," T-Bone said, and Broxton remembered him floundering around in the ocean, hanging on to those cockpit cushions when most men would be struggling for a line, wanting out of the water as quickly as possible and damn the cost. T-Bone, he decided, wasn't always logical.

"So what do you want to do?" Broxton said.

"Well," he said, and he was quiet for a few seconds. "We could run from it."

"Turn our backs on the storm?" Broxton shook his head. T-Bone's clear eyes were like twin lights in the darkening dawn. Forked lightning split the sky and Broxton shivered with anticipation.

"Best way to learn to sail," T-Bone said, "riding out a storm."

"I know how to sail."

"You learned a lot in a short time, yeah, and you're good, but we survive this and you could be great. Think about it."

"You're crazy."

"Yeah." He grinned like a retarded child, eyes twinkling.

"Just turn away from it," Broxton said, spinning the wheel.

"I better go down and get some heavy weather gear," T-Bone said and he slipped below as lightning cracked overhead, thunder boomed and the rain poured down. Too late for a raincoat, Broxton thought, and T-Bone was back up the hatch like a rabbit shooting out of a hole in an earthquake.

"Put it on." He handed Broxton a harness and a tether. Broxton slipped into it as if he was putting on a vest, then he clipped the tether to it. Then he clipped the other end onto the binnacle. He wasn't going anywhere.

Lightning blasted the sky again. Thunder pounded. There was no counting between the sound and the flash. They were in it. Five foot rolling seas turned into ten foot breaking seas in minutes. The wind grew from fifteen to thirty-five knots and Broxton tightened his hands on the wheel, both to steady the boat and himself.

"We're gonna have to get some of the sail down," T-Bone said. "Keep it as steady as you can." Broxton nodded and T-Bone went forward, He clipped onto the butt bars, took the main halyard off the self tailing winch, lowered the mainsail to the third reef point, and tied it off. He did it without effort as if he'd been born to it. The ten foot waves coming at the stern exhilarated him. They terrified Broxton.

T-Bone dropped to his knees and crawled back toward the stern, reaching the safety of the cockpit as *Obsession* flew over the top of a breaking wave and slammed back into the water. "Whoa, Danny boy, head up a little coming down or we'll pitchpole."

"Pitchpole?" Broxton said loud enough to be heard over the rising wind.

"Bow plows into the water and we flip, end over end. Very bad," T-Bone said, and Broxton shook.

"How far up?"

"Ten, fifteen degrees, not much, just enough to slow us down a little and keep us on the wave," T-Bone said, and the next wave was under them. But this time as they were coming off the top Broxton turned slightly toward the wind and *Obsession* surfed down the wave. Broxton felt like he did all those years ago when he used to surf the Southern California beaches.

"Atta boy," T-Bone said. "They don't teach you that in school." He looked at the windspeed indicator and pointed. Broxton nodded his head. Forty knots. T-Bone slapped a handle in a winch and rolled in the jib.

They crested another wave, and again Broxton headed up as they surfed down the slope. T-Bone sat in the cockpit, face to the weather, long hair whipping and flying in the wind, enjoying himself, and Broxton settled into the groove, riding up the waves, tail in the wind, cranking the wheel a little to the left and surfing down. His adrenaline was flowing. There was something about being pitched against the elements, watching T-Bone laugh, cajole and curse at the wind and the waves. His fear took a back seat and he started enjoying himself.

Thirty minutes later the wind picked up to fifty knots and a wave slammed into them from the side. Water rose straight out of the sea, covering the deck with frothing white foam.

"Hard starboard!" T-Bone screamed. Broxton cranked the wheel to the right. For an instant it looked like the rudder was overpowered, but the boat turned and Broxton readied himself for the next wave as the frothing water rolled off the deck.

With the boat back in control, Broxton turned back to port and resumed surfing the waves, but the wind crept up to fifty-five knots, the seas to twenty feet and he wasn't able to keep *Obsession* from crashing and slamming.

"Head up a little more," T-Bone said, and Broxton surfed down the next wave, twenty-five degrees into the wind, coming smoothly off of it. He straightened the boat, took the next one, then went back on the wind and once again he was in the groove.

He was pumped up, heart, nerve and sinew working together despite the riveting rain and the biting cold. When the wind picked up to sixty knots and the seas were too high to think about, he headed a little more into the wind when he surfed down the waves.

"Don't head up too much," T-Bone yelled, "or we'll be broached."

"Broached?" Broxton yelled back.

"Wave slams into the side and knocks us down. Not good."

And for another half hour Broxton fought the waves, staying in the groove. Fingers and toes numb, legs like jelly, face and arms raw from the pelting rain, thighs quivering, lungs demanding more air with each breath, arms straining and T-Bone never once offered to take a shift at the wheel and Broxton never asked.

Then the wind dropped back down to forty-five knots, then thirty, then twenty and the sea turned from breaking to rolling. Broxton felt like a high school kid who had just made the game winning touchdown. He was driving the boat up and down long rolling seas that only two hours ago would have terrified him.

He laughed as life came back into his arms and legs. He was getting the air he needed to calm his rocketing heart and each deep breath he took seemed to heighten the wave of sexual satisfaction that blazed through him.

Then as quickly as it was on them, it was over. The seas were calm and the wind was moderate. They were miles from land, though. T-Bone pushed himself off the cockpit seat and stood. He had spent the storm laughing at the weather, trusting his boat to Broxton. He moved behind the wheel, slapped Broxton on the back and said, "You're a real sailor man now, don't let no one tell you different."

"Thanks," Broxton said, and he flopped down on the cockpit seat and stretched out. He fell asleep to T-Bone whistling, *Popeye the Sailor Man*.

Broxton was jerked from his sleep by the crackling radio, "Will the sailing vessel *Obsession* stand by to be boarded." T-Bone was asleep on the cockpit seat opposite him. *Obsession* had been merrily sailing north under automatic pilot.

"What is it?" T-Bone wiped the sleep from his eyes with curled fingers.

"The Coast Guard," Broxton said.

"Shit," T-Bone said. The cutter loomed large next to *Obsession*. The water was calm, the winds slight. The *Puerto Rico* was close enough to touch.

"I repeat," the familiar voice boomed over the radio, "Will the sailing vessel *Obsession* stand by to be boarded."

"Do you remember his name?" T-Bone asked.

"Andrews," Broxton said.

"Yeah, that's it," T-Bone said, through clenched lips.

"Good thing we tossed the drugs."

"Hey, yeah, that's right." T-Bone's tight frown turned into a wide smile. "We got no drugs."

"What about the guns?"

"Shit, they don't care about guns. Every American boat out here is armed to the teeth."

"But our guns have killed people."

"Aw, shit, that was up north." He picked up the mike and clicked the talk button. "This is the sailing vessel *Obsession* standing by to be boarded, and a fine,

fine morning to you, Captain Andrews. Will you be coming over for that drink now?"

"Yes, I believe I will," Andrews answered.

Broxton and T-Bone watched as the cutter backed off and lowered its launch. Three young sailors and an older man in an officer's uniform climbed into it and in seconds it was alongside.

"I'm Andrews," the captain said, holding out his hand. Broxton shook it. A young sailor followed his captain aboard. The other two waited in the launch.

"I'm T-Bone Powers." T-Bone held out his hand. Andrews released Broxton's hand and took T-Bone's.

"Why do I have the feeling I've been blind sided?" Andrews said.

"I don't know," T-Bone said. "Cause you were?" Broxton blanched. He'd forgotten that Andrews would naturally associate his face with T-Bone's voice.

"What were you carrying that you didn't want me to find?" Andrews asked.

"Nothing, not a thing," T-Bone said. "It was a bad blowing day and if you'd have seen me on deck, you'd been a boarding, admit it."

"Whatever it was, it's gone now," Andrew said, "because you're being too damned accommodating."

"Danny boy, you wanna pop down and get us some beer," T-Bone said. Then he turned to Andrews, "Don't suppose your men can have one."

"No, and I won't either. Another time." He looked hard at Broxton for a second, then shook his head. He turned to the sailor, "You can wait with the others, Craig."

"Yes, sir," the sailor said, and he grabbed onto the port shroud and climbed over into the launch.

"You kind of look like a man in a picture I've got on board," Andrews said, looking at Broxton.

"What kind of picture?" Broxton said.

"Dead or alive kind."

Broxton shrugged.

"What are you, some sort of vigilantes?"

Broxton met the captain's stare, but stayed silent.

"The four in Antigua. The German nationals had arrest records that would reach down to Davey Jones' locker. One of the Colombians was Sierra Salizar, Hector Salizar's baby brother."

"I told you they were Colombians. He thought they were Cuban."

"You're not helping me here, T-Bone," Broxton said.

"Oh, relax. If he was gonna take you in, you'd be in irons by now. Me too."

"And firing and sinking *Snake Eyes* and *Challenge* in Rodney Bay, you get around. That was a DEA man tied to the mast. Do you have a death wish?"

"If you knew he was DEA, why didn't you board us with guns and haul us away?" Broxton asked.

"Because I know who the Salizars are what they're capable of. Now I want to know why and what you know."

"Karl Schneidler worked for the DEA, true, but he also worked for the Salizars. He killed a friend of mine. I did him. It was personal. How'd you put it all together?"

"You don't check in at Antigua, and several boats report seeing *Obsession* off the coast the day a speedboat with four dead bodies comes floating in. Then you don't check into St. Lucia and various yachties report *Obsession* sailing away as two boats are burning and sinking. You don't need to be bright to add one and one and get two."

"What are you going to do?" Broxton asked.

"Nothing, not a thing," Andrews said, mimicking T-Bone's words and his drawl. "Everybody in the world knows you didn't kill Chandee, and if it ever got to court you could probably prove it. I'm not going to be the one to bring you in so that you can be murdered in protective custody."

"That's good news," Broxton said.

"The bad news is that the whole world is out looking for a boat named *Obsession*."

"Hey, I got stick 'em letters on board. That name comes off. I'm not married to it," T-Bone said.

"Why am I not surprised." Andrews laughed. "I'll need to know the new name, so I can get that drink you owe me someday."

"*Voyager*," T-Bone said, eyes twinkling.

Andrews shook his head, laughed again and turned to go, stopped and turned back toward Broxton. "The hair works. I'd never have given you a second look if it wasn't for the boat. You got a good passport?"

Broxton nodded.

"Good. Grow a mustache, stay in the Caribbean awhile, people will forget soon enough."

Captain Andrews was at the port shroud, hanging on, about to jump into the launch when he shouted back to the men in the cockpit.

"You're not going to keep heading up north are you?"

"Sure are," T-Bone said.

"You have an SSB?"

"No sir."

"So you don't know about the hurricane?"

"Wait a minute," T-Bone said scurrying over to Andrews. "What hurricane?" Broxton was right behind him.

"Darlene, headed for the islands. South is the place to go. It's where I'm heading."

"We'll give it some thought, Captain," T-Bone said, and the two men watched as Andrews lowered himself into the launch and it motored toward the cutter. Then Andrews put it in neutral and shouted over, "What's it all about?"

"Damsels in distress," T-Bone shouted back.

"When we have that drink you'll have to tell me about it," Andrews shouted, laughing. Then he put the launch in gear and headed toward the *Puerto Rico*. In minutes the cutter was steaming away. Broxton and T-Bone stood at the shrouds and watched as it headed south.

"I don't like hurricanes," T-Bone said.

"I gotta go north," Broxton said.

"I know," T-Bone said. "We got no choice."

"Thanks."

"Hey, Danny boy. You'd do it for me." T-Bone's smile was radiating, his eyes were glowing. "Besides I want to do one really good thing before I die, and you've given me that chance."

"I don't understand," Broxton said, though he thought he did.

"Damsels in distress, we're gonna save 'em, you and me."

CHAPTER
SEVENTEEN

HURRICANE DARLENE RODE *around the southern part of the Bermuda High, gathering ground speed on her curving northwestern path. The thunderstorms swirling around her center lashed each other with lightning and the cracking thunder was loud enough to wake God.*

Darlene continued to push bad weather on ahead, smaller storms, water spouts, foaming and confused seas, all dire warnings of what was to come. The winds roaring around her center were approaching a hundred and fifty miles an hour and every ten minutes Darlene spat out enough energy to supply the whole world for day.

"Hey, Julie!" Darla yelled from the front of the dinghy, waving an arm that looped through the air like loose spaghetti. Her father was driving. His smile matched hers, only larger. There were two duffel bags in the rubber boat. They were coming to stay awhile, and that was fine with Julie.

"Hey, Darla." Julie waved back.

"Wanna buy some tomatoes?" the girl squealed.

"Anytime, wise guy," Julie reached out to grab the dinghy painter as Darla handed it off.

"We're going up north with you," the girl said.

"That's what I hear," Julie said.

"Do I get my own cabin?"

"No," Julie said. "You have to share with Meiko."

"Will I like her?" Darla climbed on board.

"You better, you little squirt," Meiko said, "or I just might throw you off in the middle of the night."

"Oh, yeah, I'm gonna like her." Darla giggled.

Henry handed up Darla's bag, then his.

"How long before you'll have the engine running?" Julie asked.

"About a minute," he said. "Then you can haul anchor."

"No you can't," Meiko said. "Somebody ripped the wires off the windlass motor, remember?"

"That's right," Julie said. "I'd better get a wrench and go down and fix it." Then she stopped short. She remembered the two dead men in the hot forepeak. She remembered the smell.

"I'll do it," Meiko said. "Just tell me how."

"You can do that?"

"Killing him was a problem for me, because I think life, all life, even his, is sacred. But he's dead now. I'll be all right. Don't forget, I'm around dead people all the time."

"All you have to do," Julie said, "is loosen the two nuts on the bottom of the motor and attach the red wire to the nut that has the large red wire attached to it, and the black wire—"

"To the nut that has the large black wire attached to it," Meiko said.

Julie nodded her head and Meiko went below and came back up with a crescent wrench. Then she went forward and down into the forepeak. Julie didn't know how she could do it. She'd have to stand on top of the bodies to reattach the wires.

"Okay." Meiko climbed back out of the hatch as if she'd done nothing more than screw in a light bulb. She bent and closed the hatch. "Want me to bring up the anchor, Mom?" Meiko giggled. She knew Julie didn't want anything to do with the front of the boat until those bodies were off of it.

"Yes," Julie said. "You do that."

Henry started the engine and took the wheel. Julie couldn't help but notice the glint in his eyes as he turned on the GPS. Then he ran his hands along the stainless steel. She knew at once that Henry Waller was a sailor and that he was in love with *Fallen Angel*.

Meiko pointed left and Henry turned the wheel, added a touch of power, then backed off, moving the boat over the anchor. Meiko toed the button and the anchor chain rolled over the bow roller, falling into the chain locker in the forepeak, with the two dead men.

Henry put it back in forward and kept the wheel spinning to port and pointed *Fallen Angel* toward the open ocean. "We should go out to sea and take care of the dirty business, before we trek up north," he said. Julie nodded, feeling comfortable with him behind the wheel.

Julie went below and stretched out in the salon. The forward motion of the boat forced a gentle breeze down the overhead hatch and it washed over her body, cooling her and calming her. That, combined with the lullaby rocking of the boat, had her asleep in minutes.

She woke when the rocking and creaking stopped and the cool breeze died. She yawned, stretched and sat up. She'd needed the sleep. More than the sleep, she'd needed the rest. It was the first time since leaving Trinidad that she was able to close her eyes and sleep the sleep of the just. No more looking over her shoulder. No more worrying about someone trying to steal her home out from under her. She yawned, smiled and pushed herself to her feet.

It was over. Someday she was going to have to look up Broxton and find out what his part in the whole thing was, but first she would get the boat peacefully at rest in the St. Martin Yacht Club. She'd be safe under the Dutch government. Dieter wouldn't dare send someone after the boat up there, and probably, after he found out what happened to his twin hijackers, he'd forget the debt and forget about her.

She heard footsteps overhead and then she knew why they had stopped. It was time. She climbed out the companionway, shielding her eyes against the bright sun. Darla was wearing her sunglasses and looked so cute in them. She couldn't ask for them back.

Meiko was up front, opening the forepeak hatch.

"How are you going to do it?" Julie asked.

"Easy," she said. "Henry and I have it all worked out. I'll go below and tie a line around the bodies, under the armpits. Then I'll loop the line and clip a halyard on it and we'll haul them up one at a time and lower them into the sea."

"What about Darla? She should be below," Julie said.

"No, not me. I've seen dead people before and I want to see these two turned into shark food."

"I should get to it," Meiko said. Don't want to wait till rigor sets in. Stench is going to be bad enough as it is." She hopped down the hatch, dragging a halyard after her and in less than a minute she yelled out. "Okay, Henry," and Henry winched Harris through the hatch.

Meiko scooted through after the body and guided it toward the starboard side of the boat. "It would have been easier if one of you could have done this part."

"No way," Darla said.

"Same goes for me," Julie said. "No way."

Meiko pushed the suspended body toward the side and Henry lowered it into the water. Then Meiko unclipped the halyard and the body floated next to the boat.

"Where's the sharks?" Darla said.

"You didn't really think sharks were going to rise up out of the sea and rip the bodies apart, did you?" Meiko laughed.

"I did." Darla pouted.

"Sorry, that's only in the movies," Meiko said. Then she went back down the hatch and repeated the procedure with Harris' boss man, Kurt.

Then Henry turned the boat out of the wind and they started to pick up speed as he pointed *Fallen Angel* north. "We'll spend the night in Fort de France in Martinique," Henry said, "and with luck we'll make a hundred miles a day, anchoring at night." We should be in St. Martin just in time for Meiko's flight."

So, Julie thought, Meiko had been talking to Henry. She'd wanted Meiko back in the States for so long that it was hard to adjust to not wanting her to go. And it wasn't only because she was going to be seeing Victor. Julie was going to miss her, but she was done trying to influence her daughter's love life. Whatever was going to happen, was going to happen, *Que sera, sera*.

Julie sat back in the cockpit and looked out over the sea. It was nice to be able to enjoy sailing for once.

"Whale!" Darla screamed and Julie turned her head in time to see the great tail flap in the air, then slap the sea as it splashed back into the water. "Did you see it?" Darla exclaimed. "It was huge, and boy does it smell." She put fingers to her nose, pinching it closed, and Julie laughed.

The wind picked up and Henry sniffed the air. "We better shorten sail," he said, greeting Julie's gaze with a smile. "It's nothing to be concerned about. I've been through countless Caribbean blows, I know what to do."

"I wasn't worried, Henry," Julie said, and she was surprised to find that she meant it. She wasn't worried. Henry radiated confidence.

"You wanna take the wheel while I go up and take care of the sail?" he asked. Julie nodded and relieved him as he grimaced and moved up toward the mast. His legs must hurt awfully, but he never brought it up. If Darla hadn't told her, she'd never have known.

She watched as Meiko helped him with the sail. He brought it down and was showing Meiko how to tie in the reef lines when the wind picked up a little more. He turned his face into it, the way a dog does when it sticks its head out of a car window. Then he looked at the jib, yanked on the reef lines, started to tighten it and stopped.

"I think we should drop it," he said, "and tie it off good."

"All right," Julie said, and Meiko took the main halyard off the winch and dropped the sail. The lazy jacks kept the main from spilling off onto the deck, and the two of them started tying sail ties around it, cinching it to the boom.

"Okay," Henry said. "Let's get ready for a blow." Then he went back to the cockpit and started rolling in the jib.

"Are you going to take it all the way in?" Julie asked.

"No," he said. We're going to heave-to."

"Without the main?"

"Julie, that sail is in such bad shape. I think it would blow right out. But the jib's okay, we'll be fine." He turned the wheel hard to leeward and lashed it to a winch.

The boat fell off the wind and the partial jib backwinded. "The goal here," he said, "is to stop all forward movement. The boat will drift with the wind and create a drift slick on the water, breaking up most of the wave's meanness."

The boat slowed almost to a stop. The wind started to howl. The seas started to break. Henry sat behind the wheel and watched the waves and felt the boat's reaction to them.

"I don't suppose you have a sea anchor on board?" he said.

"No," she said. Meiko and Darla sat in the cockpit, taking everything in, Darla's eyes as wide as Meiko's. The black horizon moving toward them riveted their attention on Henry.

"If you had a spare sail on board I could make one."

"No spare sail," Julie said.

Henry looked out over the sea and studied the rapidly moving darkness. "It will be here in a few minutes. It's going to be a big one." He was quiet for a few seconds, staring at the oncoming storm. "We need to stop the boat from moving forward."

"But it's not going very fast," Julie said.

"It will when that wind picks up." He must have seen the concern on her face, because he said, "Hey, don't worry, didn't I promise it would be all right? It will be, but we have things to do and not a lot of time. How many buckets do we have?"

"Four."

"Good ones?"

"Plastic, good enough I guess."

"Okay, get the buckets. Meiko, get all the line you can out of the forepeak. Darla, you help her, and bring all the fenders back here, too." Seconds later he had everything he asked for in the cockpit and the women watched as he tied the buckets to the end of the line, then he tied on five floatable fenders and the two life rings.

"Is your second anchor on rope?" he asked.

"Thirty feet of chain and three hundred feet of rope," Julie said.

"Excellent." He began tying long lines to the fenders and buckets. When he'd finished he dragged the whole mess up to the front of the boat.

He unshackled the Bruce anchor from the chain and tied a bowline through the shackle, attaching his makeshift sea anchor to the boat. Then he tossed it in the water. They waited and watched and after a few minutes *Fallen Angel* stopped her forward movement and sat still in the water, drifting with the waves.

It wasn't long before the full force of the storm was upon them, large rolling, then breaking, seas, and winds up to forty knots. But they rode out the storm, hardly moving at all.

Static electricity charged the air and lightning cracked overhead, stealing the dark of the storm for a fraction of a second as it pitchforked into the water around them.

"Jeez, that was close," Meiko's hair was sticking out and Julie felt electric tingles on her arms.

"I need wire, quickly now," Henry said.

"Main halyard," Julie answered.

Henry went to the main and climbed up the mast steps, unhooked the wire halyard from the sail and jerked it down. Then he ran it around the mast three times before taking it to the side and dropping it in the water.

"I don't know if the boat was properly grounded," he said, "but it is now."

They were all on deck and the rain came on them, fast. In seconds they were drenched.

"Okay," Henry said. "Let's go below, get dry and have some coffee."

"That's it?" Julie yelled.

"The rest is up to the boat," Henry yelled back. Then added, "She's a good boat, don't worry."

"I know," she said., "We'll be fine."

Henry nodded.

Two days later they set anchor in Simpson Bay, a short dinghy ride from Princes Julliana Airport on the Island of St. Martin. They'd had four brisk and windy sailing days after the storm, and she'd learned so much from Henry.

"I know you two want to be alone for Meiko's last day," he said, "and I have some old friends that need seeing. Darla and I will come say goodbye before we head back down island."

"I'll miss you guys," she said. She hugged Darla, and Henry gave Meiko a giant bear hug.

Then Henry's face lit up with a smile that looked like it was going to rocket off his face. "Captain Tanaka, it's been a pleasure sailing with you." He stuck out his big hand.

"Thank you, Henry," she said, taking his hand. "And especially thank you for the captain part."

"You earned it," he said, and she fell into the embrace of his giant arms.

"Mom, Look!" Meiko pointed. They were walking along Front Street in downtown Philipsberg. Julie turned to look. "It's Tammy."

They walked over to the poster. "Tammy Drake, world famous calypsonian, appearing nightly at Maggie's Starlight Lounge," Julie read.

"I can't believe it," Meiko said.

"That pretty much decides what we'll be doing before you leave tonight," Julie said.

"Yeah. I love to watch her sing, but I didn't know she was famous outside of Trinidad," Meiko said.

"It's because she's so well known outside of Trinidad that she's so famous in Trinidad. She's been World Calypso Queen for the last three years running." It was strange, Julie thought. Her daughter idolized Tammy, but didn't really know too much about her.

"I've never even heard her sing calypso music," Meiko said.

"And you probably won't hear it tonight. She mostly sings pop outside of Trinidad. She's got a lot of CDs out."

"I know that," Meiko said. "I've got several." When had she bought them? Julie had never heard her playing them.

That night they were seated at a front row table in the dinner restaurant when Tammy took the stage.

"I guess Hurricane Darlene has kept some people at home," Tammy said into the mike. Then she winked at Julie and Meiko and went into her set, singing pop, blues, and country and western songs. She ended the show with a bluesy version of Bob Dylan's *Knockin' On Heaven's Door* that had everybody up and clapping.

"Wow, she can really sing," Julie said.

"Remember," Tammy said from the stage after the applause had died down. "My compact discs are on sale by the cashier for only fifteen US each. Buy a couple and keep a girl like me in mink." She laughed and the audience laughed along with her. Julie saw several people get up and start for the cashier.

"I was wondering when you were going to come walking in." Julie and Meiko turned to the sound of the familiar voice. Tammy bent and kissed them both on the cheek, before she pulled up a chair and joined them.

"You were great," Meiko said.

"Thanks kiddo, but I've been a lot better. It's hard singing to a half empty house."

"Yeah, you said something about a hurricane? What was that?" Julie asked.

"Hurricane Darlene, just a day away from wiping us all out, or not." Tammy laughed.

"What do you mean?"

"It's out there in the Atlantic headed toward the islands. It'll turn north, they usually do, but it's got the cruise ship people frightened. They don't bring their ships and my audience goes to hell. It sucks."

"What if it doesn't turn north?" Meiko asked.

"Honey, if it doesn't turn, it doesn't turn. We'll still be okay. It's a big ocean, we're on a small island, the chances are a million to one."

"Are you sure?"

"Honey, I'm Tammy Drake. Do you think I'd be sitting here if I thought there was any chance at all of a hurricane messing with my future?" She laughed, and Julie and Meiko laughed along with her.

"Now," Tammy said, "tell me all about your adventures."

And they did.

"You killed him?" Tammy whispered, when Julie got to the part about Kurt in St. Lucia.

"We didn't have any choice," Julie said. "It was him or us. He was crazy insane. You wouldn't have believed it."

"I can't believe Dieter would actually send someone to hurt you. I could see him maybe trying to steal the boat out from under you, but not that," Tammy said.

"I'm not so sure," Julie said. She remembered the day out at the Five Islands, when Dieter was screaming and cursing and she had to cower and hide with Meiko in the hot sun till he left.

"Hey, I know," Tammy said. "You can spend the night with me."

"Can't," Julie said. "We have to leave after this set. Meiko's heading back to the States on the ten-thirty flight to Miami. I'm sacking out in a motel by the airport and I guarantee you five minutes after that plane leaves the ground my head is hitting a pillow."

"That's okay," Tammy said, "I have a date. This way I don't have to break it, but starting tomorrow you're staying with me, okay?"

"I was going to stay on the boat," Julie said.

"You'll love my place. It's huge, big window overlooking the ocean. Honey, it's a girl's dream. How long can you stay?"

"As long as you'll have me," Julie said, giving up. There was no point in arguing. Tammy always got her way. "If the boat's okay anchored in the lagoon. This hurricane talk has me worried."

"The lagoon is the safest hurricane hole in the Caribbean, completely surrounded by land. So your boat is perfectly safe. But just to be sure, you call me when you wake up and we'll go out to the boat together. Okay?"

"Tammy, you're a life saver," Julie said.

"Hey, what are friends for?" she said. "Whoops, there's my date, I gotta go." The women stood and Tammy gave each one of them a hug. Then she hustled across the room to meet just about the handsomest man Julie had ever seen in real life.

CHAPTER EIGHTEEN

JULIE WOKE WITH THE HOWLING WIND. She sat up. She'd slept in her clothes. Her stomach growled and she remembered the donut shop in the airport. It was closed last night when she saw Meiko off. But it would be open now. She pulled her sandals on. The airport was only a five minute walk from the motel.

A grey sky greeted her when she stepped outside. She judged the wind to be about twenty-five knots and she was glad that *Fallen Angel* had an all chain anchor rode and that she had plenty out. She'd paid in advance for the room so she didn't have to check out. She started toward the airport with the wind at her back. It looked like rain, but she was confident she could get to the airport before it started. She'd get a cab to the dinghy dock after the squall had passed.

She was thinking of Meiko when she entered the airport lobby. She hated it that she was going to have a schoolgirl fling with Victor in Miami. She was half convinced that he was taking advantage of her. She couldn't imagine him walking away from Charlene Heart and all of her father's money. But maybe, she told herself, he was doing well enough in the yard to step out from Charlie Heart's shadow.

Maybe he really loved Meiko.

She bought two glazed donuts at the small pastry shop and went out to the lobby. Curiously the airport was almost deserted. She decided to sit down and eat her donuts. They tasted like heaven. She hadn't had a donut in over two years. When she finished she closed her eyes for a second and thought about Hideo. The last time she'd had a glazed donut was with him, at a small donut shop in Miami, just before they bought the boat. She felt like she was going to cry.

"Are you okay, Miss?" a wide-eyed young black woman with a honey voice asked her. "You looked so peaceful. I hated to bother you." Julie noticed that she was wearing a uniform. She had a gun. She was a policewoman.

"I'm sorry."

"Don't be."

"I have to go to the bathroom." She didn't know why she said that. It made her seem vulnerable, like a little girl. But it was how she felt. Wide open. Lost. Alone in a strange airport.

She bit her lip in a vain effort to fight back tears, and the policewoman offered her a handkerchief.

Julie noticed the finely manicured nails and the genuine smile, coupled with the very real concern in her eyes. She took the handkerchief and offered a half smile in return.

"It's very nice," she said.

"A gift from my husband," the policewoman said.

"I can't," Julie said, and then the dam broke and she cried. Big, wracking tears. Stomach wrenching sobs. The policewoman sat down next to her and took her hand. Julie looked into her full, brown eyes, eyes that they had seen it all and still had plenty of room for compassion. Her smile faded a little, covering sparkling teeth under a concerned tightening of full lips. The policewoman cared and Julie badly needed someone who cared.

"Is there anything I can do?" the woman asked, and Julie wrapped her arms around the woman's strong shoulders and tucked her head under her chin, unable to stop crying.

"My husband died." She sobbed. Julie clutched onto the strange woman as if she were a lifeline. The woman put her arms around Julie's fragile frame and let her cry it out.

The tears didn't go away quickly, but after a short while the river turned to a trickle. The policewoman gave her a final hug, then drew away from her.

"Do you feel better now?"

"I loved him so much. I was so angry that he'd gone. It wasn't his fault, I know, but I couldn't deal with it. So much was happening. I chased my daughter away. I've made a mess of my life."

"I'm sure it's not that bad. Now that you've cried it out you can start to put your life back together again." The woman spoke with a soft island accent and the smile was back, full as before. She couldn't have been more than twenty-five or thirty, but she seemed oh so wise.

"You're right," Julie said. "I'll start to get my act together."

"That's the way," the policewoman said. "Here, let me show you to the bathroom. You need to wash your face and begin the first day of the rest of your life."

Julie stopped and looked at the woman. The overused phrase seemed fresh coming from her, and it was true, she had the rest of her life ahead of her, but it seemed that the best of her life was behind her.

The policewoman stood and helped Julie get up.

"Thanks."

"Over there. Second door on the right. You're going to be okay now," she said.

"I'll be fine. Thank you for the shoulder."

"You're welcome," the policewoman answered and Julie made her way to the bathroom.

It wasn't until she had splashed water on her face and was staring at her puffed up eyes in the mirror that she realized she hadn't gotten the woman's name. She ran her hands through her hair, wishing she had a comb or a brush. She gave herself a smile. She'd get the policewoman's name and thank her properly when she left the bathroom. She'd get her address, too, and she'd send her a nice gift. The woman was a lifesaver.

Satisfied that she was looking as good as possible under the circumstances, she gave herself one more quick glance, then left the bathroom. There was no sign of the policewoman. She looked around the bare lobby, but she was gone. She promised herself that she'd contact the police department in Philipsberg and try to find out who the good Samaritan was.

She sighed and left the lobby. Outside she found the taxi rank empty. She waited for a few minutes as the sky darkened. She thought about going to a pay phone and calling for a cab, but she'd been at sea for so long without a chance to stretch her legs. She decided to walk, hoping she could beat the storm.

"Time to get yourself together, kid," she said to herself, aloud. Then she threw her head back and marched out into a windy morning. She had a three mile walk to the drawbridge, with the lagoon on her left and the airport runway on her right. Once past the runway it was just narrow road, the lagoon on one side, the bay on the other, almost all the way to the bridge.

The time had finally come to put Hideo away. He would always be with her, in every word she said, every flick of her wrist, every toss of her head. He was her smile, the sparkle in her eyes, the spring in her step. He was all that, and more, but it was time to move on. She'd lived with the lump in her heart and the ache in her breasts for too long. Hideo wouldn't want that. The time for mourning was over.

But she was going to take one last cool walk with him before she moved on with her life. The rain started to fall, mingling with her tears. But that was okay, because these were cleansing tears.

She looked to her right, across the airport runway. The field was empty. There were no planes at the departing gates, no tractors pulling baggage trailers, no men with flashlights guiding the big planes. The field was naked as a ghost town.

What did they know that she didn't?

Was the hurricane coming?

Was it close?

She shivered and quickened her pace.

She heard a car coming from behind and turned. Although only drizzle wafted down from the big sky, the road was already wet. The car fanned spray from its tires as it raced toward her from the airport. She kept her eyes on it as it approached and decided to flag it down and ask for a ride. She raised her hand as the car drew close, but the driver must have thought she was waving, because he honked his horn as he sped by.

Damn, not quick enough, but it wouldn't have made any difference, because the car was chock-a-block full, three in front, as many or more in back. They looked as if they were wearing coveralls and that worried her, because that meant they were airport employees, going home. The airport was closing.

There'd be more cars soon unless they all went the other way, to the French side of the island. She'd have to stop the next one, no matter how full they were. There was always room for one more. Especially if a hurricane was coming.

Thunder cracked the sky, lightning bolted overhead, and the heavens opened. The wind blew hard from the ocean, whipping her long hair in its wake and slapping it across her face. But she barely noticed, because she was concentrating on the churning sea and the boats, dancing and jumping around on their anchors, in the bay.

She put a hand up, shielding her eyes from the driving rain, and looked left. The boats in the lagoon were rocking with the chop. She hoped *Fallen Angel* was all right, but none of the boats appeared to be dragging. That was a good sign.

She wanted to get back to *Fallen Angel*, make sure she was secure, maybe let out a little more chain, maybe put out a second anchor, put some fenders out and stay in the cockpit in case someone dragged down on her.

She heard another car coming. She turned and saw a bright blue Land Rover. She was determined to stop this one. It was a big car, they'd have room. She gasped. It was coming toward her way too fast.

Something was wrong. Water splashed from the tires, sending spray out several feet, giving the off-road vehicle a surreal look as it flew through the rain, sliding as if the road was made of ice.

For a second she thought the top heavy car was going to tip and roll as it slipped left, then right, and she felt a momentary surge of relief when it didn't. She started to raise her hand. Something was still wrong. She expected the driver to slow down, but he surprised her by accelerating. She shuddered as the car charged closer. Then she figured out what was wrong. It was on the wrong side of the street.

She held her breath. The clean smell of electricity charged the hairs on the back of her neck. She felt sweat under her arms despite the rain, and a fear she'd never known rattled through her.

Time went out of kilter. The car was both charging fast and moving in slow motion. She leapt aside, rolled in dirt and mud, only stopping when she collided with the chain link fence that separated the airport from the road.

She tasted dirt and was trying to spit it out and breathe at the same time as the car shot past, churning up more mud, flinging it in her face. Thunder cracked again, but it didn't disguise the sound of the squealing tires as the driver mashed the brakes. Julie forced herself up, squinting through the rain, and saw the Land Rover going down the road sideways. Once again she thought the car was going to tip and roll, but the driver jerked the wheel to the right, forcing the car to spin around, facing her.

Then he turned on his bright lights, catching her like a rabbit as he stopped the car's backward motion. She had less than seconds. Her back was against the fence. The car was stopped, engine running. It was waiting. For what? Then she knew. It was waiting for her to make a mad dash across the road, but the only thing on the other side was a few feet of shoulder, then the lagoon.

She stared across the street, wiped her face with the back of her hand, preparing herself for the run. She'd be safe once she made it to the other side. A quick dive into the water, a short swim to one of the anchored boats and she'd be away from the Land Rover. She stopped herself. It's what he wants, she thought.

Then she broke for the road and the Land Rover burst forward. When she reached the asphalt she spun around and darted back in the direction she'd come, but either she hadn't fooled him or his reactions were super quick, because he adjusted the Land Rover's charge, and again screaming tires were coming for her as she jumped out of the mud and clawed her hands into the chain link fence.

She pulled herself up, hand over hand, feet kicking out, scrabbling for toeholds, arms burning, she dragged her weight higher in her frantic bid to get away from the car. Her right foot found purchase in chain link, her right hand closed on the top.

She was ten feet in the air, hanging on the top, stomach muscles contracting, pulling dangling legs up and out of the way, when the Land Rover careened into the fence, screeching along its side, sending sparks flying, despite the rain.

The fence shook like a California earthquake. She wrapped a naked leg over the top and flung herself over the fence and onto the airport side. She landed on her side, slapping her right arm on the ground and rolling. She forced her head around and watched the sliding car screech along the fence with its driver fighting the wheel.

The Land Rover mangled the fence and the fence mangled it, but the driver forced the automobile out of the muddy shoulder, away from the fence and back onto the road. Once again he spun the vehicle around, and once again he caught Julie in his headlights.

She pulled herself onto her hands and knees. The driving rain pelted her, stinging with the force of a thousand bees, as she dragged herself to her feet. She put a hand over her face, squinting through the squall, and felt a surge of relief. The fence had held. She was in. The Land Rover was out. But her relief faded when the Land Rover's tires started to spin again.

She watched as it crashed into the fence. For a second she thought the fence would hold it back, but it folded and seemed to wrap itself around the truck. Even the storm couldn't muffle the caterwauling sound of metal ripping against metal as the vehicle grated its way into the fence, forcing it to rise out of the ground, scratching and digging into the Land Rover, before it burst apart.

Then it was inside, stampeding toward her, plunging through the rain like a fire breathing dragon, steam hissing from its hood as it chewed up the ground. She rolled to the left and was splattered again as the truck roared by. She continued her roll, jumped to her feet, taking off on a dead run. The wind stole her breath and the mud grabbed onto her sandaled feet, sucking away her speed. She risked a glance over her shoulder and saw the car sliding and turning. She kept running from it, every stride a struggle, as she pumped her arms, forcing her legs to match their rhythm. The strap on her left sandal gave way and it was lost to the grabbing mud.

I'm gonna make it, she thought, but her breath was coming in wracking heaves. Pain shot from her heels to her heart every time her feet slapped the ground, but she kept running from the car.

The Land Rover's engine roared in protest as it slid round for another run at her. Her right foot slammed hard on a sharp rock and she went down, losing her other sandal. She slapped her arm against the wet earth and tried to push herself out of the way of the car headed for her. Just a slight change in direction and it would have her and she was powerless to do anything about it.

She stared at the oncoming beast, caught at last, bracing herself for the final blow by digging her teeth into her lower lip, drawing more blood. Thunder cracked the sky again, once, twice, three times in rapid succession. The back window on the driver's side blew out, the Land Rover went into a spin, shooting mud from its tires as it swerved and sloshed. Then the driver had the car under his power again, but instead of turning back toward Julie, he accelerated away, racing down the runway toward the airport.

She watched till the car drove between two aircraft hangers and was out of sight.

It was over.

She stood, ignoring her pain, and tried to shake off her fear.

And a car came at her through the rain.

"Shit," she said, but before she could flee the car spun sideways and slid to a stop. She smiled and exhaled a breath of relief. It was a police car.

The passenger door opened and a voice yelled above the wind, "Get in." She half ran, half limped to the waiting car. She felt the mud squish between her toes as she made the dash, felt the rain at her back, felt the wind trying to knock her down as she jumped into the car, slamming the door after herself.

"Thanks," she said.

"You're welcome," Broxton, the DEA man answered. She saw the riot gun, centered in the rack between the driver's and passenger's seats. She felt the barrel. It was hot, and she knew who had chased away the metal dragon.

"I like the hair," she said.

"Seatbelt," he said. She nodded and buckled up.

"Police car, very strong," he said. "We'll be okay."

"Where'd you get it?"

"Stole it," he said. Then he put the car in gear and started for the hole in the fence. "Hurricane coming," he said.

"I think it's here." She wiped her muddy hands on her halter top. Then she grabbed onto the safety bar and Broxton plowed the car through the fence and fought it onto the road.

The wind was whipping along the road coming from the airport, so Broxton turned the other way, driving like a mad man on the narrow stretch of land between the lagoon and the sea. Waves were cresting and breaking over the pavement and Broxton was at constant war with the wheel.

"I can't keep it on the road any longer," he said. He was past the narrow strip of road and now there were businesses on each side of the street. He aimed the car toward a row of buildings on the lagoon side of the road, and roared through a driveway, turned right, and raced along a small wharf with both sail and powerboats tied to it.

"Need protection," he said.

"There." She pointed and he risked a quick look after her pointed finger. "The space between the buildings," she said. The space between the two buildings was wide enough for the car to fit into, but there was a three foot barrier between them and it.

"We'll have to go around," he said. He downshifted into second, the car bucked, and they flew past a video shop, a liquor store, a small bank and several other businesses, before he was past the building, turning right, through another driveway. He didn't slow for the locked gate and Julie braced herself as the police car smashed through it.

Back in the wind, he cranked the wheel right again and roared past the front of the businesses, not hitting the brakes until he was almost at the slot between the buildings. Then he pumped the brakes and slipped the car into the slot, stopping inches from the short wall in front.

"Safe," he said, shutting off the engine.

"Really?" she said.

"Depends on the surge," he said.

"What's that?"

"The hurricane will push a wall of water in front of it. We're maybe one or two feet above sea level. Twenty foot surge and we're screwed, five or six, we'll be okay.

"Then we have to get out of here," she said, but it was too late.

"Hold on," he said and the wall of water smashed into the back of the car, slamming it forward into the safety wall in front despite his full pressure on the brakes.

Julie screamed as water flew by, splashing above the windows. He reached over and squeezed her hand. "It's going to flood us!"

"No," he said, as the water drained out of the slot, "We'll be all right now. If that didn't push us over the fence and into the lagoon, the winds won't either."

"What do we do?"

"Wait."

The joining roofs overhead kept most of the rain out, offering them a front row seat to one of nature's horror shows. Boats were tossed about the lagoon like toys in a bathtub. Millions of dollars wiped out in minutes.

"Duck!" he yelled. A deck chair flew, missile like, up from the lagoon, heading straight for their front window. She jammed her eyes closed and dropped, winding up tangled in his arms as the chair hit, shattering the window and turning the view off.

For three hours the car shuddered and shook as the wind funneled rain through the slot. She clung to him the whole time, digging her nails repeatedly into his arms. And then suddenly, without warning, it was over.

CHAPTER NINETEEN

"It's eerie," Julie said. They were captured by the quiet. "We have to get out of the car. I want to see." She pulled up the door handle and pushed against it. "It's stuck," she said. She popped the door with her shoulder, but still it refused to give. "Come on, we have to get out."

Broxton, tried his door and it opened with no trouble.

"Hurry," she said, and he scooted out of the police car and stepped into the clear, crisp quiet. Julie slid across, grabbed onto the steering wheel, and pushed and pulled herself out of the car.

Broxton ran both hands through his hair, starting at the front, stretching his fingers and scratching the back of his neck with his thumbs. He turned away from the lagoon and started toward the street. Julie followed. She wanted to see, and she didn't want him to get too far away.

Water skimmed along the center of the road, rushing toward the lower ground at the airport. They were circled in gray twilight and the wind was calm, but they could see it off in the distance, a moving black wall of haze, blocking out the sun, turning the day somber, murky and dark. Broxton left the protection of the two buildings and walked into the street.

The businesses on the ocean side of the street, a pizzeria, an ice cream parlor, and a tee shirt shop, were devastated, but still standing. The windows that hadn't been boarded were blown out. A man stumbled out of the ice cream parlor, dazed, holding on to the door jamb for support. Broxton guessed that he'd just had his business destroyed. He hoped he had insurance. Three other people emerged from the pizza restaurant. An older man and a woman, Italian looking, with a younger woman who looked like them both, their daughter.

Broxton stared at a child's stroller, smashed flat by a heavy white door that had been torn from a walk-in ice box. He hoped the child was somewhere faraway, someplace safe. Down the street he saw two youths running from an electronics store, one black, one white. Both were carrying portable televisions. Looters. It happened everywhere.

He looked up. Julie stepped alongside, took his hand, and followed his gaze. The thick moving gray-black cloud wall had them surrounded and locked in. It grew from the ground, like Jack's beanstalk, into the heavens, a swirling, churning, devil's brew that snapped and sizzled. Julie shivered, but she wasn't cold.

"It's like we're caught under a giant bowl, like insects, and there's a huge kid up there, sliding it around, toying with us, before he pulls off our wings," Broxton said.

"Brrrrr." Julie shivered more and clutched his hand tighter.

"Are you okay?" he asked.

"For a while there I didn't think we were going to make it." She ran her tongue along her swollen lip and tasted the dried blood.

"We haven't yet," he said, and she shivered still more, because she understood.

"We have to go through it all again, don't we?"

"I think so," he said and she looked out at the swirling wall of thunderstorms and she knew it was true. Just as surely it was moving away from them, it was moving toward them as well, coming from behind.

"Look at that," he said, his voice filled with awe. She hadn't let go of his hand and she squeezed even tighter, just for a flash. Then she eased off the pressure and followed his gaze.

Several boats had been thrown from the sea and were beached along the road, gaping holes in their sides, masts and rigging bent and broken, radar antennas, life rafts, sails ripped from their decks — sucked up into infinity.

"*Fallen Angel*," Julie gasped, and she tugged at his hand, pulling him back toward the space between the two buildings. He went along with her, holding her hand, the way school kids do that are going steady for the first time. She pulled him past the battered police car to the dock beyond.

Five boats had been tied up there. Two sailboats and three sportfishers. For three hours they had been slamming into each other. Fiberglass sides were holed. The masts on the two sailboats were twisted and bent out of shape. One of the sportfishers was on its side, another was overturned on the shore.

"Oh, God," Julie moaned.

The lagoon was rimmed with boats ripped from the water by the storm's fury and thrown onto the shore. Three hours ago there had been over a thousand boats, anchored, moored, tied down and docked in the safest hurricane hole in the Caribbean. Now, barely any were still floating, and the storm was only half over.

"She's gone," Julie said, and Broxton looked out to where *Voyager* had been anchored. She was gone, too.

"They all went down," he said. Tall masts poked from the shallow lagoon, jutting at every angle. "It reminds me of a forest after a fire," and the stark truth of his statement made her shudder.

"We have to find some cover," he said. The swirling grey eye wall was moving steadily closer. In minutes it would be on them.

"Where?" Julie said.

"Inside," he said, and a quick look told them that the first floor of both buildings offered no hope. They were retail shops with large window displays in front and back, opening on both the road and the lagoon. The storm surge had washed right through, taking out the bay windows and cleaning out the merchandise, like a fire sale in a New York department store.

"Upstairs?" she said.

He nodded and they chose the building on the left, taking the steps two at a time. The businesses upstairs were insurance brokers, real estate brokers, travel brokers and a new age church. They were all locked. Broxton kicked open the door of the church.

"Oh, no," she said. The roof was gone, there was no protection there. She heard the swirling wind as the eye wall came closer.

"Next door," he said, and he turned and flew down the stairs. She screamed as a large rat scurried between her legs, then she chased down the stairs after him. She saw him jump over another one that was running up the stairs as he was going down. She saw it coming toward her, beady eyes, tiny teeth. She yelped again and jumped over it, losing her footing.

She screamed as she landed badly, stumbled and started rolling down the stairs. He stopped her fall with outstretched hands.

"Are you okay?" he asked.

"Rats. I hate rats."

"They're trying to survive. Just like us," he said. "Can you walk?" The raging wind in the eye wall was swirling closer.

"It hurts, but I can put some weight on it," she said.

"I'll help you," he said. He wrapped his arm around her waist. She responded by winding her arm around his and they moved toward the building next door, hobbling fast, like a boy and his father in a three legged sack race.

"I can get up the stairs," she said. He nodded, and led. She followed by supporting herself on the rails, using them like crutches. She heard a wailing sound, like an army of cars honking their horns off in the distance. She turned toward the sound. The eye was across the street, coming for her, a giant wall of dark.

Broxton kicked the first door open and pulled her inside. She nearly passed out with the pain as her foot hit the tiled floor, but she didn't yell out. She kept her eyes on him and the advancing black beyond the door.

"Quick," he said, and he grabbed her hand and dragged her across the floor of a beauty shop. It felt like he was pulling her arm out of its socket as he pulled her past a row of hair dryers and wash basins, through a door to an attached apartment. He threw himself on top of her as the hurricane burst in the open door of the beauty shop.

The dry room went wet and the sheer force of the moving air made it almost impossible to breathe. She felt like she was super charged, on fire, about to explode. Broxton, still on top of her, shook and his chest jammed into her and she knew that something flying around the room had hit him. He was protecting her and he didn't even know her.

"Can't breathe," she forced out, her mouth at his ear.

He sucked in a great gulp of air and brought his mouth down to hers and blew in. She took it in and coughed. He did it again, then again. She was in the throes of a full panic seizure, shaking and clutching her arms around him like a little girl holding on to a Raggedy Ann doll during a thunderstorm.

He squeezed her tightly into himself with all his strength, clamped his lips over hers and forced another lungful of air down her throat. Then he put his lips to her ear and said, "It's going to be all right. I'm here and I won't let anything happen to you."

She stopped her shaking and forced herself to relax. She attempted a breath, inhaled some air, exhaled. "I can breathe now," she said, and he rolled off of her. The initial force of the eye wall was past, but the winds were still raging outside.

She watched as he slithered across the floor toward the door to the apartment. The wind wasn't blowing directly toward it and he was able to struggle it closed. Then he sat up with his back against it. "It's not strong," he said, "but as long as the wind doesn't blast straight in, it should hold."

Outside the wind howled like banshees roaming through a graveyard. Inside the apartment was relatively calm. The windows had been boarded against the storm and the glass was still intact, despite the blast of wind that had come in through the beauty shop. The floor was covered with books, magazines, newspapers, clothes, blankets, sheets and pillows, but there was no major destruction.

"Will the building hold up?" she asked. She was speaking loudly, to be heard above the blowing wind outside, but she wasn't shouting.

"It's brick. Solid. It made it through the worst of it. It should stand." His confident voice gave her hope.

"If it doesn't?"

"It will," he said, smiling.

"You're hurt." She slid across the floor toward him. His left side was covered in blood. She looked around the room and saw a wooden clock on the floor over by where they had been lying.

"That's what hit you?" she said.

"I think so," he said, looking down at his side, He touched it with his fingertips and brought them back up and looked at the blood on them.

"Let me help you get that shirt off," she said, and he scooted away from the door. He winced as he raised his arms and she pulled the bloody shirt over his head. Then she used it to dab the blood away. "It's not bad, just a small cut. It's going to be a huge bruise though."

Something slammed into the side of the building with a thundering crash that blasted through the room like a vibrating cannon shot. She screamed and threw her arms around him, hugging him tight. Her breasts mashed against his chest. She rolled on top of him. Her pelvis ground into his groin and then her lips sought his and she was kissing him, wide and open mouthed, drawing his tongue deep inside.

His hands slid up under her halter top and she shivered at the touch of them on her bare back. She ground her pelvis into him in hard, heavy thrusts. She moaned into his mouth and darted her tongue inside, breathing deep into him and sucking his breath into her own lungs.

He ripped her halter top apart, baring her breasts without breaking the kiss. She quivered when they pressed into his bare chest and she reached down between his legs to feel his hardness and he groaned. He was wearing Levi's, very unyachtie, she thought, as she fumbled with the belt buckle.

"Easy," he said, breaking the kiss. "I have a hand-held radio clipped to it." He unbuckled the belt and she helped him get the pants down, but they jumbled up around his ankles.

"Shoes," she said, and he kicked them off. Then she stuffed a foot between his feet and pushed the jeans and underwear off. Now he was completely naked and she still had her shorts on. His lips were back on hers as she stuck her hands into the elastic waistband and struggled out of them.

He knew exactly what to do with his fingers to send her into a quick, spasmodic orgasm. "Oh, yes," she moaned into his ear, and she grabbed him between the legs, fondling him, as tiny explosions of pleasure rippled through her, starting between her legs and zapping the chill zone up and down her spine.

He stood and picked her up and carried her to the bed. Her eyes were wide, staring into his, as he climbed on top of her and she rocked with pleasure when he entered her.

He took her with the force of the hurricane outside, slamming and pounding into her. He had his hands wrapped around her buttocks and she had her hands wrapped around his, not wanting him to slip away.

"Yes, yes, yes," she shouted with each stroke and he increased his tempo as the wind howled outside. The power of her need blocked out the frightening fury of the hurricane. She bucked under him, matched his hammering thrusts with undulating thrusts of her own until she screamed with ecstasy and he blasted into her and it was over.

"Man, oh man," she moaned as he eased over and lay beside her.

"Yeah," he said.

"Man, oh man. Just man, oh man."

He sat up. The wind was still howling.

"I like you much better with hair." She sat too, and ran her hands through it. He wrapped a hand behind her neck and drew her into a long and still passionate kiss. "Again?" she said.

And this time he took her slowly, as if he had the rest of his life.

She drank in his smell, inhaled the pleasure, closed her eyes and kissed him deeply. She felt herself building to orgasm and miracle of miracles, she felt him shoot into her as her own orgasm, greater than before, greater than anything she'd ever felt before, thundered through her. She screamed into the night, but the raging storm swallowed up the sound and nobody heard.

When it was over, they lay side by side, sweating and spent, listening to the thunder boom over the island. They lay without talking, holding hands, till the worst was over.

"What's it all about, this crazy thing that brought us together? How do I fit in, how do you fit in? How did you find me?" She asked him.

"One of Dieter's trained twins told me where to look for you," he said, and he told her about the drugs so skillfully hidden throughout *Fallen Angel*. How Dieter Krauss was laundering drug money and smuggling drugs into the States. About Michael Martel the Magic Man, and how he moved money back and forth. About how Martel was double crossing the Colombians, and about how he had a key to a luggage locker full of money.

He went on to tell her about how Kurt's brother murdered his friend and former partner in the States, and how he swore he'd get even, how he killed Karl Schneidler in Rodney Bay by lashing him to the mast of a burning, sinking ship. He didn't leave anything out. She grimaced when he told her about the seizing wire.

"And they think you have the key," he said.

"So that's what he was looking for," she said, and she told Broxton about the intruder on her boat the day after they found Martel floating in the Gulf of Paria. She fingered the Kennedy half-dollar hanging between her breasts, then she lifted it off and handed it to him.

"2124," he said, and smiled.

"What?" she said.

"Have you ever heard of the magic trick, Scotch and soda?"

She shook her head.

"It's called Scotch and Soda because it was designed to be played in a bar, for a drink. The magician shows two coins to the bartender, a silver half dollar and a bronze Mexican peso. The peso is smaller then the half, about the size of a quarter. Then the magician says, 'I'll bet you a Scotch and soda that if you put both these coins in your hand, you can't put your hands behind your back and separate them, the silver one in your left, the bronze one in your right.'

"The bartender, or any other mark, looks at the two coins and sees the difference in size, then he takes the bet. The magician puts the two coins in the mark's hand and the mark puts his hands behind his back.

"When the mark holds his closed fists out in front of himself, the magician taps the mark's left hand and the mark opens it revealing the half dollar. The magician plucks the half out of the mark's hand and drops it in his pocket.

"'Now for the Scotch and soda,' the magician says and the mark opens his hand, showing not the bronze peso, but a US silver quarter.

"Naturally the mark realizes it was a trick of some kind and wants to know how it was done. The magician doesn't tell and when the mark wants to see the fifty cent piece, the magician pulls it out of his pocket and tells the mark to keep it."

"It's a different coin," Julie said.

"Yes," Broxton said, smiling, "but do you know how the trick was done?"

"No," Julie said.

"The half dollar is hollow. The peso is a two sided coin, one side is the silver *tail* side of the half dollar, the other is the *head* side of the Mexican peso.

When the magician shows the mark the two coins in his open hand, the quarter is resting inside the half dollar, when he folds the coins into the mark's hand he slips the quarter out and presses the peso firmly in place into the half, and presto a bronze coin has changed into a silver one."

She thought for a second, then she held out her hand palm up and he dropped the coin into it. She looked at it, front and back, studied it closely. She smiled, "I think I see it," she said, and she unhooked the clasp on the chain and pulled it out.

"Hold the coin in both hands and press on Kennedy's head with your thumbs."

Julie did it, "Look," she exclaimed, as the back side of the coin fell out. "The key," she said.

"The key," he echoed, "and very nicely done." The bottom part of the key, the part that goes into the lock, was neatly secreted in a cut-out inside the coin. "Mr. Martel hid the key in plain sight. He wore it right out front, where nobody would look." Broxton took the back part of the coin from her and turned it upside down. The key fell out. Broxton squinted and looked at it in the dim light. "Look here," he said, showing her. "The initials SXM scrawled on the side of the key."

"What's it mean?" she asked.

"It's a three letter airport code. LAX, Los Angeles, SFO, San Francisco, JFK, New York."

"And SXM?" Julie said.

"St. Martin."

"Ah."

He got up from the bed and started toward the closet, "We need clothes," he said, "and you need shoes." He slid open the door and laughed. "Shoes won't be a problem, there must be twenty-five pair here."

She hopped off the bed, padded over to the closet and looked in. "They're men's. What kind of person owns this beauty shop anyway?"

"A man." Broxton took a safari jacket from a hanger. He slipped it on over his bare skin.

"They're way too big," she said.

He bent low and picked up a pair of used running shoes. "Stuff some tissues in them," he said, handing her the shoes.

He went back to where his Levi's were discarded on the floor and put them on. After cinching up the buckle he took the hand held radio out of its holster and pushed the talk button.

"*Voyager, Voyager*, It's Broxton," he said.

"Danny Boy, how ya doing?" T-Bone's voice crackled over the radio.

"Looks like you lost the boat," Broxton said.

"Like hell, I took it out of the lagoon, she's fine. It blew like a mother, but we made it."

"You know that stretch to the airport between the sea and the lagoon?"

"Know it well," T-Bone said.

"Ten, maybe fifteen minutes I'll be going down it in a battered four-wheel drive."

"How will I know it?"

"It's a cop car."

T-Bone laughed into the mike. Then said, "The damsels?"

"Safe so far."

"If I turn my head sideways and squint I can almost see land through this pissing rain. I'll keep an eye out for you."

"I'll be in touch."

"What was that all about?" Julie asked.

"Friend of mine. I came in on his boat."

"The damsels, I mean," Julie said.

"Damsels in distress, we came north to save them," Broxton said.

"Us, you came up to save us?"

"Yeah," Broxton said as he rummaged about the closet, then he started on a chest of drawers.

"What are you looking for?" she asked.

"Clothes for you." He turned and tossed her a sweat shirt and a pair of jeans that were only a little too big. "We have to get going," he said.

She gave him a quick kiss, then stepped into the jeans, surprised to find they fit. The sweat shirt was a touch large, but that was okay. She felt funny with the big shoes, but they were better than nothing at all.

"It's time," he said, and she followed him out the door and into the wind and the rain.

CHAPTER TWENTY

JULIE CAME DOWN THE STAIRS with an arm around
Broxton's shoulder for support. It was pelting rain,
but at least the hurricane force was gone from the
biting wind. She stumbled and he held her up. Her
foot hurt, but the pain was manageable.

"Just a little farther," he said.

She tightened her grip on his shoulder, looked
out at the road and gasped. It wasn't there. "How are
we going to get through that?" The ground—earth,
driveway and road—was covered by the ocean.

Two more steps and they were at the bottom and
they stepped into the water. "It's only a few inches
deep," he said.

"But you can't see the road," she said. It may have
been shallow, but those few inches joined the ocean

to the lagoon. The airport a quarter mile away looked like a small island. The underwater pathway was marked up ahead, at the halfway point, by a few restaurants on the right side of the road.

He helped her into his side of the car and she slid over. "Will it start?" she asked.

"Should," he answered. "Four wheel drive, Mitsubishi Montero, built for the police department. If this baby can't get us there then nothing can."

"But it's so beat up," Julie said, "and you can't see out." The front window looked like a carnival of crazed spiders had crisscrossed it at every angle, drunkenly laying their webs as they passed.

He turned the key and the engine purred to life. Then he leaned into the back seat, brought out a policeman's nightstick and punched a hole in the sticky safety glass, then another and still another.

Julie looked around the car and spied a laptop computer on her side of the back seat. She grasped onto it and used it as a battering ram, poking at the glass, helping Broxton to remove the window.

"I always hated computers," she said when they were finished.

"Me too," he said.

She laughed and sailed the laptop out the front window and they both watched it hit the water and sink.

"You know all the info on the hard drive will be lost," he said.

"Let's go see what's in that locker," she said.

"I'm with you." He put it in reverse and eased the battered police car out of the protective shelter of the two buildings.

"Scary," she said.

He laughed, but looked tense as he felt for the road under the sloshing water. He found it, backed onto it and shifted into drive. Rain pounded them through the front window.

Julie was horrified at the total destruction. The lagoon was a Sargasso Sea of floating vegetation, raw sewage, the wreckage of broken homes, broken lives and sunken ships—catamarans, schooners, sloops, yawls, trawlers, sportfishers, and million dollar mega yachts—all now worthless.

She was captivated by the palm trees in the distance, still bending with the wind. Then she turned around and saw it, coming fast, water splashing out from its four tires.

"Oh shit," she said. "The Land Rover is back."

Broxton looked over his shoulder, saw it and added gas, but he wasn't quick enough and the car smashed into to their rear. The Land Rover was trying to drive them into the sea. Broxton jammed on the brakes, but the driver of the four wheel beast behind was a step ahead of him. He backed off the gas, then rammed them again.

The crunching impact ricocheted through the car and sent it spinning sideways toward the airport. Broxton was working the wheel like a demon possessed and Julie saw the Land Rover back off. He was gloating, Julie thought, sitting back, watching and waiting. Spastic thoughts riddled and ran through her brain at lightning speed as Broxton fought to keep the car on the road.

Meiko's face flashed before her, then Hideo's, then Tammy's. Tammy. What was it about Tammy?

Then Broxton yelled out, "I got it!" He spun the wheel one last time and they were again headed toward the airport. They were firmly on the road.

"Put the pedal to the medal, Danny boy," T-Bone's sweet bass voice boomed from the front pocket of the safari jacket. Broxton jammed on the gas and the Mitsubishi squished and slid as he worked the wheel from left to right and back again, fighting to keep the car on the sunken pavement.

"What are you doing?" Julie asked.

"Trusting a friend," he said, and then they heard it. The unmistakable sound of an outboard motor with the throttle wide open. Julie looked toward the sea, toward the sound, and widened her eyes at the sight.

A wild man, long hair and beard flying in the wind, bright yellow Hawaiian shirt open and flapping, was tilting the engine up in a fast moving dinghy as it charged toward the road. She gasped as he whirled around and grabbed onto the painter with his right hand as if it were attached to a pair of galloping horses. His left hand started spitting fire at the Land Rover behind them.

The dinghy shot out of the ocean as it flew between the two moving cars. T-Bone was whooping like a cowboy on a bronco as he poured lead from the thirty eight into the front window of the Land Rover.

Julie spun her head around and saw the wild man, still standing as the rubber boat barreled into the lagoon. He was facing backwards in the dinghy, still shooting at the Land Rover.

T-Bone let out a rustler's yell as the Land Rover lost control and flipped onto its side. Then the Land Rover slid into the sea, and was gone.

Broxton slammed on the brakes and the car slipped and squirmed to a stop.

T-Bone dropped the engine back in the water and brought the dinghy around and throttled back as he neared the land under shallow, shallow water. He cut the engine, pulled it back up and jumped out, splashing through the water as he pulled the inflatable up onto the road, and dragged it up to the driver's window.

"The nick of time," Broxton said. "Like in the movies."

"Man, you should've seen it," T-Bone said. "All those guys fighting to get in the lagoon, I just wanted out. I don't care how good a hurricane hole it is, if there's a thousand other boats in there with you, it's no hurricane hole."

"*Voyager's* all right then?" Broxton asked.

"I laid out all three anchors, put on a diving mask and snorkel so I could breathe, and spent the most fabulous six hours ever, keeping her pointed into the wind. God, it was fucking beautiful. I just wish you could have been there."

"I'm sorry I missed it." Broxton laughed.

"That one of the damsels?"

"It is," Broxton said.

"We save her?

"We did," Broxton said.

"Her boat?"

"Gone."

"It's for the best. Grass, okay, but the white powder belongs on the bottom of the ocean," T-Bone said, then added, "Sorry, ma'am."

"It's all right, I understand," Julie said.

"You get the key?"

"I did."

"Listen, Danny Boy," T-Bone said. "If I had to bet, I'd bet that in about an hour or so the Dutch government is going to close this island down tighter than a shivering Eskimo's ass. Nobody in, nobody out."

"Why would they do that?" Julie asked.

"They won't want the tourist industry to see what a hurricane can do to paradise."

"We should hurry," Broxton said.

"My thinking exactly," T-Bone said. "How long you think you need?"

"Not long."

"I'll have the dinghy by the end of the runway. Be quick." Then he looked at Julie, winked, turned, and dragged the dinghy across the road, back to the ocean side. He hopped in, started it up and paced them until Broxton swung the car into the airport parking lot. Julie watched as he drove the dinghy out toward the runway's end.

Broxton jumped out of the car into six inches of water and she scooted over and he helped her out.

The electric door into the terminal had been blown away. Large bay windows were devoid of glass, water sloshed across the floor, wind ripped through the building. Julie half expected the hurricane to start back up again and she took Broxton's hand as they entered the departure terminal.

"The lockers are over there, on the way to the departure gates," Broxton said. They picked and splashed their way across the terminal with her leaning on him for support. The service counters had been ripped from the floor. The computers that once sat atop them were broken, smashed and littered throughout the room. The rank of chairs Julie had been sitting in earlier was twisted and bent. The contents of all of the airport shops were littered everywhere.

It would be a long time before that bakery made any more donuts, Julie thought, and she squeezed Broxton's hand. Who could ever dream such a thing could happen?

"Hold it." The familiar voice jerked Julie aware. She turned. "So you had the key all along," Victor said. He was standing by the luggage lockers, gun in hand, pointed at Broxton.

"It was you," Julie said. "The rudder leak, the furling line, the water in the diesel tank. You even told Kurt where to find us. It was all you."

"The key," he said.

"I don't know what you're talking about," she said.

"Give it up, or I'll shoot your friend."

"Then you'll never get the key, because I have it," Broxton said.

Victor held out his left hand, shaking it.

"Wait," Julie said. "Not yet."

"You're pushing it, Julie." Victor moved the gun away from Broxton toward her.

"Just one thing," Julie asked. "Dieter doesn't speak German, does he?"

Victor laughed, "You're pretty good. No, he doesn't. He needed a place to hide and I provided it. He was wanted for murder and drug smuggling in the US. The DEA," Victor nodded at Broxton, "would never suspect that a German managing a shipyard in Trinidad was actually Eddie Fitch."

"I've never heard of him," Julie said.

"Number one US importer and money launderer for the Salizar family. Not a nice man," Broxton said.

"And my partner," Victor said. "If you don't hand over the key, you'll be dealing with him. And I'm sure you know how he operates."

"No," Julie said.

"Likes to pull out fingernails," Broxton said.

"Oh," Julie said. Then she turned back toward Victor, "But you were doing so well. You have the biggest yard in Trinidad. I don't get it."

"It's my name, but Charlie Heart's money. I don't want that. Fitch showed me how to launder money and I helped provide him the perfect cover."

"You stuffed my boat full of drugs," Julie said.

"And they're perfectly safe, thanks to Hurricane Darlene. When they salvage the sunken boats, we'll buy *Fallen Angel* and ship it to Miami for repairs." It was at that moment that Julie knew for sure that Victor was going to kill them.

"And Meiko," she said, playing for time.

"I'll join her in Miami tomorrow and we'll live happily ever after. Ironic, isn't it?" Victor was still shaking his hand and Broxton tossed him the car keys, high and to the right. Victor stretched and grabbed them out of the air.

And Broxton started his run, head down, running hard, splashing water. He was running against the odds. Even without the water it would have been close.

Julie screamed, distracting Victor for an instant, giving Broxton the small edge he needed. He slipped to the floor, landing on his buttocks, legs extended, like he was sliding into second base to break up a double play.

Victor started shooting, but Broxton was faster than his aim and the bullets whizzed over his head and sizzled into the water covered floor.

"You fuck!" Victor screamed as Broxton's extended feet smashed into his knees. Victor went flying backwards with Broxton grabbing and clawing onto him.

Julie looked around for a weapon as the two men rolled around on the floor, pummeling each other and fighting for the gun. One second Broxton was on top, the next Victor. She had no illusions as to what would happen if Victor won the fight.

She hobbled over to a floating piece of wood, about a square foot in measure, part of a counter top, plywood, covered by white Formica. Not much of a weapon, but better than none at all. She hobbled toward the men, but as she approached they rolled away, two gladiators locked in mortal combat.

Julie struggled on, but they were all over the room. They both had their hands on the gun and it went off. The bullet smashed into the wood she was carrying, knocking it out of her hand.

A second shot rang out and bits of the ceiling rained down on her. She was confused. Who was pulling the trigger? She needed her weapon. The gun went off again, the bullet scorching by her, blasting into a computer half buried in the filthy water.

She dropped to the floor as the gun went off for a fourth time, landing on her wooden square. Again the gun went off, but she didn't see where the bullet went.

Then she heard the staccato stutter of an automatic weapon. She scrambled on hands and knees through the water and squirreled behind a fallen ticket counter. Out of sight, on her belly in the water, she peaked around the counter.

Dieter was standing, framed by the light coming in through the blown out windows, hair and clothes rippling in the wind. He was holding a Mach Ten machine pistol. He fired again, splashing bullets into the water around Broxton and Victor. Then they hit home and she watched in horror as Dieter pumped several rounds into Victor's back.

"No!" She still had the Formica covered piece of plywood in her hand and she stood, whipped her arm back, like she was throwing a Frisbee and sailed the board toward Dieter.

Alerted by her scream, he ducked and the spinning board flew over his head. She was dropping back to the floor even as he was bringing the gun to bear on her and a single shot rang out.

"Shit!" Dieter screamed as the bullet socked into him. The machine pistol went flying and Broxton was rising from the floor with the pistol in his hand. Dieter's body spun around as he thrashed and splashed across the lobby, finally coming to rest face down in the water. Broxton pointed the gun at him and pulled the trigger and Julie heard the clink as the hammer fell on an empty chamber, but the body didn't move.

"Looks dead to me," Julie said.

"Me, too," Broxton said.

Julie slogged across the lobby and picked up her wooden Frisbee. "I almost got him," she said, tucking it under her arm.

"You're going to keep it?"

"I have a feeling," she said. Something was niggling at her mind. She looked at Dieter or rather Eddie Fitch, face down in the muddy water. Quiet and still in death. It had something to do with him. She held tighter to the plywood, digging it into her side. It would come to her.

"This way," Broxton helped Julie out of the lobby and toward the departure gates. "There," he said, and she saw them, two rows of luggage lockers.

Julie, excited, let go of Broxton, and stumbled ahead, clenching her teeth against the pain shooting from her ankle. "There," she said, "2124."

Broxton inserted the key. "I can't turn it," he said. "The back has been cut off so that it could fit inside the half dollar." But Julie wasn't listening, because she had a flash, a lightning bolt to the brain. It hit her hard, the thing that had been bothering her.

Without thinking she shoved Broxton aside as bullets blasted into the locker where he'd been standing, and she spun around, pivoting on the oversized running shoes, flinging the plywood with all her might. Tammy Drake was caught off guard as the spinning wood slammed into her stomach, knocking the wind out of her.

She doubled over, but kept her hand on the gun. She was about to fire from a bent over crouch, when a crazed yell echoed though the departure hall, and before she had a chance to pull the trigger again T-Bone dove on her and ripped the pistol from her hand.

Tammy thrashed in the muddy water, but T-Bone grabbed her by the hair and shoved her face in the muck. "I'll let up if you stop," he said, and she went limp. T-Bone stood, holding the pistol in his left hand and Tammy's hair in his right, keeping her down on the ground, her head at his knees.

"How did you know?" Tammy said, wiping mud from her face.

"I remember you said you'd overheard Dieter and Kurt speaking German. He doesn't speak German, he's American. I just figured it out."

"Who shot Victor?" Tammy said.

"Dieter," Julie said. "He was trying to kill Broxton and missed."

"Hey, we don't have all day here. Let's get the show on the road and blow. There's dead bodies out there, there's gonna be cops. Lots of 'em. We gotta go," T-Bone said. Then he added, "Danny Boy, can I have this woman?"

"No you can't," Tammy said.

"She's yours," Broxton said.

"You can't do that, Broxton," Julie said. "It's like rape."

"Does my man get a share of what's in that locker?" Tammy said.

"He does." Broxton said.

"Then let's get the damn thing open and get out of here. There's a nail clippers in my purse. It's over there, she pointed to a counter by the departure gates that was still standing. She pushed herself up and sloshed over to the purse and pulled out the clippers, came back and handed them to Julie.

Julie pressed the clippers, like a small pair of pliers, around the bit of key that was sticking out of the keyhole and turned.

The locker opened.

"Briefcases," Julie said. "Five of them."

"There's two million in each one. US dollars," Tammy said.

"Holy shit," T-Bone said.

"It's drug money," Julie said. "It got Hideo killed and ruined thousands of lives. I don't want it."

"She's right," Broxton said. "I couldn't live with it either."

"Well, I can," Tammy said, bringing a small twenty-two automatic from her purse, but a shot thundered through the room. The gun flew from her hand as she jerked up and landed on her back, a bright red stain spreading between her breasts.

"We could have been so good together," T-Bone said, his thirty-eight smoking in his left hand.

"What do we do now?" Julie said.

"We'll take the money to the boat. Then we'll motor round the island to Grand Case. It's a small anchorage. I got a house there, woman friend of mine watches it. I'll take the money ashore and you two can sail *Voyager* off into the sunset. We'll meet up again in a couple of months."

"You serious?" Broxton said.

"Hey, don't look so disappointed, I'm not gonna keep it."

"What are you going to do with it?" Julie asked.

"When I was a kid there was show called the *Millionaire*. It was about this rich guy who went around giving a million bucks anonymously to folks who needed it. Kind of a stupid show, but I liked it. Now I'm gonna be him. I'm gonna give money to folks that lost their boats, folks that couldn't afford the rip of insurance rates. I'll find the ones that need it the most and find a way to give it to 'em so that no one finds out."

"I think that's a fine idea," Julie said.

"So do I," Broxton said.

"Then let's get the fuck out of here," T-Bone said.

They grabbed the briefcases, two for each of the men, one for Julie, and started toward the exit. Julie carried her case in one hand and used Broxton's shoulder for support with the other. Outside the wind was calm as they ran across the field to the runway and the dinghy beyond.

Read more of DEA Agent Bill Broxton's Adventures in Jack Stewart's first book, SCORPION, out now on Bootleg Press.

Following please find the first chapter of SCORPION.

"A terrific, spine tingling, sea-going yarn." —Ken Douglas

JACK
STEWART

SCORPION
A NEW MILLENNIUM THRILLER

CHAPTER ONE

THE PLANE JERKED with the thundering sound of the explosion, cutting off all talk in the cabin. Broxton grabbed his seatbelt and cinched it tighter. Cold chills laced along his spine. A stewardess going by with a drink tray stumbled. He lashed out with his left arm, circling her waist, and pulled her toward him, spilling the tray from her hand, showering nearby passengers with Coca Cola and orange juice.

"Hey," she said, resisting and pushing against him, but he was stronger. "No," she said, as he pulled her down into his lap.

"Bomb," he whispered into her ear. Her body sagged as he wrestled her into the empty window seat next to him. She grabbed behind herself with both hands, searching for and finding the seatbelt. She buckled up and Broxton saw the color fade from her face. She grabbed onto the armrests, her skin pale as the sky on the other side of the window, her lower lip quivering, her eyes wide.

"Oh, lord," she said, as oxygen masks dropped down from above each passenger, orange, with clear plastic tubes, bouncing and jiggling, like hula dancers on parade. They were flying at thirty-five thousand feet and losing pressure. Broxton reached up, grabbed the mask and slipped it over his head. The stewardess next to him did the same, her hands shaking.

"You okay?" he asked, voice muffled by the mask.

"Yeah," she nodded, but he didn't believe her. She sucked her lower lip between her teeth and clamped down on it to stop the quivering, her auburn hair, long and perfect only an instant ago, now seemed wild and untamed, her flared nostrils accented the freckles around her nose. She had a fawn like quality that startled him. He forced himself away from the terror in her eyes and looked over her shoulder, out the window. The mammoth wing shuddered and he was afraid the powerful engines were going to break away, but the shaking stopped as the wing tipped earthward, seeming to drag the rest of the plane with it.

"My God!" he said as the plane shuddered again, a great spasm running through it, like a death rattle, as the 747 lurched earthward, seeming to pick up speed. The clouds below were moving in a circular direction, but the pilot straightened the descent, added power and pulled back on the yoke. For a few seconds they were in a steep climbing turn. Broxton felt the G force as the plane fought the pilot. He was sucked into his seat, jaws, arms, hands, even fingers weighed down. He dropped his head, forced his mouth open, fought an urge to scream and grabbed oxygen into his lungs.

Then the plane lost the will to climb and started downward again.

He reached into his pocket, feeling for the engagement ring. He slipped the tip of his index finger through it, satisfied that it was still there. He prayed the pilot would bring them in safely. He twirled the ring around his fingertip. Dani, he thought, and he felt the familiar ache in his heart. He should have married her all those years ago.

The plane shimmied to the left, pulling him out of his reverie as the descent steepened. He was afraid it was too much for the plane. He looked out the window, half expecting the wings to rip away, turning the plane into an aluminum tube, spiraling and spinning toward the ocean below. Then the nose eased up, the pilot had slowed the rate of decent, but the sinking feeling in his stomach told him that they were still going down.

The stewardess gripped his hand, nails digging into his palm. He turned to look at her and she relaxed her grip for a second. He couldn't see her mouth through the mask, but he could tell by the crinkles around her eyes that she was attempting to smile. He forced himself to smile back and he gave her hand a gentle squeeze. He noticed the bruise under her right eye. She'd tried to cover it with makeup. He wondered how she'd hurt herself.

A baby cried, the pressure loss playing havoc on its eardrums. He squeezed his nose, held his mouth shut, and tried to breathe out, equalizing the pressure in his own head. He saw the stewardess imitating him, felt her sigh as the pressure equalized.

A woman's scream shrilled up from deep in second class and it gave him the excuse he needed to turn away from her. He looked around first class. The orange oxygen masks hid the lower half of the faces, but they couldn't hide the furrowed brows, eyes clenched shut against reality, or the stiff hands gripping armrests. Many were holding their breath. But there was no panic. There was no point.

He felt the pressure on his hand lessen, then increase. He turned back to look at the stewardess, caught in her Christmas green eyes, and he tried to imagine what he looked like to her.

Did his eyes show the freezing spark that was running up and down his spine? Did they betray the electric tingling at the back of his neck? The tight heat in the pit of his stomach? Did she know he felt like voiding himself at both ends? Could she feel the invisible claws raking over his skin?

The plane jerked and the luggage locker overhead popped open. He ducked as a briefcase fell out, bouncing off his shoulder, sending a stab of pain through his arm. He saw her wince, as if she felt it too. The briefcase hit the floor and sprang open. Papers, a cellular phone, a pocket calculator and a Barbie doll rolled out. The traveling executive had a little girl.

The doll rolled against his foot. He bent over and picked it up. Wherever this Barbie was, it was always summer. Her hair was always blond, always long, her eyes always blue and she always had on that pert summer dress. Barbie never worried. Barbie never had clammy skin, and Barbie never died.

He inhaled the oxygen, closed his eyes and wrapped his fist around the doll, tiny breasts digging into the palm of his left hand as the stewardess' nails dug into his right. He squeezed harder.

"Hurts," she whispered.

"Sorry," he said and he relaxed the pressure on both her hand and his eyelids. The interior of the plane slid back into focus. They were still going down, but the angle of descent had eased even more.

He began to hope as he slipped the Barbie doll into the magazine pouch on the seatback in front of him.

There. She was safe and warm and away from harm.

He leaned his head back against the seat and rolled it slightly to take in the passenger across the isle. She was old, with rouged cheeks and blue rinsed hair, sitting next to a man who looked like he'd been her husband for several generations. Like himself and the stewardess, they were holding hands. She was looking into the man's eyes. The man took off his mask and mouthed the words, "I love you," and Broxton felt the stewardess squeeze his hand. She'd seen it, too.

The plane leveled off after what seemed like a forever down slide on the world's longest roller coaster.

"Ladies and gentlemen," the captain's voice boomed over the plane's speaker system, "I don't know what the problem was, but we have it under control. We've had some sort of malfunction in the rear of the plane that caused us to lose cabin pressure, but we have the aircraft under control."

He was repeating himself. He didn't know what he was talking about. He was lying.

The stewardess squeezed his hand again and he turned toward her. She slipped her mask off and the hairs on the back of his hands started to tingle when she smiled. Full lips, no lipstick, she didn't need it, perfect teeth. She was gently biting down on her tongue, as if she wanted to say something and was holding back.

"What?" He pulled his own mask off. He inhaled and smelled a whiff of her perfume mingled with her fear. It assaulted him like a patch of wildflowers on a windy summer day.

V

"You didn't check on them?" the stewardess said.

Broxton smiled. "You're very observant."

"I'm married to a cop, it goes with the territory. You've been watching them. Sneaking peaks whenever you think you can get away with it. You're not very good. If they were criminals they'd be on to you." She had a slight Mexican accent that didn't go with her pale skin and green eyes.

"I'm supposed to see that nothing happens to them." He turned and looked over his shoulder at the last two seats in the center of the first class section.

The prime minister's face was ashen, and he was gripping his seat with an intense fervor. His gray skin and gray hair gave off a death-like pallor, only the beads of sweat dripping from his hair line and the weak rising and falling of his chest told Broxton that there was any life there.

By contrast, the attorney general, in the seat next to him, was taking long, slow breaths, sucking the life-giving oxygen deep into his lungs and exhaling in an almost leisurely fashion. He's accepted his fate, Broxton thought, he knows it's out of his hands. He'll take whatever is dealt. He won't show fear. He's a strong man. The prime minister is not.

"He's a good man," the stewardess said. "Tough too. You'd never know he'd had open heart surgery last year."

"I didn't know that." Broxton took another look at the prime minister's face. He was grimacing, but it could be pain, not fear. Maybe he'd been too quick to judge.

"Looks like he might be in some pain," Broxton said.

"I wouldn't be surprised," she said.

"The attorney general looks pretty calm, though."

"He was an athlete. World famous."

"I've never heard of him."

"Actually neither had I, but the two Trini flight attendants are both gaga over him. He was a cricket player."

"That explains it. It's a sport I don't keep up on."

"They say he's a real ladies man, Trinidad's most eligible bachelor."

"He looks the part," Broxton said, noticing the dark man's expensive suit and salon haircut.

"Are you some kind of bodyguard?" she asked. He turned back toward her and again she was looking deep into his eyes.

"Kind of. I'm supposed to keep Prime Minister Ramsingh alive, only he's not supposed to know it."

"I don't understand," she said. Her nostrils flared, just a little, and the wrinkles around her eyes scrunched together. Little crow's feet. He guessed her to be in her mid-thirties, about his age.

"Someone wants him dead. Attorney General Chandee doesn't take the threat seriously. My boss does." He couldn't believe it. He was telling her about the job. That was forbidden, but he didn't care. They were talking to take their minds off the horrible reality around them. They were whispering.

"Who do you work for?"

"The United States Government."

"Oh," she said.

He turned to look over his shoulder again.

A well built man pushed through the curtain from second class. The sun shining in through the windows on the left side of the aircraft reflected off something shiny in the man's hand. A knife?

Broxton flicked open the seatbelt and charged down the aisle. The man was leaning over the prime minister. Broxton pulled him off and slammed him across the laps of two priests sitting in the seats opposite. The man had a shocked look on his face. Broxton raised his hand to strike, then he saw the chrome flask in the man's hand.

"Sorry," Broxton said, "I thought it was a knife." He held his hand out to help the man up. The grip was strong and firm and a smile glinted out from his pale blue eyes, but it vanished quickly, turning to a cold stare. Not a man to take lightly.

"Brandy," the prime minister said. His mask was off and in his hand. "If I have to take the heart medication I like to enjoy it going down." Broxton noticed the liver spots on the prime minister's hands.

"Bill Broxton," he introduced himself. "Again, I'm awful sorry about the mistake. For some stupid reason I thought I saw a knife. I feel like an idiot."

"Kevin Underfield," the man said. "I work for Minister Chandee." Broxton had to think for a second, then he remembered that in Trinidad the cabinet members were also elected members of parliament.

Broxton turned back toward the prime minister, who continued talking as if nothing had happened. "I used to drink more than my share, enjoyed it. I liked the way it made me feel and usually I could handle it, but from time to time I'd make an ass out of myself. That was before I came into politics, but the press never lets one forget his indiscretions, so now the only time alcohol touches my lips is when I have to take the damn medicine. They still write about my drinking, but now it's a plus because it's the old Ramsingh they're writing about and everybody knows it except them."

"So you turned your drinking and past indiscretions into an asset. It can't be easy to live with."

"So you see the two edged sword."

"I see it," Broxton said. "As long as you don't drink you can shrug off the past and any man that writes about it unwittingly reminds his readers how you overcame your problem to become prime minister, but if you ever get tanked up again it'll all blow up in your face."

"Yes, they would see me as nothing more than a common drunk."

"A hard way to go," Broxton said. Ramsingh looked up at him through gray eyes that danced around his smile. The man radiated honesty and Broxton couldn't help liking him.

"Are you a cop of some kind?" Underfield asked. He had a British accent and that puzzled Broxton.

"DEA."

"I thought we made it clear to your government that we understand the threat and don't desire any of your help." The attorney general's voice was muffled by the oxygen mask. Broxton was finding it hard to breathe, but not impossible.

"I don't know what you're talking about," Broxton said. "I thought the man had a knife. I recognized the Prime Minister of Trinidad. I made a mistake. I said I was sorry."

"If you're not here to watch over the prime minister, why are you on this flight?" Chandee pointed an accusing finger at Broxton.

"I'm going to Trinidad to get married," Broxton said, adding, "if she'll have me."

"And the lucky woman is?" Now Chandee had his mask off, too. He pulled his finger back and laced his hands in his lap. He was addressing Broxton as if he was on the witness stand, but it didn't matter, Broxton had an answer for him.

"Dani Street," he said.

Chandee's snarl shifted into a smirk that turned Broxton angry. He wanted to slap it off his face, but he held himself in check.

"The ambassador's daughter?" the prime minister said. "Maybe we've been too quick to judge Mr. Broxton, George. I've told you before, you have to watch that." The prime minister looked at Chandee like a benevolent parent does a wayward child, and the man visibly withered under his stare. His fingers stiffened in his lap as he turned away from his boss and toward Broxton, offering him a thin lipped smile.

"I think I'll just go back to my seat," Broxton said.

"That would be best," Chandee said, his face tight.

"The ambassador's daughter?" Underfield said, almost laughing.

Broxton nodded, then the plane hit a patch of turbulence and he stumbled, but caught himself, gripping the back of the prime minister's seat. Several of the passengers gasped, but nobody screamed. Most of them kept their masks on.

He looked at Chandee, met his eyes, smiled and said, "You know, George, you really should watch that temper. One of these days it's going to land you in deep shit and the prime minister won't be around to help you out."

"There's always me," Underfield said, his gaze turning to knife blades.

"Right," Broxton said. And he turned away and started back toward his seat.

"I work for the attorney general, you know."

"You said that," Broxton said, without turning around. And he quickly forgot about Underfield when he eyed a little girl sitting next to her father. Her hand was clasped tightly in his and her lips were moving. She's praying, he thought. He smiled at her and she smiled back, lighting up her freckles. Then she gave him a thumbs up sign. He stuck out his right thumb and flashed it back.

He returned to his seat, thinking about the Barbie doll. He took it out of the magazine pouch and fluffed the doll's hair with a finger. Then he straightened her dress. He felt the stewardess' eyes on him. He didn't even know her name.

"Yours?" he said, smiling at the girl. She nodded and he handed it back to her. He was rewarded with a smile back. Would the girl's mother be waiting for her husband and daughter at the airport? Would the airline tell waiting friends and relatives about the trouble on board or would they just say the plane was delayed? Would they make it to Port of Spain at all?

"It'll be okay," the stewardess said, as if reading his mind.

"I know," Broxton said, but he didn't know.

"I'm Maria," she said.

"Bill," he said, "but most people call me Broxton."

"You made an enemy back there," she said.

"Sometimes I have a big mouth, like today. My job is supposed to be kind of secret and not one day into it and I've not only told you, but I've managed to get in an argument with the attorney general."

"It looks like Mr. Ramsingh's being well taken care of."

"You mean the muscle man?"

"He looks like he can handle himself."

"He does at that," Broxton laughed, "and I guess I've upset him a little, too."

"It would seem so," she laughed, and he swore her eyes were sparkling.

"Ladies and Gentlemen," it was the captain's voice over the speakers again, "we're flying at eight thousand feet and although it's possible to breathe without your oxygen masks I would recommend you keep them on. Our speed is two hundred and fifty miles an hour, less than half of our normal cruising speed, and I'm afraid that will put us forty-five minutes behind schedule for our landing in Port of Spain. So our new ETA is 2:45, If you haven't already reset your watches, now would be a good time to do it."

Maria took his hand again and he felt her leg pressed up against his.

"I'm sorry, I shouldn't kid you," the captain continued, "we have a problem and we don't know what it is, but we seem to have control of the aircraft. I don't want to risk climbing or adding any more power. The situation is delicate, but I'm confident we will arrive safely, and in that light I'm requesting that you all, flight attendants included, stay seated with your seatbelts securely fastened until we are on the ground and the engines are off. Thank you very much."

This time he was telling the truth. Broxton preferred the lie.

"It's going to be a pretty tense hour and a half," Maria said. She was still holding his hand. She gave him a half smile, as if she just realized it, and relaxed her grip. He noticed her face turning the embarrassing shade of pink.

He smiled back, "Thanks for the moral support," he said. "I don't know what I would have done without you."

"Thank you for that," she said, her color returning to normal. Then she asked, "Will she be waiting at the airport, your girl?"

"No, she doesn't know I'm coming. It's a surprise. How did you know about her?" he asked.

"You were fiddling and fidgeting with that engagement ring, like it was a hot rock burning your fingers, all during take off, remember?"

"I've known her all my life." He let go of her hand and dug the ring out of his coat pocket. He looked at it, turned it over in his fingers. "Our folks always assumed we'd be married, but things just didn't work out."

"What things?" she said. She pulled her long hair back and met his eyes.

"Another woman," he said.

"Ah," she said.

"But that was over a long time ago."

"She knows this, your girl?"

"Dani? Sure. She never stopped loving me and I guess I never stopped loving her. She's been part of me almost as long as I've been alive. When someone's been that close for that long, well, I took her for granted. I'll never do it again."

"Good for you," Maria said, "I hope it works out for you." And she started to get up.

"Where are you going? The captain said we should stay seated."

"Someone has to check on the passengers. I'm the senior flight attendant."

"But the captain said."

"He's got his job and I've got mine, and besides you sure didn't stay seated." She smiled.

He unbuckled his belt and stood to let her pass.

"I'll be back soon," she said, squeezing his arm. He watched her make her way back toward second class, working her way down the aisle, steadying herself by grabbing on to the seatbacks.

Then the plane jerked to the right and started to go down again.

The Bootleg Press Catalog

Ragged Man by Jack Priest
Bootleg 001 — ISBN: 0974524603
Unknown to Rick Gordon, he brought an ancient aboriginal horror home from the Australian desert. Now his friends are dying and Rick is getting the blame.

Desperation Moon by Ken Douglas
Bootleg 002 — ISBN: 0974524611
Sara Hackett must save two little girls from dangerous kidnappers, but she doesn't have the money to pay the ransom.

Scorpion by Jack Stewart
Bootleg 003 — ISBN: 097452462x
DEA agent Bill Broxton must protect the Prime Minister of Trinidad from an assassin, but he doesn't know the killer is his fiancée.

Dead Ringer by Ken Douglas
Bootleg 004 — ISBN: 0974524638
Maggie Nesbitt steps out of her dull life and into her dead twin's, and now the man that killed her sister is after Maggie.

Gecko by Jack Priest
Bootleg 005 — ISBN: 0974524646
Jim Monday must rescue his wife from an evil worse than death before the Gecko horror of Maori legend kills them both.

Running Scared by Ken Douglas
Bootleg 006 — ISBN: 0974524654
Joey Sapphire's husband blackmailed and now is out to kill the president's daughter and only Joey can save the young woman.

NIGHT WITCH by Jack Priest
BOOTLEG 007 — ISBN: 0974524662
   A vampire like creature followed Carolina's father back from the Caribbean and now it is terrorizing her. She and her friend Arty are only children, but they must fight this creature themselves or die.

HURRICANE BY JACK STEWART
BOOTLEG 008 — ISBN: 0974524670
   Julie Tanaka flees Trinidad on her sailboat after the death of her husband, but the boat has a drug lord's money aboard and DEA agent Bill Broxton must get to her first or she is dead.

TANGERINE DREAM by Ken Douglas and Jack Stewart
BOOTLEG 009 — ISBN: 0974524689
   Seagoing writer and gourmet chef Captain Katie Osborne said of this book, "Incest, death, tragedy, betrayal and teenage homosexual love, I don't know how, but somehow it all works. I was up all night reading."

DIAMOND SKY by Ken Douglas and Jack Stewart
BOOTLEG 012 — ISBN: 0974524697
   The Russian Mafia is after Beth Shannon. Their diamonds have been stolen and they think she knows where they are. She does, only she doesn't know it.

BOOTLEG BOOKS ARE BETTER THAN T.V.

THE BOOTLEG PRESS STORY

We at Bootleg Press are a small group of writers who were brought together by pen and sea. We have all been members of either the St. Martin or Trinidad Cruising Writer's Groups in the Caribbean.

We share our thoughts, plot ideas, villains and heroes. That's why you'll see some borrowed characters, both minor and major, cross from one author's book to another's.

Also, you'll see a few similar scenes that seem to jump from one author's pages to another's. That's because both authors have collaborated on the scene and—both liking how it worked out—both decided to use it.

At what point does an author's idea truly become his own? That's a good question, but rest assured in the rare occasions where you may discover similar scenes in Bootleg Press Books, that it is not stealing. Writing is a solitary art, but sometimes it is possible to share the load.

Book writing is hard, but book selling is harder. We think our books are as good as any you'll find out there, but breaking into the New York publishing market is tough, especially if you live far away from the Big Apple.

So, we've all either sold or put our boats on the hard, pooled our money and started our own company. We bought cars and loaded our trunks with books. We call on small independent bookstores ourselves, as we are our own distributors. But the few of us cannot possibly reach the whole world, however we are trying, so if you don't see our books in your local bookstore yet, remember you can always order them from the big guys online.

Thank you from everyone at Bootleg Books for reading and please remember, Bootleg Books are better than T.V.

JACK PRIEST
ST. MARTIN, 2003

Printed in the United States
29612LVS00007B/4-12